W9-AFY-574

<u>Dedication</u>

This book is dedicated
To my husband, Paul.
Without his love, support and encouragement,
Casey Quinby would not exist.

PROLOGUE

He opened the back door leading from the garage to the kitchen of the white picket-fenced house he now shared with no one. It seemed so empty. Once there was family and laughter and happy times. Now it was just a place to 'hang his hat' as the old saying went. He checked his watch and saw that it was ten minutes to ten. The Channel Seven news will be on at ten. He wanted to make sure the reporters on the scene gave an accurate description of the accident. After all, it was just that, 'an accident.'

The clock on the mantel struck ten. Right on cue the evening news anchor, Tom Eckhart, opened with a breaking story about a tragic accident that occurred earlier in the evening. "It appears one person, believed to be a young girl, was walking along a remote section of the Scenic Highway in Bourne. She was found face down in a shallow ditch on the side of the road. A cell phone, presumably hers, was recovered approximately ten feet from the body. The victim was taken to Memorial Hospital, where she was pronounced dead on arrival. Since no identification was found on her person, the Bourne Police Department is attempting to use the cell phone to help them ascertain her identity. The name of the victim is being withheld pending notification of next of kin."

News reporters, Tony Thomas and Vickie Roper, reported from the scene. They gave their renditions of what happened. A heartbreaking hit-and-run, they called it, where the driver of the alleged car failed to stop. Both reporters asked the public to come forward with any information that could be helpful in identifying the person, or persons, in question.

He watched the tag-along cameramen filming the scene that was surrounded by Bourne Police and Sheriff Department vehicles. Law enforcement teams were using spotlights in an effort to detect any skid marks or signs of a vehicle. The Bourne PD investigator was concentrating on a specific spot near the body, while the Sheriff's personnel expanded the circumference of the search. It was hard to tell if they were successful in locating or identifying anything relevant.

Just the way he planned it.

The emptiness of his house didn't matter anymore. He lay back on the couch and closed his eyes. He could see her face. She was a mere child. That's what made her so beautiful. He could hear her whisper his name ... James. She always called him James, never Jim or Jimmy. James seemed more mature. Jim was short and harsh. Jimmy is what his mother called him. And Becky definitely was not his mother.

CHAPTER ONE

James spent the night curled up in a fetal position on the couch. With the burden of Becky's demands lifted from his shoulders, he succumbed to a deep, bottomless sleep. He awoke startled by a beam of sunlight that snuck through the ever-so-narrow opening between the living room curtains, and danced on his closed eyelids. Mother Nature had planted him in her spotlight. Relieved it wasn't an intruder, or worse, an investigator from the Bourne Police Department, he wiped the sweat from his forehead.

His mother's patchwork quilt had slid off the back of the couch and onto his legs. She was so proud the day she finished attaching the last button.

He closed his eyes, not to sleep, but to reflect on the memory of another car accident – one that had haunted him for 20 years.

It was Thanksgiving Day. They were on their way home from Aunt Betty's house in Plymouth. His dad wanted to get home early to watch the end of the Cowboy/Redskin's game. He was pushing the radio search knob on the dashboard trying to catch some of the commentary. His mom had unbuckled her seat belt to turn and tell James and his siblings to stop their bickering.

It had been a long day and they were all tired. His brother, Billy, was in between his sister, Sally, and him. Billy would move his legs from side to side – first to bump Sally, then James. She'd complain, but he would just bump back. Billy was only seven and kind of a skinny kid. Billy was smart though, and knew how to worm his way out of trouble, smiling unnoticeably when Sally and James got blamed for something he did.

Sally was only a year younger than James, but she was already two inches taller. That bothered him. They shared the same reddish-brown hair, freckled noses and dimples. The only difference was he had two and she only had one. She could throw a mean baseball and was pretty darn accurate. Maybe his mom should have called her Sal. She was okay for a girl, but she was his sister, so he couldn't let her know that. His mom's reprimand didn't stop him from reaching behind Billy to pull Sally's ponytail.

The next thing James remembered was waking up in a room with what seemed like an army standing around in a circle, all watching him. Tubes, beeping machines and bottles hung over him. He was eleven and old enough to know the people in the circle were nurses and the guy was probably a doctor.

There would be no more bickering, or bumping, or hair pulling. He would never watch another ball game with his dad, and his mom would never make another quilt.

James slowly slid his feet from under the quilt, swung his legs over the front of the couch, and sat in a crunched position with his head in his hands.

CHAPTER TWO

It was Monday morning, time to fall into his regular everyday routine. The shower was cool and refreshing. The water cascaded down his body. It felt good. The clean citrus smell of the soap transported him to an imaginary tropical island far away from Cape Cod.

His mind traveled long enough. He knew he had to let go, to move on. What happened twenty years ago and, more important, what happened yesterday could not be changed.

He shut off the faucet, shook the excess water from his hair, and stuck his arm out the end of the shower curtain to grab a towel. He'd done laundry yesterday morning and forgotten to hang fresh towels on the rack. Still dripping wet, he pulled back the curtain and carefully stepped out onto the linoleum floor. The linen closet was just outside the bathroom door. To get to it he had to pass in front of the mirror on the wall over the vanity. James had put up the four-by-five-foot mirror two years ago when he remodeled the bathroom. He glanced at himself, and then stopped to admire his reflection. He liked what he saw: the six-foot-two-inch frame with a perfect thirty-six waist and flawless muscular thighs. In his eyes, the perfectly formed bulging biceps looked like they were stolen from Charles Atlas. And, the six-pack he sported would lure any girl into his hidden den of iniquity. Smiling like a Cheshire cat, he winked as an imaginary sparkle appeared on his left front tooth. "Those years of braces and trips to the gym all paid off." James caught himself talking to his image. Without realizing it, a little puddle of water had formed at his feet. He almost slipped when he turned away from the mirror and started toward the door.

He toweled off his body, blow-dried his hair, and sprayed the necessary body stuff that would get him through the day. Just in case, he gave himself an extra spray to insure his internal stress would stay just that, internal. He walked into the closet, picked out a freshly laundered shirt and pants and proceeded to get dressed.

For twelve years, James had been employed by the Massachusetts court system. It was a prestigious position that demanded the best in work and appearance.

How impressive.

He stood admiring himself in the full-length hall mirror. His uniform was a picture of exactness. His sparkling white, impeccably-starched shirt displayed two prominent state seal patches. He reached down to stroke the perfectly-trained crease in his pants.

I do look good, even if I say so myself.

He certainly portrayed an image of accepted accomplishment. His promotion last August to Chief Superior Court Officer was well deserved and he knew it. A job envied by many and held by only a chosen few.

He was living his dream.

He always had a special feeling for the Superior Court building. Even when he was just a kid, that big building on the hill fascinated him. As a boy, somewhere around six or seven, his dad took him fishing at the harbor. Billy, just a baby, stayed home with his mom. They always invited Sally, but she never wanted to go. She'd make a face, then walk away mumbling that she'd never touch a funny feeling, ugly fish. She was about nine when she changed her mind and even learned how to gut them.

Almost every Saturday on the way to the harbor, James and his dad would pass by the big building on the hill, the one with a huge replica of a cod fish mounted above the door. They'd watch as the intricately sculptured scales danced in the reflection of the sun. That big fish sure appeared to be moving. It seemed as though it always tried to be the one that got away.

Someday, he'd catch one just as big and not let it get away.

He loved that big building high on the hill, maybe because it was part of a memory, a memory of his dad. Now look at him. He's part of that building.

It was too early to get to the Courthouse, but he didn't feel like making breakfast. Besides, like a robin red-breast, he wanted to be out among the locals to strut his ever-so-striking facade.

Yesterday, he accomplished an amazing feat. He faced a dilemma head on and skillfully executed a plan to eliminate an out-of-control problem. As he stepped outside, the warmth of the sun embraced him. It was too hot for a jacket, but he took one anyway, carefully folding it so that the embroidered badge lay visible for all to admire. He picked up his two-way radio, car keys and an Almond Crunch bar, for his afternoon snack, and headed for the garage. "Good morning, my friend," he said as he patted the right front fender on the way by.

CHAPTER THREE

Nancy's Donut Shop was in the Village across from the Court House. As James opened the door, a little bell attached to the top of the door jamb jingled. Nancy, who was middle-aged, slight in structure and very sweet, just like her donuts, was refilling the napkin holders. He couldn't help but remember how hard she and her husband Ned had worked their whole life, living humbly, saving for the day they could kick back and retire to the life on the beach they'd always dreamed about. That life never came.

Ned had been a rugged, burley guy with a smile that would make a fish jump into a frying pan. James remembered how Ned handed out warm apple cider and cinnamon sugar donut holes to the hardy souls wandering the street singing carols during the Village Christmas stroll. He was a good man, one of the best. He suffered a massive heart attack last September and never made it to the hospital. James was glad everybody in the Village, and Nancy's customers, rallied behind her. They became her extended family, helping with her decision to keep the shop open.

"Good morning, Nancy," James said smiling. "Do you have any of those thick, sweet cream creations of yours ready?" He towered over her. His eyes traveled back and forth, scanning the shelves in the donut case. "They always give me a burst of energy to start the day."

She looked at James, took a deep breath, tilted her head slightly sideways, and let her mind recall her childhood when she'd go to the penny candy store. Gramma Allen had made a small candy store in a backroom of the Allen homestead. Nancy's mother would give her fifteen cents to buy whatever treats she wanted while her mother visited with Gramma. With bag in hand, she methodically searched the shelves for the perfect picks. "Some things never change." Nancy leaned forward on the glass case next to the cash register, "For you, Jimmy, anything."

"What was that?" he said, cupping his hand behind his ear.

"Oh, nothing," Nancy said, eyeing James with admiration. He was the son she always wanted, but never had. "What's on the agenda for today?"

"Well, let's see. I think we're starting jury selection for a drug-trafficking case. You know the one – the fishing boat that was catching more than lobsters and clams. The one allegedly picking up sealed boxes of marijuana in the shallow waters around Squaw Island."

Nancy's body stiffened, her tone hardened as she tapped her fingers on the counter. "If you ask me, it's a slam dunk, open and closed case," she said. "Those whatever you call 'ems, they think they can pretend to fish our waters and be our friends. But what they don't know is we're a special breed and they'll never fit in. My Ned was a real fisherman. It was his love."

James watched Nancy wipe a couple tears from her eyes.

"Justice will take care of those guys, don't you worry," he said, putting his hand over hers.

"I've got a morning paper here, if you'd like to take a look." She pulled her hand back and gave the already-been-read paper to him.

"Thanks, you wouldn't be a good juror, too biased." He reached over and took the paper. "I've got some time to kill," he said with a sneer, careful to not let his hidden emotions ooze out into his speech.

Nancy laughed quietly, poured James a cup of coffee, picked up an empty donut tray, and turned to walk back to the kitchen.

With coffee in one hand and his donut dish balanced on the newspaper in the other, he made his way to the little two-seater in the back corner of the shop.

The front page of the Cape Cod Tribune was unremarkable. He sipped his coffee as he glanced at the stories. Most were human interest: pictures from a 5K March of Dimes race on Saturday, a story about declining real estate prices, and an article about construction plans for the Bourne Bridge. This was good. He leaned back in his chair, lifted the paper, and turned to page two. There – the story he was looking for. He read about a tragic accident on the Scenic Highway in Bourne last evening in which a young girl was killed by what appeared to be a hit-and-run. His eyes blurred to the bold black print of the newspaper; it was his mind telling the story. After all, he was there.

For a moment he remembered 20 years ago.

He had been knocked unconscious, so the details of the accident that wiped out his entire family, he learned from his Aunt Betty. It was hard for her, losing her only sibling, his mom, but it was harder for him. He lost Billy and Sally, and his dad and mom too. Unlike now, the newspaper print he read then jumped off the page and became embedded in his head forever. It was an ugly picture. His dad never saw the car coming.

CHAPTER FOUR

"Hey, buddy," a voice called from the counter. James jerked his head sideways to see Barry Binder, his courtroom counterpart. He gathered up his thoughts quickly, and stored them in a secret compartment in the back of his head. Hoping his expression didn't arouse any unwanted curiosity, he greeted Barry and an unknown female companion with a two-finger salute.

There was a world of difference between Barry and him. He was 'Mr. Particular' and Barry was 'Mr. Here I Am'. James imagined that Barry's morning routine consisted of a half-hour bathroom stay that included everything. He knew Barry's shirts were worn at least twice because he came in to work one morning with the same dirt smudge he had when he left the day before. He probably would have worn it a third day if he hadn't missed his mouth with a catsup-covered French fry. He was a piece of work, but all in all, he was an okay guy.

They'd worked together for almost seven years and traveled with the same Village groupies and co-workers. James let Barry think he knew more than he really did about his personal life. It was better that way. He never confided in Barry about his relationship with Becky or any of the other girls. That was his secret and he wasn't about to let anyone in on it. Now, more than ever, he was glad he didn't.

11

He stood and extended his hand.

"James, I'd like you to meet my cousin Marnie Levine. She's visiting for the summer from Long Island. For some reason Marnie thinks she'd like to go into the *law business*." He gloated as he spoke.

Poor Barry, James thought. *Always trying to make himself the man of the hour and far more important than he really was. But this was Barry's home turf, so let him be.*

Marnie just rolled her eyes.

"He's your cousin, Marnie Levine. All yours," James said watching her eyes respond to Barry's remarks. What beautiful eyes, robin-egg blue and so piercing. He wondered if she was wearing those color-changing contacts.

Nancy looked out through the kitchen door.

"Got a second?" Barry asked her. She came out to greet them.

"This is my cousin, Marnie. You'll probably see a lot of her. When we were kids she had quite a sweet tooth as I recall."

"Glad to meet you," said Nancy, wiping her hands on her apron. "These two are my boys. Most mornings, I make sure they have enough energy to start the day. I hope you join them." Nancy reached out and shook Marnie's hand. "I better get back to work before the tourists want their treats." And with that, she scooted back into the kitchen.

James tried to study Marnie without drawing any unsolicited attention. She was attractive – no beautiful. He figured her to be about five-four or five-five and in her early twenties. Her long red hair was pulled up with one of those clip things. She could have doubled for Ariel in Disney's *Little Mermaid*. The only difference: Marnie had legs. She wore a pair of cream-colored Capri's with a turquoise print top and sandals to match. Her shoulder bag was soft brown leather that reminded him of an expensive attorney's valise.

She's a lot like me ... coordinated and confident ... well put together, James thought, as he silently continued to give her the once-over.

12

He wanted to tell her that living with Barry in a one bedroom condo was going to be an experience, but decided it was better left unsaid. Barry had help furnishing and decorating it from an old girlfriend, so at least the living should be comfortable. It was relaxed and inviting, and decorated in a nautical motif, not unique to many Village residences, since they were so close to the beach.

James remembered that Ned had given Barry a couple of old fishing buoys he'd found in his beach travels. Ned said they were a housewarming present. Barry kept them rustic because Ned believed every stain and chip in the paint told a story of the sea and to change them would change a tiny part of Village history. Barry did, however, have them made into lamps and told Ned that when they were lit, they showed him the way, like a beacon from a lighthouse.

James envisioned Marnie being ushered about by Barry. Heads would turn as he walked this red-headed beauty along Main Street, pretending to show her the local sights. James knew he certainly could show her sights much more interesting than Barry could.

"Marnie is going to sit in for the morning court proceedings today," Barry said.

James already assumed that.

"So you're studying law?" James quickly interjected. This would let him know approximately how old she was. He guessed early twenties before, but Barry gave him an opening so he took advantage of it.

"Yes, I graduated last May from Huffa Law School in New York City. Barry's been after me for a couple of years to visit him on Cape Cod. So here I am. Have you lived here long?"

"I'm a lifelong Cape-y," beamed James. "Been here for 32 years, if you count seven years over the Sagamore Bridge in Plymouth, and I intend to stay at least that many more."

James' mind drifted back. *The first six or so months after the accident, he wasn't able to move around very well. He could walk with help, but easily tired. His Aunt Betty tried her best to help him move on, but he never felt completely comfortable away from home. Almost every weekend, they'd pack a lunch and make the hour long drive from Plymouth to Sandwich. His family's home, only two miles from the center of town, had been left to him as the only survivor. It was his job to mow the lawn, rake the leaves, and plant the same scarlet-red geraniums his mother planted every year. At first it wasn't easy, but gradually, as he regained his strength, he looked forward to it. Aunt Betty would dust and vacuum as if there were people still living there. In his eyes, there were. For seven years, it was the same routine. On his eighteenth birthday, he packed his bags and Aunt Betty drove him home.*

"You'll find a much more laid-back style of living than you're accustomed to. Some night when you can't sleep, take a walk down to the beach, sit in the sand, and watch the stars twinkle above you. If you close your eyes and listen to the waves break, you'll be transported to a special place where dreams are made. You can get caught up in these dreams and if you believe, you can make them come true."

"Earth to James, Earth to James," Barry piped in, breaking James' train of thought. "My, aren't we the great philosopher," he continued.

"Have you ever tried it?" James asked.

"No, and I don't know if I ever will," chuckled Barry.

James, frustrated with Barry's arrogant remarks, looked at his watch, nodded and motioned toward the door. "Marnie, if you'd like, we can continue this conversation later. Right now we need to get a move on. Court doesn't wait for anyone."

CHAPTER FIVE

James, Barry and Marnie waved to Nancy, who was stacking to-go cups alongside the coffee machine. James did his usual flick of the bell before opening the door for Barry and Marnie.

The threesome made their way across the street toward the steps of the Courthouse. "Watch out for cars," said James. He held his arm out in front of Marnie. "If people left their houses five minutes earlier, they wouldn't have to speed to get to work on time."

He watched Marnie scan the façade of the building they were about to enter. "Is this the Superior Courthouse?" She stared in awe at the beautiful granite structure, the epitome of strength and stature.

"Yes." James provided a little history as they continued up the steps. "It's typical Greek Revival-type construction, built in 1831. When we walk though these ornate carved oak doors, I want you to imagine right under your feet, in the catacombs below, are the ghosts of many who've passed through its gates. To this day, if a record stored in the basement needs to be retrieved, two people go down there to fill the request. There's lots of history around the Cape. I'm kind of a buff, boring to some, but to me, I love it."

James led the trio up the stairs to the second floor. "The Clerk's Office and the Planning Department, among others, are on the first floor. The second floor is home to the main and secondary courtrooms, judges' chambers, jury room and our office."

James had given many visitors, both young and old, tours of the Courthouse. It was on one of these tours that he saw Becky.

His mind raced fast forward, then withdrew into the past. *At the beginning of June, the sophomore class from Bourne High School scheduled a tour in conjunction with a Cape Cod history class they were taking. This wasn't supposed to happen. She wasn't supposed to know who he really was. He had been so careful. This changed the plan.*

"Are you okay?" Barry walked over to James, while Marnie sat down on a bench in the hallway. "You look like you just saw one of the catacomb ghosts."

"I'm fine." James unlocked the set of huge polished mahogany doors that led to the courtroom. He gestured for Barry and Marnie to go inside. "I'll be right back. I need to open the jury room." Beads of sweat formed on his forehead. He quickly detoured into the men's room to splash some cold water on his face. He stared into the mirror.

You've got to let go, he thought.

He met up with Barry and Marnie inside the courtroom.

Marnie did a three-hundred-sixty-degree sweep of the walls where original oil paintings of past Superior Court justices hung. "I can feel their eyes watching me." She shivered and pointed to one of the pictures. "The look on his face is scary. The pictures may be intimidating, but the furnishings are impeccable and the drapes are absolutely beautiful. I've never experienced such a vision of grandeur in a courtroom before. The ones in New York are brash, cold and lack character." She turned to the guys and said, "How weird, that a place where lawyers fight for a murder conviction is so warm and embracing."

Barry pointed toward the viewer's seats against the wall, "Why don't you sit over there. Usually they're reserved for the press, but there won't be any today. From there you can see everybody seated in the audience: the witnesses, the attorneys, the accused, the judge and, of course, the Court Officers."

Marnie took Barry's advice and selected a seat half way into the courtroom. From this prospective she could draw a mental picture of her entire surroundings. Reaching into her valise, she took out a notebook and pen. One of her most important learning tools as far back as junior high school was her daily journal. There was no reason for her not to continue this practice. She was always driven by desire to absorb knowledge and wisdom that would help her make challenging, life changing decisions.

At exactly 9:00 am, James announced, "All rise." Judge Richard Thompson entered the Courtroom. Judge Thompson walked up the four steps to his desk and responded with, "Be seated." He was a big man, a bit intimidating to some, but known to be gentle and compassionate. With all the formalities aside, the Court Clerk called the first case. James had it right. The jury for the fishy marijuana case was going to be picked. He moved through the doors at the back of the courtroom, across the hall and into the jury room. Forty-five people in the jury pool were waiting to be questioned by the judge and the defense and prosecution attorneys.

They certainly were a diverse group. James could never understand how someone could come to court to be considered for a position as important as a juror wearing ripped jeans and a tee shirt. And then there was the gum chewing, big-rim-glasses lady, wearing a tight mini-skirt and a blouse that looked like the buttons would pop if she breathed too hard. She irritated him because each time he turned away she'd snap her gum.

"All those in groups one and two, please follow me," James said as he motioned them toward the door. There were a few grunts and groans, but all did as instructed. Fortunately, the gum chewing lady was in group six and, hopefully, wouldn't be called. Once inside the courtroom, each one of the eighteen people was questioned and either retained or released. This went on all morning until all parties involved were satisfied they'd assembled an impartial jury.

Marnie watched as the attorneys did their respective song and dance routines. She knew each juror filled out an information card before they were assigned a number and told to show up on a certain date. It seemed like a fruitless effort and waste of time for all involved to have the retired policeman, or the correctional officer that worked in the jail up the hill from the courthouse, or the secretary to one of the judges at District Court get called to appear. Such a misuse of public money; the defense attorney would never agree to accept any of them for trial. It was a game, always a game. Marnie glanced up at the clock on the wall to her left. She moved forward in her seat and leaned her palms at the edge of the bench on either side of her lap to balance herself. She knew when she became a practicing attorney she'd play the game too.

James noticed the occasional glance she gave him. He thought he even detected a slight smile. At precisely 12:00 noon, the Judge summoned the Court Clerk to the front of his desk. He bent forward to speak quietly to only her, then stood up and announced that court was adjourned for the day.

James stood up. Confused, both he and Barry waited for the judge to exit through his office door before moving toward the jurors.

"What do you think?" Barry said puzzled by what just happened. "Not like him to do this, especially Judge Thompson. It's only Monday … sometimes on a Friday, but never on a Monday.

"Oh well, he is the boss," said James.

As he escorted the jurors through the doors in the back of the courtroom, James reminded them, "You need to be back in the jury room no later than 8:30 tomorrow morning." He bid the attorneys a good day and proceeded to lock up the courtroom. Barry and Marnie were already in the lobby waiting for him.

"Do you need me to do anything?" asked Barry.

"No. Why don't you guys meet me outside? I'll finishing locking up and file the day's paperwork with the Clerk. It'll only take me a few minutes." James watched as they went downstairs and walked outside. He took a deep breath, headed down the stairs, and went into the Clerk's office. "Judge Thompson adjourned court for the rest of the day. I've locked the courtroom. Barry and I are leaving now. See you tomorrow." With that he handed the paperwork to the counter clerk that was standing closest to him.

Several of the girls behind the counter gave him a puzzled look, but knew better than to ask why. Even if James knew, he wasn't about to feed into their gossip mill, especially if it was a personal matter concerning the judge.

Once outside, he spotted Barry and Marnie standing in the lower lot by his car. Paranoia set in – that wasn't a good place for them to be waiting. James raced down the stairs and over to where they were.

"Real exciting day, huh," James said then, continued without hesitation, "So you want to be a lawyer?"

"If that's all I have to do to earn money, damn straight," Marnie responded. Barry wasn't paying much attention to James and Marnie's conversation. Instead he was rubbing what appeared to be a smudge on the front passenger side of James' car.

"Barry, I thought you said you had an exciting job?" Marnie said turning to face her cousin.

"Okay, okay, knock it off you two," Barry said shaking his head. "Hey James, you're slipping. Where'd you get these scratches? I thought it was dirt so I tried to rub it off ... just so you don't think I did it."

James' eyes darted to the fender.

Before James could speak, Barry shifted back to Marnie. "Tomorrow will be a better day. By the way, James, would you do me a favor? A couple of weeks ago, before I knew Marnie was coming to visit, I made some plans. Could you entertain my cousin tonight?"

"You're a real piece of work," said James nervously looking around to see if anybody was near. "And that's being kind."

Marnie, standing with hands on her hips, glaring at her cousin, stepped forward. "You two are talking about me like I'm not here." Her foot tapped rapidly on the ground. "I'm a big girl and perfectly able to fend for myself. I live in the big city … remember."

James put his hands behind his neck, locked his fingers together, and rocked slightly up and down on his toes. He felt embarrassed, not just for himself, but for Marnie.

He took a deep breath. Hoping he wouldn't get rejected, he extended an invitation, "Come on Marnie, you and I will have some dinner and conversation tonight, then maybe I'll show you that beach with the stars. Let me offer you some real Cape-y hospitality. What do you say?" James' face softened as he looked into her eyes.

The corners of her mouth curled up to form a smile.

What a pretty and delicate smile.

"I would be delighted to dine with you this evening, Sir James," Marnie whimsically proclaimed, batting her eyelashes, and teasing like a pampered princess.

"Okay, then dinner and conversation it is," said James as a smile spread across his face. "I'll pick you up at Barry's around seven pm. Nothing fancy, just a typical Cape-y atmosphere with great food. I forgot to ask, do you like seafood?"

"If I don't, then I don't belong on the Cape, do I?"

James nodded in agreement. "Catch you later," he said as he got into his car.

Barry never drove his car to work: a perk of living in the Village – everything was within walking distance.

CHAPTER SIX

It had cooled a little, enough that he rolled down the two front windows of his car instead of turning on the air conditioning.

He closed his mouth and inhaled a lungful of air through his nose. "Smell that salt air." He found himself singing an old Patty Page tune, "If you're fond of sand dunes and salty air …." It was one of his mother's favorites. He still had her old forty-fives, but the record player was long gone. Now he only remembered coming home from fishing, hearing *Old Cape Cod* playing and her singing.

"That stupid squirrel," James yelled as he slammed on his brakes. "He should have paid more attention. Too bad, he'll never run across a road again."

His mood darkened. He reflected on last night's fatal meeting with Becky. Things got out of control. He recalled their conversation earlier in the afternoon. She wanted some kind of commitment. Imagine a sixteen-year-old girl asking for commitment! They had an arrangement and commitment wasn't part of it. "Not an option," he murmured. "She's gone and that's good." He'd be all right. James felt assured that he'd made it through the day without a hint of guilt or remorse getting in the way. Now it was time for him to move forward.

He pulled into his driveway and glanced at the over-grown grass and weed-filled flower beds. "Guess I know what I'm doing next weekend," he said out loud. That reminded him – he'd need to get some gas for the mower. He hesitated by the flowerbed, bending down to pick off a couple dead leaves from the geraniums.

He had a few hours before heading back to the Village, so he decided to sit out on the deck, go through his mail, and relax with an icy cold Budweiser Select.

An ad for a new car wash got him thinking about his car and how Barry noticed some scratches. He was sure there was some rubbing compound and a tin of wax in the garage. Last night he was able to pull out the two dents from the impact using an old fashioned toilet plunger. He remembered watching his father remove a couple dents from their family car after a deer ran into the side of it. It worked back then and, thank goodness, it worked last night. The last swallow of beer went down smoothly, maybe too smoothly. He thought about having another, but decided instead to clean up his car, take a shower, and get ready to pick up Marnie.

The scratches weren't deep and came off easily. "Nobody ever notices scratches on Barry's car cause there are so many, but you are is my baby," he said as he lovingly patted the fender.
"Now that you're all gussied up for our big night, it's my turn. Hang tight, we're doing the town later."

He had taken his watch off when he washed the car.
Wow, I lost track of time. I've got to hustle.

He didn't want to be late, so his usual make-me-beautiful routine had to be cut short. A hot shower and a quick fluff and buff were all he had time for. He slid on his new Polo jeans and pulled an orange-colored pocket tee over his head. Before he left his bedroom, he stopped in front of the mirror. "Lookin' good," he said as he gently smoothed a couple of hairs back into place.

He picked up his car keys, cell phone and money clip from the counter, crossed through the kitchen and out the door into the garage.

"I feel like David Hasselhoff in Knight Rider and you're my nearly indestructible car," James marveled, as he spoke to his shiny black Mariah. He talked to it half expecting it to talk back. "If only you could speak, what stories would you tell? Forget it, I don't want to know. Cancel that thought. Let's get going."

The ride to the Village was uneventful. He chose to ignore the squished squirrel that was now part of the pavement. His fingers tapped in time on the steering wheel as he listened to the latest single from Carrie Underwood.

CHAPTER SEVEN

At exactly 7:00 pm, James lifted his hand to knock on Barry's door. Before he could get the first knock in, the door opened. "Right on time," said Marnie. "I like that. Actually, I'm really hungry, so I'm glad you're not late. There are only two beers and a stale greenish-looking loaf of bread in Barry's refrigerator. I'm sure the green is not in the pistachio family. I can see that I'm headed for the grocery store in the morning." James stepped into the condo. At a quick glance, he wondered how Barry could keep his living quarters so neat and clean and himself so ... well, clean, yes, but the neat part left something to be desired.

James didn't want to linger in his friend's apartment without him being there, so he hastened the conversation along and headed back toward the open door. "At least for tonight, Marnie Levine, I can whisk you off your feet with a fabulous fried clam roll, a loaf of onion rings, and a frosty mug of beer at Seafood Harry's, if the lady permits?"

"Let's get going." Marnie, not to James' surprise, was again dressed to perfection. Instead of her hair being clipped up, it was flowing gently down her back. She wore a pair of skinny jeans. He was sure were designer, but didn't want to stare at the back pocket for the name, and a white sleeveless jersey with a flowery ruffle on the top right side. Her purse, that was hanging on the back of the dining room chair, and her sandals were navy with white polka dots.

Her closet must look like his, with a place for everything and everything in its place.

Marnie was ready. She grabbed her purse and closed the door, making sure it was locked. James engaged her in small talk as they drove the ten miles to Seafood Harry's. "So you grew up in Long Island?"

"Yes and no. Until I was fourteen, my dad, my mom and I all lived in Long Island. My parents got divorced around that time and Dad moved to New York City. He spent more time in the City anyway, so I wasn't surprised. After about three years, my mom remarried. Nice guy and all, but by that time, I was thinking about college and getting out on my own. I'd stay with my dad for the summer. Most days I'd go into the office with him. He'd keep me busy with filing and stuff." She looked at James. "Am I boring you yet?"

"Not at all, I'm envious. I've never been any further than Boston. New York is a foreign land to me. Keep going." James was intrigued by his new friend.

"The law business grew on me. Some of it is dull, but it can be very exciting too. All depends on what phase you want to commit to, and for the most part, I like the criminals. I find them more challenging. Every case is different. Every person is different. Every outcome is different in some way. It really is a study in psychology and how the human mind works. You meet good people and bad people. Truth sometimes gets tangled up with lies, but that's when the challenge begins. Corporate law is boring and Real Estate law falls into that same category as far as I'm concerned. Besides, I can do a lot more talking in the courtroom than I can sitting behind a desk with stacks of papers and piles of books. And, in case you haven't noticed, I like to talk."

"You'll have to slow down for a few minutes, 'because we're here."

Marnie was excited to see the restaurant was situated right beside the water. There weren't many cars in the lot, so they were able to park two spaces from the door. Judging from the other patrons, James was right; it was a jeans and jersey kind of place. He knew the owner, Harry, and most of the girls that worked the registers. "During the summer months the restaurant gets pretty crowded, but since it's a Monday night and 7:25, we won't have to wait to place our order."

When they reached the register, a tall, burley, middle-aged man came around the corner from the kitchen. Marnie couldn't help but notice him. He had sandy-blond hair that was tussled a bit, his skin was tanned, the shade of the weave in a Longenberger basket, and he was dressed in well-worn jeans and a navy Nautica jersey. He could have walked right out of an ad in the Cape Cod Life magazine.

James leaned over, "Don't pay much attention to Harry. He can be pretty forward and sometimes a bit crude."

"James, my friend, it's been far too long. Whatcha been up to and who's the looker with you?" Harry grinned and gave Marnie a little wink.

"I told you," James said. "Harry, this is Marnie. She's visiting her cousin in Barnstable Village. I decided her first dining experience on the Cape should be at Seafood Harry's. Don't you agree?" James gave Harry little time to respond. "Now let's get some food going. I wouldn't want her to pass out from lack of nourishment."

James and Marnie placed their orders, picked up their beers and moved to a window-side table.

"The only problem with the view is the sun doesn't set over the harbor," James said looking out over the water. "We need to flip the island over to experience one of nature's true wonders. For this evening, you'll have to take my word for it."

"Sunset or not, it's like a postcard," remarked Marnie. "The sky's a soft reddish hue, mixed with calming shades of blue and lazy daubs of white. Listen to me, talking like I was an artist."

"Red skies at night, sailors delight; red skies in the morning, sailors take warning." said James. "That's an old saying and as corny as is sounds, it's right most of the time."

They looked away from the window when a young girl approached the table with their food. Marnie's eyes widened and James chuckled, "Harry is trying to make a move on you. He's doubled the size of the clam roll. Some guys have a pickup line, but not Harry. He lets his clams do the talking."

Marnie picked up her clam roll, "You certainly don't get seafood like this on Long Island, even though it's surrounded by water just like Cape Cod." She savored every tasty morsel. "These clams are the perfect size and fried to perfection. This won't be my last visit here, that's for sure."

"So you concentrated in criminal law?" asked James.

"Yes. My ultimate goal is to open an office specializing in criminal law. I know I have to take baby steps before I can walk in the big shoes, but that's my plan." Marnie continued between bites, "What I need to do now is learn more, not in the classroom, but out in the real world. And you, James, what's your plan?"

James sat up a little straighter in his chair. He had a plan; it started when he was seven and up until last Sunday, he felt he was right on track. "I have always admired the big building up on the hill – the Superior Courthouse. My dad and I rode by it almost every Saturday on the way to our favorite fishing spot. He'd tell me about its history and what it stood for." James felt more relaxed. "It was my goal to someday be a part of that building, and here I am."

Marnie sipped her beer as James continued, "My dad was a history buff. That's probably why I've always been so intrigued with history. When we rode by some place he thought was of interest, he'd give me the low down on it. I remember the day we rode through Hyannisport and he pointed out the Kennedy Compound. I was really too young to know what he was talking about, but in a funny way, I was drawn into his stories. I decided that someday I'd learn more about the Kennedy's and maybe even

27

get to visit them. Remember I was only seven and at that age, anything was possible."

Marnie laughed quietly, "Did you ever get to visit them?"

"Not yet, but I'm still working on it. Maybe you'll get lucky and join me. Enough about me." James stopped. Out of the corner of his eye, he saw Harry coming toward them.

"And how's the food, little lady? Do I pass your taste test?"

Marnie had seen his type many times at the beach bars in Long Island, so without hesitation she replied, "The foods great, but do you do dishes?"

James couldn't help but laugh. Harry got caught up in his own game. She was sharp and James liked that.

Harry shrugged his shoulders and looked at James. "You've got one up on me. Later." He left shaking his head as he walked back to the kitchen.

James could see the girls drumming their nails on the counter, anxiously waiting for them to leave. "Guess Harry's getting ready to close," James said looking around. "We're the last ones here." With Harry nowhere in sight, they waved good-bye to the girls and headed for the door.

CHAPTER EIGHT

James glanced at his watch, it was only 9:30. He rubbed the back of his neck and wondered if it was early enough to suggest they visit to the beach.

What the heck, thought James, slowing down to a snail's pace.

"Would you like me to show you the beach I was talking about earlier this afternoon? It's not far from Barry's place."

He lifted his right arm up and pointed toward the sky. "Before you answer, look up. See those stars? From here they're just stars, but from the beach they're special. You'll have to judge for yourself. What do you say?" His arms were now crossed in front of him waiting for Marnie to accept his invitation.

She remembered how he spoke of the stars and making a dream. He said if you believe in your dream, then maybe it will come true. "Of course I'd like to see the *beach* stars," Marnie said. She wrapped her arms over her chest, gave herself a comforting hug, wrinkled up her nose, and headed to the passenger side of the car.

James melted. Her voice cast a luring spell over him. Her lips moved some more, but he couldn't hear anything coming out. He wanted to pull her close and kiss her, but he couldn't. That would spoil everything.

Slow down, he thought. *All in good time.*

He scurried to catch up with her, then reached out and took her hand as they walked quickly to the car. He opened the door and waited until she was comfortably inside, then gently closed it. Taking his place behind the steering wheel, he fastened his seat belt, raised his arm up and said, "Buckle up girl 'cause we're off to the beach ... to the beach." With a turn of the key and the hum of the engine, off they went.

On the way, James told Marnie about Kelly's Landing. "This is one of the best kept secrets around these parts. Kelly's Landing is a public beach, mostly used by the locals. Because it's on the harbor side of the island, it's sheltered from the open ocean, making it much warmer." James' voice stopped, but his mind didn't.

It's warmer in a lot of ways, certainly much more intimate and most importantly, not patrolled by the police at night. He never, or nearly never, heard of any problem with kids drinking or partying. He pulled into the lot and parked near the steps leading to the beach. It was the perfect spot for ....

His thoughts were interrupted when Marnie poked his side and, in a split second, she turned and unbuckled her seatbelt. "Are you ready to show me the *beach* stars?" she teased, then opened the door, and swung her legs out. She leaped from the car and scooted down the short flight of well-worn wooded stairs leading to the sand. At the bottom, she kicked off her sandals and started running toward the water. The sand was cool and soft and felt good on her feet. James caught up to her just as the water rolled up over her toes. It tickled and she giggled.

"James, you were right. These *beach* stars are different." Her head was bent back looking straight up toward the heavens. She blinked her eyes rapidly. "They jump in and out of their sparkle, daring you to choose a special one ... the one that's going to follow you until your dream comes true." Marnie, now with eyes wide open, reached toward the sky to catch her special *beach* star.

James spun around, ending up in front of Marnie. He was taken aback by her childlike sweetness. He remembered Becky. The difference: Becky was a child and Marnie was not. He needed to get himself back in the moment, this moment. Forget about Becky. She was gone and Marnie was here. He closed his eyes and thought about his *beach* star: the one he'd reached for many years ago.

"A penny for your thoughts," Marnie murmured.

He shuffled forward. James could no longer control his desire to kiss Marnie. Gently he wrapped his arms around her. She welcomed his embrace, clasping her hands around the back of his neck. It would just be a kiss, a gesture of friendly affection, the perfect close to an amazing evening. His face tilted downward, his lips closed. He was ready.

The sudden reflection of car headlights skimming off the water brought James and Marnie back to reality. They bounced back on their heels and became two individuals joined only by a hand.

James kicked at the sand, "I feel like two little school kids sneaking a first kiss and getting caught by our parents. We didn't even realize the tide has started to come in." They both laughed out loud. As if intoxicated, they lost their footing and fell down onto the soft, inviting sand.

Immediately James jumped up, reached for Marnie's hand, and helped her to her feet. The cool wet sand had attached itself all over their bodies, leaving only clean faces. "We look like two pieces of sandpaper," Marnie laughed, brushing the sand from her legs and clothes. "Looks like I'll have to travel with a towel from now on. Is this my Cape-y initiation?"

"You bet it is," James replied. "It's only the beginning and don't you forget it."

"I didn't get my *beach* star yet. I haven't decided which one to choose." She cupped her hands behind her neck and rocked back and forth. "This is a very important decision and I don't want to be hasty."

"So that tells me you'd like to come back to explore the possibilities?" He knew the answer before he asked, but he needed assurance.

31

"I'd like that very much." Her eyebrows lifted, "But only with someone who can help me find the right one."

They reached James' car and, as before, he opened the door for her. "You know," she said, "you're quite the gentleman and I'm impressed. Do you treat all your ladies this way?"

"Why, thank you, my dear. Some ladies require special treatment," James said as he closed the door and moved around to his side of the car. Without delay, he opened his door and slid into the seat beside her. "To Master Barry's abode," he recited like a Shakespearian actor. The radio was playing softly. He drove from the parking lot to the short narrow street that connected the beach to Route 6A. Jimmy Buffet was singing *Cheeseburger in Paradise*. The catchy tune had Marnie and James seat dancing as they pulled into the driveway beside Barry's condo. There was a light coming from the living room window. Either, Barry was entertaining or, more than likely, his evening was a fizzle and he was home alone.

Marnie was already out of the car and standing beside James' open door. He looked up at her. Before he could speak, she said, "Thanks for a great evening. I really had a wonderful time. I don't feel like a stranger in a distant land anymore. Actually, I feel quite comfortable."

He walked Marnie to the door and stood while she bent down with the key to unlock it. She cracked it open and turned to face James.

He leaned forward to give her a gentle kiss goodnight. "I had a great time myself: good food, good conversation and good company." He didn't want to leave, but knew he had to. "I'll talk to you tomorrow."

"You bet," she said. She watched him walk back to his car. "Goodnight." And with that she went inside.

James sat for a minute then backed out on to the street.

CHAPTER NINE

Once inside, she realized Barry wasn't home yet. She hung her purse on the dining room chair and collapsed on the couch. She reflected on a fun evening and hoped it wouldn't be the last. Her eyes closed. She must have dozed because she was startled when Barry came in and closed the door sharply behind him.

"My goodness, what's up with you?" she asked as she jumped to her feet.

"Good plans, bad night," he responded quickly. He opened the refrigerator and took out a beer. "Want one?" he asked, offering her the open bottle.

"No thanks. Did you come home after I went out?" Marnie questioned her cousin. "I know I shut the lights out when I left."

"Yeah, I came home … like I said, good plans, bad night. It was too early to go to bed and there was nothing on TV. I walked down to the Tavern, met up with some friends, and had a couple of beers. How 'bout you? James told me he was taking you to Seafood Harry's." Barry looked miserable, but managed a half grin, "Best fried clams around!"

"We had fun. The food was great and so was the company." Marnie caught herself beaming while Barry sat staring at the floor. "If you don't mind, I'm going to catch some shut eye," she said. "Since you're in my bedroom, could we continue this conversation tomorrow?" Marnie got up and hugged Barry, "Cheer up, cuz, better luck next time." She felt bad literally kicking Barry out of his own living room. But he was sitting on the couch and that's where she was sleeping, so he had to go.

"Night, cuz," Barry said, making his way to the bedroom. He closed the door and lay down on the bed. It was nice coming home and having someone to talk to, even if it was his cousin, he thought, as he drifted into a deep sleep.

CHAPTER TEN

James turned the radio volume up. Music played, but he didn't hear the words. He put himself out there and let her in. What was going through her mind? He hoped he made a good impression.

It was dark when he pulled into his yard. He remembered turning on the outside light before he left. The bulb had probably burned out. He'd check it in the morning. He drove into the garage and sat for a few minutes, thinking about nothing in particular. It was a good feeling.

As he turned the key to enter, he couldn't help but remember the light coming from Barry's living room window. It was welcoming, guiding, giving off a feeling of home. His house was dark and uninviting. Before he went any further, he stretched his arm out to the right until it made contact with the lamp on the table beside the door. He turned it on and in an automatic reflex scanned the room – for what, he wasn't sure. After all, he was alone.

It was still muggy and warm, a typical Cape Cod summer night, but James felt cold. It didn't matter what was going on outside, it mattered what was going on inside him. He decided to make himself a cup of coffee, take a couple of cookies out of the freezer, and listen to Jay Leno's monologue. Nights alone were always a dark time for him. Jay was his TV buddy. James felt him reach through the screen and give him an *it's okay* pat on the back. He greeted his audience with high fives, then retreated back to center stage, clasped his hands together in a firm grip and proclaimed a great big welcome. James felt that welcome included him.

Love that man.

Tonight he would sleep in his bed, comfortable and secure, knowing he'd safely tucked his little secret away from the public eye.

CHAPTER ELEVEN

Tuesday morning came much too quickly. James went through his morning routine, then headed for the Village. Nancy was busy waiting on customers. He knew they weren't regulars because of their prominent British accent. After all, it was tourist season and Cape Cod is a mecca for tourists. There were still some newspapers left in the rack so, he picked up a copy of the Tribune and headed for the corner two-seater. He marked his spot, waited for the tourists to leave, then greeted Nancy, "Here we are again, another beautiful day in paradise."

"You're early today," she answered as she glanced straight into James' eyes. He didn't like it when she did that. It reminded him of his mother.

"You know, Nancy, sometimes I think you can see inside of my head. I'm not sure you want to do that. You never know what evil lurks in the minds of men."

"You aren't old enough to be quoting *The Shadow*." She turned to get his coffee. "What'll it be today, a dark chocolate cake donut?"

He just shook his head and smirked, "Frankly, Nancy, I don't give a damn."

She laughed. "You're always a welcome start to my day, Jimmy."

As he turned to retreat to his waiting table, he saw Barry just reaching out to open the door. He was alone.

"Mornin' James," Barry chanted. "You got my cousin home a little late last night. She was up, but in la-la-land when I left."

"How would you know, you weren't home yet yourself. You must have kept your mouth shut to have a date that lasted so late," James blasted back.

"Enough, you two," Nancy chimed in. "Barry, the regular?"

"Sounds good." He moved toward the empty chair across from James.

James scowled a bit, leaned forward, and with a sarcastic note in his voice asked, "Did the yesterday's courtroom drama drive Marnie into considering a career change?"

"Absolutely not," Barry said, wondering if he should say more. "Actually, she mumbled something about green bread and said she'd see us later."

James remembered Marnie's comments about the contents of Barry's refrigerator, so he assumed she was getting ready to peruse the aisles of the Stop and Shop Market.

Barry practically inhaled his donut, then stood up, brushed the crumbs from his shirt, got a lid for his coffee, and glanced back toward James. "I've got to make a phone call before we start soul searching the jury today. See you in 15 minutes or so. Have a good one, Nance." And he was gone.

Nancy laughed and shook her head, "That's the fastest I've ever seen him move."

Finally, James could relax a bit. He started to flip through the Tribune looking for anything related to Sunday night. It seemed like eons ago, but it was still very real. When he turned to page 12, his eyes fell heavily on a picture of a young girl. It was Becky Morgan's obituary. He stared at her face. She looked back at him. He imagined her lips moving. The word *why* echoed in his brain. He read on. The family didn't want a wake, instead they were having a memorial service to celebrate her life. It was being held on Wednesday afternoon at 2:00 pm at Our Lady of the Highway in Bourne. The words gave him goose bumps.

A tap on his shoulder shocked him back to reality. "Jimmy, are you okay?" Nancy asked, sounding quite motherly.

"I was scanning the obituaries and came across one for a young girl who apparently was killed by a hit-and-run driver last Sunday night. How sad." James' face was emotionless – his words and expressions didn't match. He gathered up the rest of the paper, looked at his watch, and hurried toward the door leaving Nancy standing beside the table with a puzzled look on her face. James always nodded and reminded her to have a great day on his way out the door – but not today.

"Don't even try to figure him out," Nancy murmured as she walked toward the kitchen shaking her head.

CHAPTER TWELVE

The Clerk called the Court to order at exactly 9:00 am as Judge Thompson took his seat. The judge's face appeared troubled. There was a deep, hollow look in his eyes, one James had never seen before.

"Good morning," Judge Thompson said, acknowledging the jury, attorneys and all court personnel. "The jury is instructed to listen and to determine the innocence or guilt of the parties charged in this case, based on facts that will be presented and argued by both the prosecution and defense. Remember that the verdict should be made without any reservations of reasonable doubt. The prosecution may now begin their opening statement." With that the judge moved his arms forward in his robe and sat back in his chair to prepare for the recitation of accusations the prosecution team was about to deliver.

James leaned toward Barry and in a voice just below a whisper asked, "Does the judge look distant to you today?" Judge Thompson's eyes were dark, empty pools focusing nowhere. "He's usually sharp and right on the money."

"His mind is not here, I'm sure." Barry cupped his hand over his mouth and cocked his head slightly sideways to reply. "When I came in this morning, I stopped by the clerk's office to pick up today's docket and overhead a couple of the girls talking. They had their heads together in a low whisper, but I got the gist of what they were saying. It wasn't good. Remember that girl that was killed Sunday night?"

Just nod to acknowledge he's talking to you.

"Well, it seems she was Judge Thompson's cousin's niece," said Barry.

James' face twitched and turned pale. He wanted to turn and leave, but couldn't. It was a good thing Barry was looking down and not straight at him. The day Becky was here for the tour she did talk to the Judge more than the other kids, but he thought nothing of it. He never put Morgan and Thompson together.

"That must be why he left early yesterday," continued Barry. "He's taking it pretty hard."

James had done well up until now.

Stay calm. Don't draw attention to your shattering nerves.

The prosecution's opening just finished when James noticed the courtroom doors open. It was Marnie. She winked at him as she made her way into the back row. He nudged Barry, motioning his head toward Marnie. Now more than ever, he needed her – no, he wanted her. He didn't really know her, but he felt comfortable with her. She was strong and caring.

"It's 11:55, so we'll break for lunch." Judge Thompson read the directive with absolutely no emotion. "We'll resume at 1:15." And with that he rose from the bench and proceeded through the back door to his chambers.

The courtroom emptied, all except Marnie who waited for James and Barry.

"Lunch is on me." Marnie's face glowed like a child ready to get her first taste of ice cream. "I have an important announcement to make. Since you two are the only people I know in these parts, you have the honor of being my audience."

The guys exchanged glances with eyebrows lifted and eyes rolling back and forth. The threesome left the Courthouse and walked across 6A to Finn's Restaurant. Finn's was an icon in the Village. The weather-worn gray shingles and faded white window trim were typical Cape Cod motif.

41

James watched Marnie paint a mental picture. "This place looks more like a house than a restaurant," she said. The inside had wide-board pine floors and a navy blue chair rail, painted white below and papered with a nautical print above. "This is definitely quaint and cozy. I like it."

James turned toward the fireplace. "Wait until winter. The fireplace is always aglow. It welcomes those hardy souls who come in to warm up with a bowl of homemade *chowdah* and a chunk of crusty bread. The Cutter family has owned it going on four generations – real nice people." He kept the conversation going, "It's a gathering place for many of the locals and Village employees for lunch and well known by visitors during the summer months for dinner."

The waitress handed them menus and reminded James and Barry about the Tuesday lunch special: lobster salad on a fresh Portuguese sweet roll with curly fries and a side of home-made cole slaw.

"If you like lobster salad, then go for the special," said James. "My favorite."

Before Marnie could make another comment, the waitress appeared, "Can I take your order?"

James was first to respond, "I'll have the special, please, and a Diet Coke. Thank you." Marnie and Barry followed, both ordering the same.

Marnie closed the menu, folded her hands together, leaned them on the edge of the table, and lifted her shoulders up and forward. "I made a decision this morning." She hesitated, half waiting for a response. None. "I'm going to take the Massachusetts bar exam." Still no response, she continued, "Don't everybody speak at once. This is the quietest audience I've ever spoken to. Cat got your tongues?"

Barry got a little caught up in his words, but was the first to speak, "Hey cuz, are you serious?"

"Dead serious," said Marnie.

The waitress appeared with their order.

"That was fast," said Marnie.

James smiled. "They cater to the working customers during the week. They know that lunch hours around here are usually an hour long and that includes the time it takes to walk to and from. You might say they run on court time. I'd say about two-thirds of the people in here now are lawyers, witnesses, jurors, or other court employees."

"Smart business people," said Marnie. "Okay, back to my soapbox." She cleared her throat. "When I decided to visit you, I actually had an ulterior motive. Of course I wanted to see you, but I also wanted to check out your surroundings." Marnie was on a roll. She stopped talking momentarily to take a bite of her sandwich. "For years you've painted a picture of this island you call home. I've only seen a very little part of it and I want to see more. I want to experience the whisper of the wind gently blowing through the sea grass, the powdery sand of the dunes, the calling of the waves as they wash along the shores, the sounds of the gulls as they swoop to snatch a piece of sandwich left behind by a toddler. I want all of these things and more. Like this sandwich, for example. Mmm ... can't get this on Long Island."

Barry was still trying to absorb the sea grass, sand and waves, but James felt her words crawl up and down his spine. He couldn't help but wonder if he was a little part of her decision to stay. Does fate really work in mysterious ways? Could he really live life unfiltered and not have to screen everything? Just be happy. He quickly slid back into reality.

She noticed the concerned look on Barry's face. "Don't worry," she said, firing little punches to his arm. "I'm not asking to move in with you. I just need a week or so and I'll find my own place. Just pretend I'm here on vacation and it will end soon." Marnie laughed.

James gave her an occasional glance. He didn't want to stare. He really wanted to jump up and down like a little kid.

Control ... don't blow it.

They'd just finished lunch when James asked, "There are a couple of guys playing guitar at the Tavern tonight. Any takers?" He hesitated. "They play James Taylor type music. He's number one in my book. Marnie, did you know he spent many of his childhood years vacationing with his family on Martha's Vineyard? I believe the Vineyard and its lifestyle influenced many of his songs." James had her undivided attention. "One of my favorites is *Don't Let Me Be Lonely Tonight.*"

Marnie leaned forward on her elbows again. "I'm sure that was no pun intended. Maybe one of these days I'll let you take me over to the Vineyard. I just might get to feeling like Carly Simon and fall in love with *Sweet Baby James* myself. Of course, you know I'm talking about the song." She shrugged and continued, "I know the singer well – let me add, as an artist, not a real person. The only time I ever watched the Red Sox, when they weren't playing the Yankees, was when James Taylor performed in the second game of the 2004 World Series in Boston. I love the guy."

James cocked his head to one side wondering where this girl came from. "So, the Tavern it is," he piped in. "I think you'll like it there. More history. It's actually a 200-year-old stagecoach stop. Although some say it's haunted by a ghost, I've never bumped into her or him. It's comfortable and cozy. Come on, Barry, we have to get back. Thanks for lunch Marnie, tonight is on me."

Barry stood to one side with his hands on his hips. In a sing-song fashion, he said, "Guess I'm the old tag-along."

Since Barry lived within walking distance of the Tavern, they planned to meet James there somewhere around 8:00 pm.

"Back to work for us," said Barry. He turned to Marnie, "I'll see you back at my condo."

"I hope these lawyers are prepared. It should be a pretty simple case. They got caught red handed." Barry kept talking. "Good thinking for tonight. I forgot those guys were playing. Marnie will enjoy it, I'm sure. She's a good kid, seems to like you."

James tried to act amused. He hoped Barry was right for a change.

The afternoon was uneventful. At 4:30, Judge Thompson adjourned for the day. James went through his ritual, waited until the courtroom emptied and locked up.

"Catch you later, Big Guy," said James.

CHAPTER THIRTEEN

Back home, James took a frosted mug from the freezer and poured himself an icy cold Bud. He kicked off his shoes and stretched out on the couch. The anguish and concern that emanated from Judge Thompson's eyes was embedded in his mind. He had to change the image, change the channel, block the grief.

Afraid he might doze, he slowly sat up and finished the last couple swallows of beer before heading for his bedroom.

His closet was arranged in a manner that would drive even the neatest of people to craziness. Each pair of shoes was allotted an equal amount of space in the shoe caddy. He arranged them by color and shade, then heel to toe. The right side of the walk-in closet was dedicated to his court apparel. At a quick glance, one could image the shirt sleeves bent at the elbow as if to salute. The left side was divided into casual Cape-y attire hung in an order similar to the shoes: first his shirts and jerseys, then shorts and pants, all by color and shades. At the end of the closet, beside the shoe caddy, he reserved a small space for serious wear. He kept his marry-them and bury- them clothes hidden inside plastic bags to prevent dust build-up before the next time he'd have to wear one. His bureau drawers were the same. His underwear and sock drawer looked like a perfectly engineered three-level box of chocolates – each piece was folded the same size and had its own space.

It was still hot and muggy, so jeans were out of the question. He decided on a blue polo jersey with plaid shorts and his new Docker sandals.

He tried to shave, but the image of a stranger with a piercing glare stared back at him. He leaned on the edge of the sink and looked down into the soapy water. "Let it go," he said out loud, almost shouting. He thought he heard an unfamiliar sound and looked toward the door. "Nothing," he said and turned back to the mirror. His dark-sided imaginary vision was gone.

The shower felt good. The water was cool and calming … countering the heat running through his body. His mind wandered back to Marnie. Why hadn't he met her before – before Becky? Deep in thought and embracing every drop of water, he never heard the phone ring.

It was 7:30 pm when he re-entered his living room. The light on the answering machine was blinking. His message center was empty; apparently the caller didn't leave one. The ID information for the incoming call read *unpublished*.

Must not have been important.

He sighed, picked up his keys and headed for the garage.

CHAPTER FOURTEEN

Barry and Marnie were already at the Tavern when James arrived. Barry was across the room, introducing Marnie to a couple of their friends.

James stepped up, "We're early but if we don't get a table now, we may not get one at all, especially if we want to sit together. You know the crowd The Tavern draws when The Sandbaggers play. Everybody relates to James Taylor type music and besides, they're good. Since there's going to be at least six of us, let's get the big table along the wall. You okay with this?" he whispered in her ear.

She squeezed his hand gently, "Couldn't be better."

Barry, and their friends, Scott Weber, Annie McGuire and Katie Brennen joined Marnie and James. Scott and Katie worked at Probate Court, and Annie worked in the District Attorney's Office.

"Barry told me a little bit about you." Annie smiled as she acknowledged Marnie. "He said you're thinking of joining us permanently." Annie McGuire's brain was a storage facility. She was an energetic, enthusiastic information booth with a personality stronger than a high-powered magnet. She was a charmer all right, but a valued friend. "Have you given any thought as to what you want to do until you take the bar exam?"

Marnie wrinkled her lips as though she had just eaten a lemon. "I know I'm going to have to do something to pay for an apartment and living expenses. I'd really like to keep it within my sphere of study. My skills at waitressing or as a short-order cook are non-existent. I'm afraid you'd wear the bacon and eggs or starve to death."

"Been there, done that," snickered Katie.

"We know," said Annie, pretending to brush spilled food from her shirt.

They all laughed.

"Before I make a final commitment, I really need to have a plan. I figure I'll look around the rest of this week and get a better handle on what's happening to see if I can pull it off." Marnie answered, a little on the serious side, and then became bubbly. "But for tonight, I'm here, and I plan on staying."

James breathed a little sigh of relief. "I didn't have anything for supper. Is anybody hungry?"

"Yes," was the resounding response.

"Let's order before the music starts," he said.

"Especially the drinks," said Annie.

"How about some pickies and do a pass-around," Scott suggested.

They ordered a double of fried calamari, loaded potato skins, two dozen peel-and-eat shrimp and some hand-cut, lightly-battered onion rings, along with a couple pitchers of beer. The music started about five minutes after the food arrived. A perfect combination, thought James, good food, great friends, awesome music, and Marnie at his side.

The night ended with a rendition of *Fire and Rain*. The guys divided the last pitcher, while the girls wound up their conversation.

"The sun rises early around here," Annie sighed. "Marnie, don't forget to call me in the morning. We'll do lunch and talk."

There were hugs all around and they went their separate ways, either to the parking lot behind the restaurant or to one of the limited number of spaces in front. James, Barry and Marnie headed to the front. James reached out to shake the bartender's hand while Barry gave a half wave.

Marnie was already outside gazing at the stars, "Wonderful – the salt air and the night breeze. I had a great night. Your friends are fun."

James cocked his head and smiled, "You really need to know more about Cape Cod. This is how we live. Life is meant to be enjoyed and stress doesn't fit into the picture."

"Stick with us, cuz, and you'll know why I didn't want to move back to Long Island." Barry looked at Marnie, who's eyes were as wide as a child's watching a Ferris wheel go round.

James reached for Marnie's hand and pulled her closer to him. "Keep looking at those stars." He put his other arm around her and gently kissed her forehead. "Good night," he whispered. "I'll talk to you – better yet, I'll see you – tomorrow."

"See you in the morning, James," Barry, who had already started walking toward his condo, quietly called back to his friend. "Come on, cuz, time to go home."

"I'm meeting Annie for lunch, then I'll stop at the Courthouse. Pleasant dreams, *Sweet Baby James.*" She winked and turned to catch up with Barry.

James got into his car and watched the two silhouettes make their way to Barry's condo.

Instead of heading straight home, James drove to Kelly's Landing. The parking lot was empty. He pulled into a space near the top of the stairs, shut off the radio, and opened the window. It really was a beautiful night. Without realizing it, he was out of the car, his sandals off, and half way across the sand toward the water. He could see lights coming from the boats moored in the harbor. "Talk about a dream," he said out loud. And like he had done many years ago, he reached up to grab a star. "One of these days I'll get you." As he turned around and slowly headed for the stairs, he caught himself singing in a soft voice, "I've seen fire and I've seen rain."

He was walking to his car, kicking the loose sea shells in his path, when out of the corner of his eye he saw a vehicle that wasn't there when he'd pulled in earlier. It sat still and dark in the shadows created by the moon. The window on the driver's side showed no reflection. It must be open, he thought. Was somebody inside watching him? His guilt flared up, but only slightly. His main focus was to control his inner emotions. He made an attempt to erase the suspicion from his mind. His secret must remain intact.

He drove home slowly, glancing frequently in his rear view mirror. He was half way home when he noticed a set of headlights behind him.

Why don't they leave me alone.

Paranoia began to set in. Just as he was about to take an unscheduled right turn, the vehicle in his wake took a left. He removed the panic from his mind, but the fear still lingered.

Once at home, in his secure surroundings, he felt relief. "Tomorrow will come soon," he said, followed by a deep sigh. "Every day that passes is moving away from the past and getting me closer to the future," James continued as though somebody was listening.

CHAPTER FIFTEEN

Wednesday morning, the fog was so thick you could cut it with a knife. This weather made it difficult to drive the back road to the Village. The winding turns were exaggerated by a wall of haze, blocking the vision of anyone bold enough to venture into it. It was eerie to say the least, especially since there was a cemetery around the next corner. James shivered as he imagined the cemetery at dusk and ghost like figures rising from behind the grave stones. Finally the Court House came into view. He wanted to see Nancy, to talk to her. Today he needed to sense her motherly presence.

The donut shop was empty. Nancy, who was tying the strings of a fresh apron, heard the bell and looked up as the door opened. She remembered James' quick exit without a word yesterday.

"Wow, what a miserable ride in this morning, but I'm here now and hungry to boot."

Nancy's puzzled look changed to her usual smile. "Remember, it's that time of year when the heat lifts the mist from the bogs and lays it across the roads to remind travelers that Mother Nature still rules Cape Cod. Speaking of mother, I made your favorite cinnamon coffee buns this morning. You seemed a little down yesterday, so I thought I'd make sure you started today off right." She beamed as she slid the spatula under the biggest bun in the pan and gently glided it onto a waiting dish. "I've just made a fresh pot of coffee." She poured him a cup and handed him the dish with the bun and two pats of butter. "Enjoy."

Today there would be no newspaper. He bent down for one of the little magazines that listed places for rent in the immediate area. He'd start doing his homework, hoping to help Marnie find a place close by to live.

The gooey sweet cinnamon bun melted in his mouth. He closed his eyes and remembered how his mother used to cut them into small pieces and make him use a fork, so he wouldn't make a mess. When she wasn't looking he'd pick them up with his fingers, stuff them in his mouth, then lick the frosting from underneath his nails. He'd get in trouble every time, but she'd continue to make them for him. It was like a game between them. He told Nancy the story once and she never forgot it.

She walked over, poured James a refill, and sat down beside him. "Jimmy, are you looking to move?" she said as she glanced at the *for rent* magazine in front of him.

"No, not hardly. Do you remember Barry's cousin, Marnie? Seems we've inherited another wash-a-shore. After listening to Barry talk about his conversion from a Long Islander to a Cape-y for, let's see, he's been here 10 years now, she's decided to give it a try." James continued, "Some of it might be my fault. I started introducing her to the good life we all know and love."

Nancy watched as he spoke. "Besides I'd like to get to know her better. She's an okay chick." With that, he winked, bid Nancy *good day* and was off to greet the jurors.

CHAPTER SIXTEEN

James jogged up the stairs to his office and around the corner, just missing Barry. "Where were you this morning? You lost out. Nancy made some of her special cinnamon coffee buns, to die for … warm and gooey."

"You try sharing a bathroom with a girl, especially a girl you're not sleeping with. And, it's worse, if you're related." Barry motioned to the slight cut on his cheek. "The razor slipped when she opened the door and bumped my elbow. She's excited about lunch with Annie today. I don't know what those two have up their sleeves, but we both know Annie."

It was still early when Judge Thompson crossed the lobby and, without speaking, opened the door to his office.

The first jurors arrived at 8:30 and, as before, James directed them to the jury room. The fishy marijuana case was moving right along and by all indications, it would go to the jury on Friday, if not sooner. The facts were cut and dry. They were presented without much objection.

The three men accused of trying to smuggle marijuana into Hyannis harbor were slumped down in their seats. "You might think they'd be concerned with the witness testimony," James said to Barry. The defendants showed no emotion at all.

"That's the result of having shit for brains," Barry said.

The public defender assigned to the case knew he was fighting a losing battle. He sat behind his table, fumbling through papers, pretending to search for some vital information. It was all a ploy to stall for time. Witnesses testified. Questions were asked. And before they knew it, Judge Thompson called for a recess until Thursday morning.

James watched the Judge step down from his desk. Without talking to anyone, he exited into his chambers. James' stomach tightened. He knew the memorial service was scheduled for two o'clock.

Barry poked James' arm, "Let's go get some lunch, then I'll come back and help you lock up."

James made an excuse for lunch, so Barry left and met up with Scott at Scoops for a burger and fries.

CHAPTER SEVENTEEN

James walked down the hill to the general store and bought a bottle of water and some peanut butter cheese crackers. The morning fog had burned off leaving a clammy, clingy feeling in the air. Maybe a walk around the court house loop would clear his head. The view from the top of the hill was breathtaking. He looked out over the harbor. The deep blue water was endless as it met the complimenting hue of the sky. The tip of the Provincetown Monument could be seen pointing up through the horizon. He was in the middle; in front of him was freedom of the seas and behind him was captivity, the Barnstable County Jail. A short beep from a Sheriff's Department vehicle brought him back to reality. George, a correctional officer James had known for years, pulled up to the front door of the jail with an inmate cuffed in the back seat.

"Hey, man, you thinkin' 'bout takin' a cruise? Your mind was sure sailin' out over the harbor." He was always smiling and upbeat.

"Just doing a little sightseeing." James paused, adding, "You have to admit looking out and being able to see the P Town Monument some twenty eight miles away is pretty incredible."

"I hear ya." George opened the cruiser door and told his prisoner to get out. With eyebrows raised, he rolled his eyes toward the shabby, unshaven man now standing beside the cruiser waiting to be escorted up the stairs and into the cage.

George shook his head. "Look whose back. You remember Jeffery Fulton, don't you? Guess he figures he gets three squares a day here and look at him, he certainly likes to eat. Canteen will have to order a 4X jump suit if he don't slow down. He better be careful around Halloween, his cell buddies might think he's a pumpkin and try 'n carve him up." The prisoner narrowed his eyes with disapproval. "Catch ya later, James," George said as he grabbed the cuffed arms of the prisoner. "Come on, Jeffery, you might still be able to get a lunch tray." With that, George led him away.

James screwed the cap back on his water bottle and started back down the hill to the Courthouse.

Barry was cutting across the parking lot when he saw James. "You all right? You missed a great burger. Don't get too close. I figured I was done work for the day, so I doubled the onions."

"I'm just going to make sure the Courtroom is ready for tomorrow, then head on home." James backed up pretending Barry's onion-breath hit him like a ton of bricks. "Go on home if you like; it's only going to take me a few minutes, then I'm going home myself."

They continued along the sidewalk. "Anything going on tonight?" asked Barry.

"Not that I know of," James replied.

"Then I'll see you for coffee in the morning," said Barry as he cut to the right, continuing down the hill. James went left into the Courthouse.

The climb up the stairs to the second floor seemed long and steep, and the doors to the Courtroom big and heavy. He looked at his watch. It was already 1:55. He figured it would take him about a half hour to clean and lock up. After checking the jury room and collecting a couple of empty soda cans and several pages of a want-to-be artist's doodles, he crossed the hallway to the Courtroom. Once inside, he looked around, but nothing was out of place. Since there would be no afternoon session, the Clerk had taken all her paperwork back to her office. It was actually pretty clean so he saw no reason to stick around.

As James turned toward the door, he caught sight of Marnie sitting in the back row. He'd forgotten she said she was going to stop by after her lunch with Annie.

"I didn't notice you come in. How long have you been sitting there?" He stared into her eyes.

"Only about five minutes; you were in deep thought, so I waited until whatever you were sorting out was finished."

They moved into the hallway. He locked up the Courtroom. Marnie took a seat on one of the benches and patted her hand beside her, expecting James to sit down. "My meeting with Annie was very productive, not to mention we ate too much for lunch."

He liked her spunky attitude.

"She's set up a meeting for me with the District Attorney. I believe his name is Michael Sullivan. Seems Barry told her my dad was an Assistant DA on Long Island before he went into private practice. I don't think you even knew that. Anyway, there's more, but this isn't the time or the place. Are you done for the day?" Marnie was fidgety and spoke non-stop without taking a breath between sentences. "Is Nancy's still open?"

"No, she closes up shop at noontime. But, if you want to go for coffee, we can go to the Dunkin Donuts in Hyannis," James said. "So, daddy's little girl wants to follow in his footsteps."

"Yes and no." She hesitated, then continued, "He just has his career to keep him company and I want my career, but I want the company, too. His law practice is his whole life: boxed and wrapped up with pages from law journals and clients' files. If I hadn't told him I was taking a mini-vacation to visit Barry, he probably wouldn't have noticed I was gone. And truthfully, he may not have listened to what I said and thinks I'm basking in the sun at Jones Beach." Marnie was troubled at the recollection of her last meeting with her father before leaving New York. She let out a big sigh, rolled her head around, and said, "Okay, where were we? Oh yeah … I'm so excited, and I admit, a little scared. I think I'm going to burst if I don't tell someone." Marnie's emotions were running wild. "Let's go."

She headed down the stairs with James following close behind. Marnie hummed some tune as they crossed the parking lot. When they reached the car, he popped open the truck and pulled out a neatly folded white jersey. "I'm just going to run back up to the Courthouse and change shirts. I'll be right back." He turned the car on so Marnie could open the windows and listen to the radio for the few minutes he'd be gone.

He hurried back to the Courthouse, hoping not to bump into anyone before he reached the men's room. The corridor was empty and, fortunately, so was the men's room. He splashed cold water on his face, switched shirts and combed his hair. He didn't want to take much time, but couldn't help a short glance of approval as he walked past the row of mirrors. Giving himself a nod, he dashed back down the corridor toward the exit door. Even from a distance, he could see Marnie snapping her fingers and shaking her shoulders to the beat of the music.

When he opened the door, she turned down the volume on the radio. "Wow, aren't you the quick change artist."

"I'm ordering you decaf. Caffeine's going to put you right over the top. Strap yourself in, we're on our way."

CHAPTER EIGHTEEN

They pulled out of the parking lot onto Main Street. He wondered where all this was going. He liked her … her enthusiasm, her spark, her love of adventure. She was cute, no, more … down- right pretty.

We really make a good-looking couple.

"Annie took me to a local spot for lunch today." Marnie's voice penetrated James' thoughts. "It was different, but fun. I knew the food must be good when we walked in because it was crowded. We had to write down our own order and give it to the guy behind the register. She told me he was Bert, the owner. He was tall and lanky with a head of gray hair in need of a trim. He probably shaved yesterday judging from the five o'clock shadow. But his white dress shirt, with the sleeves rolled up twice, and permanently creased jeans were neat as a pin. I would never have pegged him for the owner. He's quite a character. If you took too long to decide, he'd hurry you along. He told me he didn't have all day, so to make up my mind." James chuckled as she continued, "Then we got our own drink. I had root beer. The best part was we had to clean up our table, even wipe it off, before we left. Bert's Back Yard is definitely on my save list."

They pulled into Dunkins just as Marnie finished her story. She looked around. For a minute James forgot she was new to the Cape. He watched her head turned from side to side, her eyes

60

opening and closing like the shutter of a camera. She was storing her personal Kodak moments in her mind's photo album.

James pulled into an empty parking space right in front. "Since it's the middle of the afternoon, it should be pretty quiet inside." He unbuckled his seat belt, opened the car door, and slid out. Marnie did the same and joined him in front of the car. They headed inside and walked up to the counter.

Marnie tilted her head back to read the sign listing the types of coffee available. "I don't think I want anything hot. Have you had their iced latte?" Before James could answer Marnie spoke again, "Actually, I think I'll have the caramel flavored iced latte. Between the caffeine and the sugar syrup, I should be good for the night."

James nodded his head in agreement and placed the order with the young girl behind the counter, "Two medium, caramel flavored iced lattes, please."

He noticed another young girl, who was filling the donut shelves, turn toward him. She seemed to have a brief moment of recognition. He didn't know her. He passed it off as a case of mistaken identity. It was the same kind of glance that led to his affair with Becky. Those days were gone.

Marnie picked out a table away from the counter where they could talk without being overheard. She watched as James picked up the lattes and headed toward her.

"Okay, let me figure out where to start." She took a sip. "Yum, these are great. They remind me of a little sweet shop in New York down the street from my father's office. It's called Seductive Sensations." She caught the look on James' face. "What, you don't believe me? I'm not kidding, that's their name. Their caramel iced latte is Touch Me Taffy and their plain coffee iced latte is Beans to the Bone. It's a yuppie upscale neighborhood. What can I say?"

James had never been any further than Boston and then only to visit the Museum of Science on a freshman class trip back in 1993. His whole life had been spent between Plymouth and Cape Cod.

"Like I said earlier, Annie set up a meeting with her boss. It's for this Friday at 10:00 am. While I was in school, I did some investigative work for my father's firm. It was interesting and I have to admit, I was pretty good at it."

James leaned forward on his elbows. "I bet you were. So, Miss Super Sleuth, tell me more."

"Don't burst my bubble, let me talk." She continued, "Anyway, there's a possibility I can do the same thing for the Barnstable DA's office as I did in New York, at least until I take the bar exam. This way I'll be able to work in the legal field and get acquainted with the dos and don'ts of the territory. What do you think?" Marnie looked at James for approval.

"I think you, Miss Marnie Levine, are here to stay. Let me be the first to officially welcome you and help you find a place of honor in the sand to leave your footprint."

She was reassured by his response. She was more and more confident that she had made the right decision.

"Things have moved much faster than I expected, but time stands still for no one. I have to discover myself. In New York, I was being stifled by an image that wasn't me. I need someplace to breathe where the air is clear and I don't have to worry about peeking around a corner before turning it." James' puzzled look concerned Marnie. "Do you understand where I'm coming from?"

"I think so," he said as he took a long slow sip from his straw, even though he really wasn't sure.

There was a short pause. Marnie thought she may have said too much. She could see he was trying to figure out what she was talking about.

He broke the silence. "So what's next on the agenda?"

"Tomorrow I'm going to check out the real estate rental ads in the paper. I don't know the area so I could use a little help. I haven't had a chance to talk to Barry yet, but I know between the two of you and Annie, of course, I can't go wrong. Maybe I can meet you guys for lunch and show you the interesting ones I found."

"Since the Judge recessed early today, he'll probably adhere to a strict one hour for lunch tomorrow. Why don't we meet you at Scoops? I'll show you where it is on the way back to Barry's place. We should be there about 12:05. If you get there a little before noon, you'll be able to get a table. Any later than that we might be out of luck."

James finished his latte. He looked over at Marnie's empty cup and asked, "You about ready?"

She crumbled up her napkin and stuffed it inside. "All done," she said.

It was almost 4:30 when they started back toward the Village.

Marnie spoke first, "I think I'll sit down tonight and figure out a timeline. If I can put this altogether by Saturday, or at least have some of it in place, I'll head back to New York on Sunday. Usually I don't sweat the details, but since I'd like to get settled in as soon as possible, I need to make some lists." Marnie took a deep breath. "I'm sure Barry won't mind if I order in tonight. Maybe he'll join me and, of course, you're welcome, too."

"Thanks for the offer, but I'll take a rain check This is a good time for me to catch up on some housekeeping duties." He glanced at Marnie for her approval. He wasn't quite sure she'd heard him. She didn't say anything. Instead, she was looking out the side window studying all the little houses they passed. "Besides," he kept on talking, "I think I'm in for a busy few days, so I better get my beauty rest now."

She smiled and said, "You have no idea what you're in for."

They pulled into the driveway at Barry's condo. James put the car in park, but kept the motor running. "I'll be home all night, so if you feel like talking give me a call. Otherwise, write your lists and I'll see you tomorrow around 12:05 at Scoops." He reached over and squeezed her hand, then turned and gave her a little kiss on the cheek.

"Thanks for your support, I really appreciate it." She gave him a quick hug then opened the car door and scooted out.

He pushed the button to open the passenger window. "Don't forget the honey-do list," he called to her as she stood searching for her key. She turned and made a throwing gesture with her empty hand.

CHAPTER NINETEEN

James drove the twenty minute ride home with a smile on his face. It had been years since he'd felt this good. Years, he thought, actually maybe never. He'd only known Marnie for three days. It sure seemed longer. She was absolutely perfect in so many ways. He found himself looking forward to her idle chit-chat and listening to her daydreams. He liked to think he'd made an appearance in those daydreams and eventually become a permanent character.

His neighborhood was quiet. It always was. He pulled into his driveway and stopped before he reached the garage. He sat and looked around. Since he had moved back some 14 years ago, there was a cloud hanging over his house. It was a haunting reminder of his past – of how his childhood had been taken from him. His memories after the age of seven were non-existent. When he moved back to Sandwich, he went from seven to eighteen, with all years in between lost somewhere in time. He put up a good front, all the while hurting inside. At first his neighbors were overly sympathetic, then figuring he'd moved on with his life, treated him no differently than anyone else. This is what he wanted to happen. He didn't want to be singled out and watched over like a hawk watches a mouse. For the last four years, he tried to experience what he'd missed. What a mistake that was. He wasn't eighteen anymore, but the girls were. Some were even younger. That was over now.

The red geraniums smiled at him. The grass looked as if it had been spray-painted green. Even the pine needles seemed strong and healthy – sporting a reddish-brown hue. His yard was alive with color ... alive with life. As he pulled into the garage, he thought he heard laughter. He laid his head back against the headrest and closed his eyes. It felt good. The imaginary laughter sounded even better. He really was back home. A couple of tears rolled down his cheeks. He reached up and wiped them away. He glanced at himself in the rear-view mirror. "Life is meant to be lived and it's time I start doing just that."

"I'm home," he announced to an empty house. He searched his CD's and found the James Taylor album that had *Sweet Baby James* on it. The volume had been turned down low the last time he'd used the player, so he reached over to turn it up. "There, now I can close my eyes and pretend Marnie's sitting beside me."

The clock on the fireplace mantel bonged six times. Maybe he should have taken Marnie up on that offer to join her and Barry for take-out. He wondered what they were having? He decided on Chinese food. He shuffled through some papers in one of the kitchen drawers until he found the take-out menu for Ming Gardens, then proceeded to call and order boneless spare ribs and vegetable lo mien.

He'd forgotten to get his mail on the way in, so after he ordered his food, he headed to the mailbox. There was only an electric bill and a coupon book put out by local businesses. Mings had a 10% off coupon, but dine-in only. It was good until the end of July, so maybe he'd take Marnie there some night when she got back from New York.

He realized he still had his uniform pants on. He quickly went into his bedroom to change into a pair of shorts before his food arrived.

Twenty minutes later, the doorbell rang. "I brought food to you, Mr. James." Chin, the little Chinese delivery boy, was standing in his doorway.

James' wallet was still in his pants pocket. "Hold on for a minute, I need to get some money." He returned, took the bag of food, and handed Chin a $20.00 bill. Chin started to make change, but James motioned for him to keep it.

"Thank you. Bye-bye, Mr. James," Chin said as he scurried across the lawn to his dull red Ford Escort. It never ceased to amaze James how that little red roller skate could move through the streets with the huge Ming Gardens sign strapped to its roof and not fall over on one of the turns.

He set himself up in front of the television. Most of the time he'd use a placemat and a plate, but tonight he decided to eat straight out of the box. Chinese food and beer, what more could he ask for? Well, maybe there was one more thing: Marnie to share it with him.

Ten minutes into the six o'clock evening news James turned on the TV. Vickie Roper was finishing up a story. It was nothing he was interested in, so he changed the channel. *Entertainment Hollywood* was flashing short clips of upcoming movies. One caught his eye. It was a trailer for a movie scheduled to be released in October. It was about the little girl kidnapped by a sex offender and hidden in plain sight for eighteen years, hence the title of the movie, *Hidden In Plain Sight*. He even fathered two children with her. How could something like that happen? It sent chills up his spine. His encounters with Becky weren't anything like that. They were different. The man in the movie was an animal.

I'm not.

James laid his fork down on the table and cradled his head in his hands.

"No, no, no," he said out loud. "You think I didn't care. I did. She demanded attention I couldn't give her. She wouldn't let it go. I had to cut the strings." Suddenly, he snapped his head back. His eyes wide open. He looked around the room. Nobody was there. He was talking to himself. Everything was okay.

Marnie, was she okay? James picked up his cell phone and punched in her number. It only rang twice and she answered. "Can I call you right back? My father's on the other line."

"Sure, I'll be waiting," he said and clicked off.

He cleaned up the table and returned to the couch to wait for her call.

Several minutes later, even though it seemed like hours, the phone rang. "Hi, I called my father when I got home and left a message. He just returned my call."

"Did you tell him about your plans?" James waited for a reply.

"Yeah, he was okay with them. I told him I planned on being in New York on Sunday and hoped we could have a late lunch or early dinner, whatever you want to call it. We're going to Raos Italian Restaurant. Usually you have to make a reservation a year in advance, but my dad has done some work for the owner, so he just makes a phone call. That's some of the stuff I want to get away from." She was quiet.

James detected a problem, so he changed the subject. "Do you have any rental places to check out tomorrow?"

"Actually I do," said Marnie. "Annie called earlier. It seems that somebody in her office owns a couple of rental units and two of them are available. They're in a duplex, just over the Barnstable line in Yarmouthport. She's going to call me in the morning and set up a time to go take a look. I've got my fingers crossed. It's almost too good to be true."

"Do you know the person's name?" James was smiling inside. He couldn't be happier.

"No, but I'll find out when I talk to Annie and let you know at lunchtime. Also, Annie asked me to go on a *girl's night out* this Friday. She has three tickets for the Beach Boys concert at some place called the Melody Tent."

"Leave it to Mother Annie. She'll take you under her wing and get you involved in lots of girl things." James was disappointed.

He wanted to spend time with Marnie. "You said three tickets. Who's the third one for?"

"She told me you know her. Her name is Casey. I think Annie told me her last name, but I don't remember it."

James stood up and walked to the kitchen. He cradled the phone between his head and shoulder and got a beer from the fridge. "I haven't seen her for a while. Her name is Casey Quinby. She's a reporter for the local newspaper. You'll like her." He tried to screw off the cap. It didn't budge. He wanted that beer. He took a bottle opener from the drawer.

Yes! Success! he thought to himself.

"First we're having dinner at a place called The Paddock. Annie's going to pick me up at 5:30. She's making reservations for 6:00. Casey is meeting us there."

"Annie sure knows how to pick them. You'll like The Paddock. The food, actually the whole place, is incredible." How can Marnie be so relaxed? She acts like she's been here for years, like they've known each other for years. He liked that. "Before you make any more plans, maybe I should ask you out on a date for tomorrow night. We'll talk about it at lunch tomorrow."

"Sounds good, I hope I'll be showing you my new living quarters. I'm going to pack for New York tonight, so I don't have to think about it later. That way you'll have my undivided attention."

James smiled, "See you tomorrow. Sleep tight and don't let the bed bugs bite."

"Bye, silly," she said and the phone went silent.

CHAPTER TWENTY

Both alarm clocks on the bedside table went off simultaneously. I sat up straight up. When I realized it was morning and I wasn't ready to face a new day, I fell back down and covered my head with a pillow. Just five more minutes, I thought, and I'd be good to go. It didn't work. Last night's sleep didn't generate sweet dreams, so I guess my psyche didn't want to revisit that dark uninviting cavity. I couldn't blame it, 'cause I didn't want to go there either. I rolled over and stared at the ceiling. It was already Thursday. Where did the week go?

My name is Casey Quinby. I'm an investigative reporter for the Cape Cod Tribune. In May, 2002, I graduated from the University of Massachusetts with a degree in criminal justice. Shortly after graduation, I applied for a position as a police officer in Shrewsbury, Massachusetts. I took the exam and passed with flying colors. My ultimate goal was to become a detective. Half way through the academy, while running a daily three mile run I stepped on a small rock. My forward momentum, coupled with the spin of the rock, sent me airborne. Before I realized what had happened, I was on the ground holding my leg and crying in pain. There was blood everywhere and my shin bone was piercing my skin from the inside out. The injury was serious and left permanent damage. Now, I sometimes walk with a slight limp.

Although I couldn't finish the academy, my perseverance and insight into situations made me a pretty good problem solver. This ability sparked a strong desire to be involved in a meaningful investigative profession.

Eight years ago I moved to Cape Cod. I love it here. For as many years as I can remember, Mom and Dad would pack up the family car and the three of us would venture down to Rogers's cottages on Grand Cove in West Dennis for vacation. There were five cottages clustered together on the shores of the Cove. Each of the five cottages had its own name and personality. We'd stayed in four of them, but the one that best suited us, especially me, was the *Hate to Quit It.* My dad always said I hated to quit doing something until I was absolutely sure I couldn't go any further. I grew up catching crabs, digging piss clams and scooping quahogs from the waters in front of the cottages. I wouldn't quit until I *knew* I'd found the very last clam. The family who owned the cottages came from Worcester. We lived in Shrewsbury, the next town over, so during the winter months we'd get together at our house. They had two sons – one a year older than me and one a year younger.

When I moved to the Cape, I found a little one bedroom bungalow in West Hyannisport, right near Craigville Beach. At one time it was a guest house located about a hundred feet behind the main house. Now, the new owners rent it out. It was a doll house, made just for me. It was a comfortable distance away from the main house, yet close enough to offer security.

For the first two years I lived on the Cape, I spent my time between rehab on my leg and studying journalism at Cape Cod Community College. I really got into the writing thing. I graduated with high honors, earning an Associate Degree in Journalism. At twenty-three, I knew it was time to take all my classroom experience and channel it down a meaningful path.

One morning while checking out the 'help wanted' ads, one in particular caught my eye. It was for a customer service representative with the opportunity for advancement at the Cape

71

Cod Tribune. It got me thinking. If I could marry my new degree in journalism to my degree in criminal justice, throw in a lot of dedication and hard work, maybe I could find a profession and not just a job.

That was six years ago. Now I'm a permanent fixture at the Trib, have my own office, embossed business cards, and the title of Lead Investigative Reporter.

I knew it was time to get up. "God, I'm tired. That's what I get for staying up late to watch the end of the Sox game. I hate it when they play on the west coast." That's the best part of living alone – I can talk out loud and not worry about anybody interrupting or disagreeing with me.

A cool shower, followed by a cup of steaming hot coffee, should do the trick. The shower did its job. The beating streams of water pumped new life into my body. I stood with my face tilted up, to catch all the drops the chrome waterfall had to offer. I felt my hair go silky straight, clinging helplessly to my back. I reached my arms up behind my head and flipped my hair from side to side. I could feel the ripples in my fingertips. They were pruning up – time to get a move on.

I grabbed the towel laying on the toilet seat, dried off, wrapped my hair in a turban, and threw on my new thigh-length lime-green and white striped robe.

I love walking around the house with as little on as possible. It's a feeling of freedom – nothing confining, no restraints. Again, the perks of living alone.

The coffee ... hmm, let's see.

My single brew coffee maker is the best invention ever. French vanilla, hazelnut, hearty roast, whatever I feel like having. Today I'm having French vanilla – my favorite. Damn it, I forgot to get milk yesterday, so no cereal this morning. English muffin. The whiff of French vanilla penetrated the kitchen air. The toaster popped up. My muffin is done and ready to take on the slab of butter waiting to seep into its nooks and crannies.

I finished my breakfast, put my dishes in the sink, and made myself another coffee. My kitchen shares the function of home office and the table doubles as a desk. This would be a good time to review my notes. It had been a tough week. Last Sunday night, I was called in to work at 8:51 to cover a story about an accident on the Scenic Highway in Bourne. I remember the exact time because when the phone rang I glanced at my watch wondering who would call me just when *CSI Miami* was revealing the identity of who murdered the detective's wife. It was a repeat from last year, but I hadn't seen it. Now, I'd have to wait for it to be repeated again.

As I took the notes from my briefcase, I remembered the accident scene. It was almost too perfect – like it had been staged. It was definitely a hit-and-run. I watched the homicide division secure the area. They measured and re-measured. They took pictures. They wrote notes. I wanted to read them. I had a good rapport with most of the Police Departments on the Cape. On other cases, they actually asked for my help in investigating clues that weren't *cookie cutter* by design.

I had wanted to view the body, but knew that wasn't going to happen. I had sized up the area. The moon was covered with a haze so distant observations were just that, distant and unclear. I had no idea why I was being kept behind the yellow crime scene tape. I was sharing space with common on-lookers. Something was wrong.

It was a dry night and according to the earlier weather forecast, there was no rain in sight. I had my camera with me. I always had it close by. I snapped a few pictures using the zoom lens. Nothing was clear except the butts and crotches of the officers bending over to pick up something and put it into an evidence bag.

If this was a random *oops-I-took-my-eyes-off the road* accident, then I should have been able to see some skid marks. There weren't any. At least none I could see or any the PD were interested in. Skid marks don't go away easily. I knew I'd be back Monday morning to check closer.

73

After standing around for almost two hours, I knew my efforts to get any information were fruitless, so I headed home.

That was Sunday night.

CHAPTER TWENTY-ONE

Monday I got up early, dressed for an outside-the-office day, and headed to Bourne. I wanted to get an early start. I needed to get to the accident scene before it changed too much. Last night, nobody would give me the time of day. Maybe today, if anybody is there, they'll share with me.

I didn't bother making breakfast, not even coffee. Instead I stopped at the White Chicken Pantry, grabbed a cup of watery, weak coffee and a prepackaged sweet bun. My cell phone was ringing when I opened the car door. I tried the balancing act and lost the coffee in the process. The paper cup was rolling aimlessly around on the ground. My efforts to catch it before it became totally out of reach under the car, were useless. Naturally, I missed the call. I tossed the pastry on the passenger seat and proceeded to retrieve my voice message.

It was Jeff from the office. He's the junior reporter I assigned to write a short rendition of the accident last night. He was there with me. I coached him on what he should include in his piece – only the facts as we knew them. There weren't many. He had, however, found out the victim's name and address. The victim was a female. She was sixteen years old. Her name was Rebecca "Becky" Morgan and she was from Bourne.

I called Jeff back. "Hi, it's Casey." I said. "Thanks for the information about the victim."

"Have you seen the morning paper?" Jeff asked.

"No, I haven't. I'm at the White Chicken, so when I get off the phone, I'll grab a copy. If I need to talk to you immediately, I'll give you a call back. Otherwise, I'll talk to you later."

I went back into the Pantry. It was early so there were lots of copies on the newsstand. Since my coffee was now part of the pavement and I certainly didn't want another, I reached into the cooler for a chocolate milk. I paid the clerk and again headed for my car. There was a maple tree shading the spaces on the side of the parking lot, so I backed out from where I was and pulled into the first one under the tree. The story didn't make the front page. The Tribune had done that on purpose. The front page would be reserved for a feature length article as soon as we had something concrete to report.

I took one bite of the stale, tasteless pastry and washed it down the some milk. I finished my chocolate milk and left the rest of the pastry on the seat until I found a place to dispose of it.

I turned to the second page. Ah, there it was – A short, slightly informative article on the accident. Jeff had done his job.

Now it was my turn to do mine.

Jeff had given me Becky's home address. It didn't ring a bell.

Normally, my first stop of the day would be the PD in the town involved in the story I was working on. They would give me directions. Today, however, was different. My GPS was in the glove compartment. It would give me directions.

My first order of business was to ride by Becky's house, make observations, take notes, and, of course, snap some pictures. I had to be discreet, and not draw any unwanted attention. According to the GPS, the estimated time of arrival to 259 Dog Leg Drive in Bourne was 9:54 am. I checked my watch. It was 9:22, so it would take about thirty minutes.

The traffic was slow, so it actually took me almost forty minutes. Dog Leg Drive was located in an older sub-division probably built twenty years ago. It consisted of well-maintained single family homes, a mixture of one floor ranches and two story capes. The rhododendrons were in full bloom and the irises were standing tall, guarding the streets from unwanted snoopers like me.

I studied the surroundings. They were warm and inviting, but something was odd. Nothing was moving, not a dog, cat, or even a person.

I slowed down as I came to number 259. There were a couple of cars in the driveway, but no signs of life. My heart felt heavy. There weren't even any nosey slimy reporters milling around. It was eerily quiet, as if time had stopped. This wasn't the time to take pictures. My mental images would be my camera and I would process them later.

I rode around the neighborhood, twice. Nothing changed.

My next stop was the accident scene on the Scenic Highway. Last night everything had been hidden in the dark. Today, maybe, I could find some key puzzle pieces.

The yellow police tape was still lying on the ground surrounding the scene. Someday the town maintenance crew will be by to clean it up. I walked over to where the body had been. Which way was Becky positioned? Was she face down or looking straight up? She was about ten feet in from the side shoulder. If she was hit from behind, she probably didn't see it coming. If she turned, she may have tried to get further in, away from the road. Either way, she was dead. No matter what she may have tried to do, it didn't work.

There were a lot of footprints, but no skid marks. There were tire prints, but those could have been made by police vehicles. My gut instinct was that this was a clean shot. Calculated and executed to perfection. I closed my eyes to imagine the darkness and experience the helplessness to change the inevitable. This was no accident.

There was a fair amount of traffic this morning, so I had to be careful crossing the street to retrieve my camera from the car. I studied the different angles the route of an approaching car might have taken. This was a two-lane highway with no center divider, so the car could have actually come from either direction. In all probability, it came up behind Becky, traveling on the same side she was walking. That would allow the driver to carry out the mission far more smoothly than veering across the road, hitting her, then, regaining control as if nothing had happened.

I took enough pictures to fill a small album. I always did. I'd print them at home, then study them looking for clues. I was good at what I did, but this one was going to test my abilities. Everything I ever learned from books and the skills I acquired working cases was going to be brought into the equation to solve this one.

It was almost noon and I was hungry, so I stopped at Manny's Fish Market to pick up a lobster roll and diet root beer. The Canal bike path parking lot was just around the corner. It was about half full of cars with empty bicycle racks. There was a nice breeze, making it a beautiful day for a bike ride. This was also a popular tourist spot for sight-seeing along the canal so, I was surprised it wasn't busier.

I pulled into a space overlooking the Canal. The water was so blue and calm. The boats glided effortlessly along leaving a perfect geometric-shaped spray behind them. I needed a break to clear my head. I finished my lobster roll, reviewed my crime scene pictures, then decided to head home.

CHAPTER TWENTY-TWO

I spent a half day at the office on Tuesday.

Laying the pictures out on my desk, in no particular order, I shuffled them around. I was trying to create a panoramic view of the scene. My notes were sparse. I had to talk to someone at the Bourne PD. Since a couple days had passed, maybe I could get a few answers or at least find out why they wouldn't talk to me.

I closed my office door and looked up the Bourne PD phone number on my rolodex. My friend Peggy answered the phone.

"Mornin', Miss Peggy," I said, trying to sound upbeat. "It's me. I need your help."

"I've been waiting for your call," answered Peggy. She sounded cautious. "I know why you're calling, and there's not much I can tell you."

"Peggy, all I need is a why. Why is the Becky Morgan accident so hush-hush?" I stopped to listen, but there was no response. I continued, "I don't think it is an accident."

"Neither do the guys." Peggy's voice was almost a whisper. "I'm not supposed to talk about it to anyone, not just you, no one."

I knew if I could talk to Peggy face-to-face she'd open up a little and that's all I needed to get started. "I've got an idea," I said. "Can you meet me for lunch? We can go to Barney's." I waited for her reply.

"Yes, I guess I could. How about 1:00. That will give you a little over an hour to get here. Since that's my normal lunch time, I won't draw any undue attention." Peggy's voice was anxious. I know she had something for me.

Knowing I wouldn't be returning to the office, so I gathered up my notes, pictures, doodles, and my camera. I stuffed them into my briefcase, and headed for the door. This could be my big break and I wasn't about to be late.

Thank God for air conditioning. It was hot. It took awhile for the cool air to start settling in. I love summer, but oh man, this one is a doozie. As I drove toward the mid-Cape highway, I tried to piece my thoughts together, hoping to make sense of the morning's puzzle. It was all fragmented. Nothing flowed in the same direction.

The parking lot at Barney's was only half full.

Good, maybe I can find an out of the way table so we can speak more freely than we were able to earlier on the phone.

I didn't see Peggy's car, but that was okay. I was about fifteen minutes early. I went inside and headed for the back of the dining room. There was a square four-seater against the back wall, out of ear shot from the bartender and the girl selling tickets at the lottery booth – both had four sets of ears pointed in every direction you could imagine. I swear they had both bought one of those across-the-room sound amplifiers from the TV infomercial on Game Show Network. If I had one of those gadgets on Sunday night at the accident scene, I wouldn't be groping around for information now. I would have heard it first-hand from one of the Bourne detectives.

The waitress crossed the room with a menu. "We'll need another one, please." As she turned toward the bar to retrieve one, I saw Peggy coming through the side door. I raised my hand to let her know where I was sitting. She looked around, then headed in my direction.

"Hi," she said as she set her purse on the empty chair beside her. "Good choice of tables."

The waitress returned with the other menu and asked for our drink order. We each got a Diet Coke.

"I think I'm going to have a clam roll with fries and slaw," I said to Peggy as I laid the menu down at the edge of the table.

Peggy was still deciding when the waitress came back with our drinks, ready to take the order. I ordered. She looked toward Peggy. "Guess it's my turn. Let's see. I'll have the same thing, only instead of fries, I'll take the onion rings. Could I please have some extra tartar sauce too? Thanks."

I cut right to the chase. "What in the world is going on with the Becky Morgan case?"

Peggy looked me straight in the eyes and shook her head. "This is a real tough one. The guys back at the office are having a lot of closed-door meetings. They are being real tight-lipped. Even the files are locked up in Sam's office."

For the files to be in the chief of detective's office was not normal. But then, I'm finding this whole case to be far from normal.

"On the phone I said I didn't think this was an accident and you kind of agreed with me. You said the guys didn't think so either."

"Casey, believe me, I tried to find out what was going on before I left. I had to be very discreet. If they knew I was meeting you, I'd lose all credibility. They know we're friends and that I've helped you out in the past. But that's just it. In the past, I knew it was okay to give you information. This time they aren't even sharing anything with those of us in the office." Peggy sighed.

"Wow, I wonder if one of their own might be involved and they need to keep things under wraps until they can actually prove or disprove it. Theory and misdirected facts can be devastating if they fell into the wrong hands." My mind was spinning. I was envisioning all sorts of scenarios – some not so good.

Peggy reached up behind her neck and stretched her head back. "That's my interpretation too."

I leaned forward, resting my elbows on the table and cradling my chin in the palm of my hands. I looked over at Peggy trying to think out loud, but nothing came out.

"There is one thing that may or may not be relevant. Just remember, it didn't come from me. They think a dark-colored, late-model car might be involved. I'm not sure why, but I did hear one of the guys talking about it. I wasn't supposed to be within earshot, but I had walked into the break room to get a cup of coffee and they didn't see me. As soon as they did, they changed the subject. That's when I figured they were talking about Becky's case."

So far it wasn't much information, but it was more than I had before. "A dark-colored, late-model car could be ...." I stopped when I saw the waitress come through the kitchen door and head toward our table with our tray of food. Peggy's back was facing the kitchen door, so I gave her a slight nod and motioned with my eyes in that direction.

We took a break to scoff down some of those tasty little morsels – hot and crunchy with a dab of tartar sauce. I gave Peggy some of my fries and took a few of her onion rings. We made small talk while we ate, catching up on the social gossip in the department. Peggy and I had both dated police officers from Bourne PD, but decided their high maintenance wasn't for us. That was five years ago and we've been friends ever since. Actually, both of the guys moved on and were now on the State Police Force stationed in the western part of the state. Since then, I've been dating Peggy's boss, Sam, off and on.

We were about done when the waitress came over with two more Diet Cokes. She took our plates and we began brainstorming again.

"Do you think they have a witness to the accident or a local that saw something out of the ordinary?"

"A witness? I don't think so. You may be right about a local though." Peggy seemed hard at work trying to tie together bits and pieces of conversations she'd heard at the office. It wasn't working. "I'm really sorry that I can't give you more. I just don't have anything. I can tell you that the Morgan family was well-respected and highly-involved in the community. They were always volunteering for various functions like the Scallop Festival and the Road Race – just to name a couple. I remember one Fourth of July, last year to be exact, Becky was crowned Miss Teenage Bourne 2010. If I close my eyes, I can see her smiling and waving as she rode through town on the lead float in the holiday parade. She was a beautiful young girl."

"Wait a minute," Peggy's face lit up. "Do you remember Mr. Parker, the guy who lives on the Scenic Highway in that rickety weather-worn house with two old lobster boats on one side and a broken down Chevy on the other?"

"Yeah, what about him?" I said. "If I remember correctly, he stuck his nose into everybody's business. And no matter what time of day or night you went by his house he was sitting in a rocking chair watching every bit of movement around. It was spooky – like Anthony Perkins' mother in Psycho."

"Well, listen to this." Peggy was sitting on the edge of her chair and leaning in my direction. "He came into the office yesterday. I didn't think anything of it. He's come in many times before with goofy stories about non-existent problems. The guys would always pacify him, take a report, and then send him on his way. Yesterday, they brought him into Sam's office and shut the door. He was in there for a good hour. His arms were flying about indicating some sort of direction. Two of the POs were sitting on the desk, one to his left and one to his right, listening   very intently."

"Peggy, do you think this has something to do with Becky's case?"

"Think about it." Peggy grimaced as she stared into my eyes. "He lives right around the corner from the accident, or should I say, the scene of the crime. Do you catch my drift?"

It slapped me up-side of my face. "Peggy, you may have stumbled onto something big. My original question still remains though." I continued, "Why is this all being kept so quiet?"

Peggy shrugged her shoulders. She glanced at her watch. "It's 2:15. I've got to get going.

I knew Peggy was worried about the guys finding out they'd had lunch.

"You're right. I'm going to drive by Mr. Parker's house and use my imagination. If I'm able, I'll snap some pictures of the area. I don't want the old buzzard to see me. He might jump in his pick-up and truck on down to the PD with another story – one that includes me."

We laughed, even though we both knew it was no laughing matter.

We paid our bills, I bought a lottery ticket, and we headed for the parking lot.

"You going to be home tonight?" I asked.

"I've got to stop at the market, then I should be home the rest of the night. I've gotten caught up in that *America's Got Talent* television show. I don't know where people get the nerve to parade themselves in front of millions with a talent like hanging stuff from body piercings or diving thirty-five feet into a kid's wading pool. Crazy, if you ask me."

I grinned and turned toward my car. "Talk to you later. Don't forget to keep that sixth sense working."

"Always," replied Peggy as she closed her car door.

I got into my car and sat for a moment. What had caused Mr. Parker to sit up and take notice? Notice enough to make a trip to the PD with a story that brought him into Sam's office with the door closed.

I pulled out of Barney's lot and headed east. When I reached the Scenic Highway, I slowed down and rounded the curve just before the accident scene. The yellow tape was still there, lying limp and ribbon-like along the ground. The memorial service was being held tomorrow. I hope it will be gone by then. I continued on less than a quarter of a mile around another small bend and bingo – there it was – Mr. Parker's house and the famous Mr. Parker rocking back and forth on his front porch watching me as I rode by. I contemplated turning around and retracing my route, but thought better of it.

I decided to head on home. I'd rather be wearing a pair of cut-off jeans, drinking a glass of white zinfandel with ice, and sitting on my back deck than cooped up in the office. Besides, I do my best thinking when I'm alone and totally relaxed.

CHAPTER TWENTY-THREE

It was still hot and muggy, but my deck was on the east side of the cottage and shaded by a beautiful big maple tree, so it was bearable. Last spring I purchased a new table and chairs, with puffy, comfortable cushions. I call it my outdoor office. Settled in, I opened my briefcase and pulled out the notes, pictures and doodles I had taken from the office earlier.

I laid out the pictures I took yesterday at the accident scene. I froze. Mr. Parker … did he see me scrutinizing the scene? I was there a long time. My mind raced to the sight and Peggy's mention of a dark, late-model car.

No, no, shake it off girl. First of all you don't have a dark-colored car, it's light green and second, it's almost eight years old. And, he can't see the actual scene from his porch. I was starting to let that old buzzard Parker creep under my skin. As near as Peggy and I could figure out, Mr. Parker was talking about the night of the accident, not the next day.

I took a long sip of my white zin, leaned back against the cushion, and tried to focus on the task at hand. Hmm, Mr. Parker didn't see me yesterday because I didn't drive by his house. He may have remembered my car, a 2003 light green Mazda Spider convertible, if I had driven by more than once within an hour's time, but I didn't. I came in from the other direction and retraced my route when I left. Good job Casey. I reached behind my shoulder and patted myself on the back.

Let's exam the doodles.

There was a time, I could paint still-life or abstract or landscape and really wasn't half bad. I was, however, never very good at detail drawing. But as I've honed my investigative career, my stick figures, fuzzy bushes, primitive structures, and arrows for direction were, in my eyes, works of art that helped me put meaning to a particular situation. They were my way of recreating a crime scene and it worked more times than not.

The only bit of information I had to go on was the car and Mr. Parker. And truthfully, neither may be of any value, but it was a start.

I was on my second glass of wine when my cell phone rang. I looked at the caller ID and saw Peggy's name. "Hey hi," I said as I glanced at my watch. "Wow, I didn't realize how long I've been sitting here."

"When I got back to the office there was a big pow-wow going on in Sam's office. Again, I wasn't privy to any of the conversation, but he was pretty animated. His arms were doing the talking and he was pacing back and forth."

"I wish you had been a fly on the wall. Something out of the ordinary is going on here. We know that. The question is 'what' and I aim to find out. How, I'm not yet sure, but I'll do it."

"Casey, please be careful. This may be something you need to stay clear of. I'll keep my eyes and ears open for you. By the way, are you going to the memorial service tomorrow?

"Yes, I thought I'd go." said Casey.

Most of the guys are going. I can't because I have to stay in the office. I'd keep my distance from them if I were you. Give them time and they may come through for you. They've valued your opinion and help in the past. After whatever is keeping this case under wraps unfolds, I think they'll include you again."

"I hope so. This one is really eating at me. I'll call you tomorrow, when I get clear of the church. "Later," I said and pressed the end button.

A gentle breeze kicked up. It felt good. I didn't know if it was the breeze or the wine, but I was completely relaxed. A couple of my pictures gently moved across the table interrupting the sequence of the scene. The sun was starting to slide down behind the treetops. I took a deep breath through my nose. Even though I lived a half mile from the ocean, the smell of the salt water penetrated the air.

I put the pictures back in order, collected all the paperwork and slipped everything back into my briefcase. Tomorrow would be another day.

CHAPTER TWENTY-FOUR

I had a hard time falling asleep last night. So much so that I got up around two am, started to watch a movie, and ended up snoozing on the couch before it was over.

I wasn't looking forward to the events of the afternoon. The memorial service was scheduled to begin at two o'clock. I decided to work from home and head toward Bourne around one. That should get me there a half-hour early. I called the office and asked Jamie to intercept my calls. I told her I'd call later to see if there were any of importance. Since this was the only story I was working on, I didn't expect the phone to be ringing off the wall. She said she'd call my cell if she needed me. I did remind her about the service for Becky and I'd have my cell shut off for a couple of hours, but would check it when I left the church.

I slipped into some jeans and a tee and made myself a cup of hearty robust. The fancy flavors just didn't sound appealing. I laid my notes out across the table. Usually at this point in a story, I've got it half written. Not this time. I settled into the chair with one leg tucked under me, leaned back and lifted up my coffee with both hands. I took a sip, but didn't really taste it.

Moments like this frustrate me.

Time passed and I was still in the same position. I'd finished my coffee and was leaning forward, resting on my elbows and re-

reading my notes for the hundredth time. I had an idea. It was far-fetched, but I had nothing to lose.

Peggy thinks Mr. Parker said something about a dark-colored, late-model car. Before the service, I'm going to peruse the parking lot. If, in fact, a vehicle of this description was involved, there should be some marks indicating contact somewhere on the front half of the car. I would have to make sure nobody was around to question what I was doing. It was a stretch. Why would a hit-and-run driver, a murderer, attend his or her victim's service? There are strange people walking around out there. Unfortunately, it happens far too often. Maybe he or she wants to make sure the intended victim actually died.

My journey into space was interrupted when the numbers on the digital stove clock changed. I must have been staring right at them. I jumped. When I tried to stand up, my left leg almost collapsed under me. I sat on it so long, it had fallen asleep. It's my bad leg and, every once in a while, it reminds me why I didn't become a full-fledged detective. It took some rubbing, but it finally came around. I shook my head, disgusted with myself.

My go-to-interview or funeral-suit was too heavy to wear, so I decided a dark brown, tailored shirt dress would be appropriate. My brown and cream colored purse matched perfectly. It also was big enough to conceal a notebook, several pens and my camera. Even though I didn't intend to use the camera, I always carried it with me.

I showered and got half dressed. I'll wait until I'm about ready to leave before I put my dress on. It was almost noon when I walked back into the kitchen. I was a little hungry. There wasn't much in the fridge. I hadn't been shopping yet this week. I opened the cupboard and gathered up the makings for a fluffernutter sandwich. I was so excited when somebody, I can't remember who, proposed this wonderful example of comfort food as the official Massachusetts state sandwich. When I was a little kid, the combination of peanut butter and marshmallow crème on soft, squishy white bread always made me feel better. It was our go-to food when things seemed out of kilter.

Wait a minute, a little kid – Becky was only sixteen. To me she was still a little kid. Now I had a new question. What would cause someone to commit such a violent crime on a little kid? Was she having trouble at school? But school was out for the summer. It appeared she came from a quiet neighborhood – a very quiet neighborhood. Anything out of the ordinary would have been noticed. Why was she walking alone in the dark on an uninhabited stretch of road? Maybe she wasn't alone. Maybe somebody dropped her off there. Maybe it was her killer.

I was coming up with too many maybes. It's like all of a sudden my mind kicked in. I wrote all my new questions down. I didn't have time to dissect them before I had to finish getting ready.

CHAPTER TWENTY-FIVE

It was just before one o'clock when I pulled out of my driveway. The traffic wasn't bad, so I got to the church ahead of schedule. There were already a lot of cars in the lot. I parked way in the back, so I could zigzag my way to the front without drawing attention. About half way up on the right side there were about six late-model dark cars all parked together. I could eliminate them because they were all unmarked cruisers. I assumed they were from the Bourne PD. Apparently, the people connected to them were already inside. That was a good thing, because I didn't want to bump into any of the guys in an open area where they could ask me what I was doing there.

I moved to the other side and weaved between a red Corvette and a white Camaro convertible. Nice cars, I thought. Beside them were a dark blue VW, a dirty gray Mazda Tribute and a spit-shined and polished black Beamer. I glanced at the VW and the Beamer, but they appeared to be fine. I continued my quest. There were a few I checked out more than others, but nothing seemed out of place or in need of front end body work.

The lot started to fill up, so I decided I'd better end my scavenger hunt and go inside. I wanted to sit in the back, so I could observe the attendees and not have them observe me. I managed to get a seat on the aisle five rows from the back.

What a beautiful church. The sunlight shimmered through the stained glass windows making the figures come to life. It appeared as though they were escorting the people as they walked up the aisles. The music was upbeat. It was fitting for a celebration of life, rather than a recognition of death. I noticed two empty sections in the front. I figured one was for family and close friends, but unsure who'd occupy the other.

The chimes in the bell tower began to ring. It was a call for those still outside to come in. Nobody, including me, wants to hurry into a memorial service, especially one being held under these circumstances. Suddenly, it was quiet. The chimes had stopped and nobody said a word. You could hear a pin drop.

The silence was broken by a rustling from the back of the church. I didn't want to seem overly inquisitive, so I waited until others around me turned to observe the processional forming in the doorway. The music started up again. My heart started pounding and tears formed in my eyes as I watched eleven young girls clad in purple and white cheerleader uniforms pass by me. I assumed Becky was the twelfth. Behind them were eight adults. I recognized only one, the Bourne Chief of Police, Peter Sutton. I assumed the group following them was Becky's family. And finally, were representatives from the Bourne Police Department, some in uniform and others in black suits.

I've attended several police funerals. I never thought anything could be more moving than those. I was wrong. This was a whole new experience. One I never will forget, and hopefully under no circumstances, will have to attend again.

The eulogy was a cheerful, positive account of her short life. The priest, who had known her since birth, recalled a story of her as a small child with pigtails and pink, patent leather shoes. She won the hearts of all the parishioners the Sunday morning she slipped out of the pew, ran to the front of the church, and stopped abruptly in front of the statue of Jesus. She looked up and in a tiny, but very loud voice said, *Good morning God*. Then, just as quickly, she turned and ran back to her embarrassed mother who stood half way up the aisle smiling and shaking her head.

More stories followed, each one just as entertaining.

Several others took a place behind the pulpit and shared stories of Becky Morgan's life. All of which brought a chuckle from the congregation.

I was a stranger when I entered Our Lady of the Highway. When I left and walked toward the parking lot, I felt like I lost a friend. My quest to find Becky's killer was now stronger than ever.

"Hey Casey," came a call from behind me.

I turned to see Sam all decked out in his dress uniform. I didn't see him inside the church. I guess I wasn't really focused on the PD.

"Afternoon, Sam," I said kind of looking away.

"What are you doing here?" His stare went straight through me. "Please tell me you know the Morgans and you weren't here as a reporter."

"I know them now, at least enough to feel their pain." I turned to face him directly. "You shut me out. I'm not sure why, but I'll find out in due time. You left me no choice, but to investigate any way I can." Sam and I had a history together. We shared an on-again, off-again relationship. Right now, it was hovering somewhere in the middle. He is a great guy and I respect him, both in his position in the department and as a person. I knew there was probably a good reason he couldn't confide in me, but damn it, I didn't care.

"Casey, listen to me," his face softened. "This case is a tough one. Give me a couple of days to sort things out and I'll give you a call. You know I value your help and I'm sure this time will be no exception."

I wouldn't let him shut me down. "I'm working on a couple of ideas myself. I'll continue, but I won't get in your way. Hopefully, we can brainstorm and something good will surface."

94

The parking lot was abuzz with people and I didn't want to bump into anyone else, so I said my good-byes to Sam and headed to my car. It was 3:15 when I slipped behind the steering wheel, turned the key to start the air, closed my eyes, and laid my head back against the head-rest. I couldn't get the grief stricken faces of Becky's family and friends out of my mind.

My cell phone vibrated. It was Peggy.

"Hi, I figured the service would be over and I wanted to talk to you before the guys got back to the office. How did it go? Did you bump into anyone?"

"As a matter of fact, I did. Sam caught me in the parking lot as I was leaving. Of all people, he's the one I wanted to see the least. It was interesting though. At first he played his usual hard ass self, then when he realized I wasn't taking orders from him, he softened. Said he'd get in touch with me in a couple of days. I told him I wasn't going to sit still and looked forward to working with him soon."

"I'll tell you," Peggy said with a snicker in her voice. "You're the only one I know who can wrap that man around a baby finger." Her voice changed back to office mode, "Gotta go, the troops have arrived."

"Talk to you later," I said as she hung up.

Since I was already in Bourne, I decided to revisit the accident scene. Somebody had placed a white cross with Becky's name carved into it, marking the spot where she died. Two scarves, one purple and one white, were knotted together and draped over the top. A small white teddy bear wearing a purple sweater with a white B embroidered on the front was sitting at the base. I smiled at the innocence that lay before me. I remembered the stories the priest told. I wondered if the eleven young girls dressed in purple and white cheerleader's outfits at the memorial had come to say good-bye to their friend.

This was a picture I needed to take, not with my mind, but with my camera. I was sure, when I printed it out, I'd see Becky standing there, trying to tell me what happened. The image on the screen appeared blurry, not caused by a camera defect, but from the tears that had formed in my eyes.

I rode by Mr. Parker's house. There he was rocking in his chair. The movement was so uniform that, I wondered if he had an electrical gadget attached to the rockers. The only part of his body that moved was his head. As I approached from the left, I watched his head swivel. He followed my car past his house and start around the bend. I tried to keep him in my sight, but I had to watch the road at the same time. Old buzzard Parker, what exactly did he know about Becky? It will be interesting if he remembers my car from yesterday. I don't think he'll report a car that's passed only twice.

Wait a minute, I thought. The dark car he reported seeing. Maybe it's been around far more than twice. That's it! He's seen that car many times.

My adrenalin was flowing. My mind was racing. I was in such a deep discussion with myself that I missed the entrance to the highway. "Oh shit – guess I'll take the shore road," I muttered.

Actually, the change of scenery might help to clear my head. I'll save all my theories and opinions until I get home, when I can give them my undivided attention.

It worked. I turned off the road into one of the tourist picture spots and marveled at the view. It was truly beautiful. And like several other of my fellow parkers, I found myself snapping pictures. I looked at my watch. I'd lingered long enough. It was time to get home.

Once inside my cozy little bungalow, I changed into my Joe Boxers and a Martha's Vineyard tee-shirt. I laughed as I checked myself out in the mirror. It was the shirt Sam bought me on one of our little weekend excursions to the island. We sure did have fun. It's times like this when I miss him most.

My stomach was telling me it was getting close to supper time. I knew there was a pepperoni pizza in the freezer and a box of mac-and-cheese in the cupboard. I stood leaning against the counter tapping my fingers as I contemplated which one to have. The pizza won out. It goes much better with wine.

I liked ice in my wine, but was out of luck. I don't have an ice-maker and, as usual, I had forgotten to fill the ice cube trays, but did remember to put a new bottle of white zin into the fridge. With bottle in one hand and glass in the other, I poured myself a drink.

I left my notes, pictures and miscellaneous stuff on the kitchen table; took a placemat, a couple napkins, a plate and my wine and headed for the coffee table. The TV news was just finishing. The oven timer buzzed. The smell of pepperoni, pizza sauce and dough penetrated the air. My gourmet dinner was ready. I balanced a couple of pieces on the spatula and headed back to the couch. *Jeopardy* was just coming on. I cringed as the host, Alex Trebek read the headings. I consider myself pretty smart, but I never get many of the *Jeopardy* questions right. Let's face it, I have a hard time with *Are You Smarter than a Fifth Grader* questions.

CHAPTER TWENTY-SIX

Three nights and three days had passed since the accident and I was no closer to an answer. I had a few clues – vague as they were, they're all I have.

I called the office. Jamie answered, "Good morning, Cape Cod Tribune. How may I direct your call?"

"It's me, Casey," I said. "Is the boss in yet?"

"No. He called. Said he had a meeting this morning with the Town Manager at 9:30, so he'd see me after lunch," Jamie always shared any information she had with me. "Do you need me to page him for you?"

"Not at all, please leave him a message that I won't be in today because I'm going to Bourne High School to see what I can find out about Becky Morgan. I'll have my cell phone on if he wants to get in touch with me. That goes for you too. I'll still check in later though."

Since I wasn't going to the office, I decided to throw on a Mickey Mouse tee shirt and jean shorts. I pulled my hair back in a ponytail and slipped into a pair of brown leather sandals.

My cell rang. "Morning Sherlock." It was Annie. "I called the office and they told me you were working the road today."

"I'm trying to fit pieces into a puzzle. I'm sure you know about the hit-and-run in Bourne last Sunday night." I continued, "I'm writing a story for the paper. The problem is: there is a who it happened to, where, what and how it happened, but no why or who did it. So at this point, I haven't got a complete story. So yeah, I'm playing Sherlock, but Watson is on vacation." I refer to my right brain as Sherlock and my left brain as Watson. When I'm successful in an investigation it's because they worked together as a team. When I'm stumped, I like to say, Watson is on vacation. Right now, Watson must be hiking in the Himalayan Mountains or walking the Great Wall of China. He certainly isn't here with me.

I wasn't sure if Annie was listening, but I kept going anyway. "I went to the memorial service yesterday. Wow, saddest thing I've ever done. Don't want to repeat that one. Of course, I couldn't take any physical pictures, just mental images. I blinked my eyes like the shutter of a camera. Now I need to figure out what they mean."

"If anybody can do it, you can." Annie always encouraged me. "But, on a happier note, I called to ask what you're doing Friday night?" She was always one to keep me going. "The Beach Boys are playing at the Melody Tent and I have three tickets. Do you want to go?"

"Know what, I have nothing marked on the calendar and I could use some *me-time*. Their music never gets old. They might, but not their music. Do you want to do dinner first? Let's do it up right. We haven't been to The Paddock since April." I was already thinking about the escargots in a buttery wine sauce finished with a light dusting of freshly-grated parmesan cheese.

"Sounds like a plan to me. It will probably be easier if I meet you there, then neither one of us will have to back track to do a drop off after the show," Annie suggested.

"I agree. By the way, you said you had three tickets. Who's the third one for?"

"Barry's cousin, Marnie, is here from New York. I met her Tuesday night at the Tavern. She's really nice. I know you'll like her. In a nutshell, she just graduated from law school in New York, but is going to take the Mass bar exam. She's going to try her hand as a wash-a-shore. She's probably looking for a place to live as we speak. As a matter-of-fact, she's going to talk to Mike Sullivan tomorrow about a job in the DA's office." Annie kept talking, "I thought she might enjoy the show. A girls-night-out and what better two girls could she team up with?"

I chuckled, "Annie, you should run for politics. You're the best front person I know."

"Yeah, yeah. I've got to get back to work, busy day." I could hear Annie draw in a deep breath and slowly let it out. "Let me know how your scouting day turns out. That accident is the talk of the DA's office. Mike was actually at the memorial service, too."

"I sat in the back of the church. He was probably down front. I only remember the looks on faces, not the faces themselves. Hell, I didn't even see Sam walk in. How bad is that."

"Hey, did you know the girl who was killed was Judge Thompson's cousin's daughter?" Annie said quietly.

There was a pause, "No, I didn't know that – different last name. I had absolutely no idea." I wondered if there was any connection between Becky and, maybe, one of the judge's cases. There I go with another maybe. "All I know is, the whole incident was unnecessary and sad beyond words."

"We've got very little information. I don't think we'll get much until they have a suspect. Although, we might get more involved earlier than usual because of the circumstances surrounding the case." Annie stopped for a moment. "Casey, I've got to go, my other line is lit up. Catch you later."

"Thanks for the invite," I said, but Annie had already hung up. I hit the end call button on my cell.

I took a fresh mini-legal pad from the bottom draw of my bureau, made sure I had sharp pencils, and picked my camera up off the kitchen table. I put everything into my briefcase, grabbed a bottle of water from the fridge, my purse from the counter and headed out the door.

CHAPTER TWENTY-SEVEN

My first stop was Bourne High School. Even though school was out for the summer there were usually some faculty, or at least the administration, around.

It was 11:00 am. There were only a few cars in the parking lot. The front door was probably locked, but that was the closest one to the office. Maybe somebody will hear me knocking or just walk by. I dug down into my briefcase hoping to find my Tribune ID on the first swipe. Got it. I slid it into my front pocket. I didn't want them to think some crazy lady was trying to get into the school and have them call the Bourne PD. That would certainly screw everything up.

I looked at my reflection in the glass, as I walked up to the door. I probably should have dressed differently. It took fifteen minutes and a lot of knocking before somebody finally heard me. A lady, about five-feet-four, slightly overweight, with short curly-brown hair came to the door, but as I expected, didn't open it. I could barely hear what she was saying. I shrugged my shoulders, pointed to my ear with my left hand, and held my ID up to the glass with my right.

She wouldn't open the door, but held up one finger in a wait-a-minute gesture, then walked back and turned left out of sight into a corridor. She was either getting permission to let me in or getting reinforcements to run me away.

I looked at my watch, five minutes had passed. I was contemplating my next move. Should I begin my annoying knocking again or would that only frustrate the situation? I was about to search in my bag for my cell phone when I noticed two figures emerge from the shadows of the inside corridor and head toward the door. When I could make them out, I saw that the little lady who first greeted me wasn't one of them. Instead, there were two male figures, one distinctly taller, older and probably twenty pounds heavier, exhibiting an air of authority through his fashion and gait. The younger gentleman was far more casual in jeans and a polo shirt. His step appeared to be continually one behind as they moved in my direction. I assumed the leader was the principal and his side-kick was either his assistant or one of the teachers.

If only I had called first, the reception committee might have been more welcoming.

Well, bring it on boys. It's going to be hard to shake me.

The door opened and the taller man introduced himself. "I'm Mr. Porter, the principal of Bourne High and this is my assistant, Mr. Bowdin." I called it – principals are a breed of their own and don't change much with the times. "What can we do for you?"

I reached my right hand out while displaying my ID in my left. "My name is Casey Quinby. I'm an investigative reporter for the Cape Cod Tribune. I was hoping I could talk to somebody about Becky Morgan."

Mr. Porter was giving me the once over.

"Please excuse my appearance. I planned on doing field research today, not interviews, hence the outfit." The men each moved to one side of the door allowing me to pass between them. "Thanks, it was getting mighty hot out there."

"Why don't we go back to my office," said Mr. Porter. "Such a tragic accident." He motioned me to follow him. Mr. Bowdin made sure the door was secure, then caught up to us. Nothing was said until we were inside the principal's office and the door was shut.

"It will be a sad day when the students return in September without Becky. You always knew when she was around. She never had a bad thing to say about or to anybody." The grief began to cloud Mr. Porter's face. His eyes looked heavy and glazed over and his mouth was expressionless.

I glanced at Mr. Bowdin. He sat to the left of Mr. Porter's desk. His expression mirrored that of the principal's.

It was evident that Becky was not just a number on a school roster. "At the memorial service, I noticed eleven girls dressed in cheerleader outfits. Was Becky the twelfth?"

"Yes, she was the co-captain," said Mr. Bowdin. "During the football games, when the team was losing, you could hear Becky's voice above all the others shouting words of encouragement. His voice grew louder, "She'd mentally push those boys into believing they were invincible and could even beat the New England Patriots. And, by God, they'd come through more times than not."

Mr. Principle lifted his head and looked around the office. "One day a week she'd volunteer for front office duty. If I close my eyes, I can see her at the copy machine or at the files. If I listen, I can hear her telling Margie, my secretary, her plans for the weekend. I remember when her class took a field trip to the Barnstable County Courthouse. She came back so fascinated with the courtroom proceedings that she wanted to become a lawyer." His elbows were resting on his desk and his chin was firmly implanted in his hands. "Just an all-around good kid."

I noted a slight smile. This was a happy recall, I thought.

Mr. Bowdin waited for Mr. Porter to finish, then turned to me. "We're planning a rally in Becky's memory the day before our first football game in September. It's only for Bourne High students, but I'm sure Mr. Porter won't mind if I invite you. It's being held in the gym. Leave me your phone number and I'll let you know the particulars when they've been firmed up."

"Thank you. I appreciate the invite and will definitely be there." I hesitated, but I had to move on. "I know this is a difficult time, but I have some questions and hope that you may be able to help me with the answers." My eyes moved between the principal and his assistant. "Remember this is coming from me, a reporter from the Tribune and not as an investigator for the police department. I do, however, have a Bachelor's Degree in Criminal Justice from U Mass, along with an Associate Degree in Journalism from Cape Cod Community. In the past, I've worked with various PDs in the investigation of cases, some current and some cold. At this point, I'm not working with the Bourne PD, I'm working for myself. This may change." I sensed I had gained their trust.

"One minute," Mr. Porter said. He swung his chair sideways to look into the outer office. Margie was busy at her desk with some paperwork. He lifted the phone and buzzed her extension. "Margie, would you please do me a favor and bring three bottles of water to my office?" I couldn't hear her reply, but was sure it was favorable. "Thank you," replied Mr. Porter. Margie nodded as she hung up her phone and headed toward a door probably, leading to the staff break room. "I would have offered you coffee, but in the summer we usually just pick one up at Dunkin Donuts on our way in."

A water did sound good. "I find it very hard to piece the images from Becky's accident into place. This is why I'm here today. I want to get to know her. I want to be able to close my eyes and see the same pictures you just painted for me. Believe me, I hope it was a tragic turn of events. I hope she was in the wrong place at the wrong time. If that's the case, then the odds are the person who hit her will feel guilty at some point and get caught. On the other hand, if it was intentional, the person responsible has, and will continue, to cover up his or her actions. In the latter scenario, Becky was the victim of a murder." I stopped, hoping I hadn't said too much.

Mr. Porter and Mr. Bowdin were so focused on what I was telling them, they jumped slightly when Margie knocked on the door. She came in carrying not only the water, but a small dish of cookies. "I made peanut butter cookies yesterday," she said placing them in the middle of Mr. Porter's desk. "Enjoy." And as quickly as she came in, she was gone, back to her desk and piles of paperwork.

Mr. Porter handed me a bottle of water and motioned for me to take a cookie. He repeated the process with Mr. Bowdin. "Do you really suspect foul play?" He appeared mystified. His face saddened. He shook his head and slid to the back of his chair.

Nobody spoke for what seemed like an eternity.

"What can we do to help?" he came back to the front of his chair. "Mr. Bowdin and I will assist you in any way we can."

"Okay, let's begin with a little background on Becky," I said as I reached down into my briefcase for a pen and my pad of paper. "Did she have an after school or weekend job that you know of?"

Mr. Bowdin took a sip of water, then set his bottle back down on the desk. "Yes, I believe she worked part time at the little sandwich/ice cream shop in the center of town. It used to be called The Tiny Cone. It was sold last January and they changed the name to The Train Stop."

"I know the one," I said. It was the same place I had gone to with Sam several times. "It's the only place this side of the canal that knows how to make a real coffee ice cream soda."

"That's it," he said looking over to Mr. Porter. "From what I've seen in my trips there, it was a gathering place for a lot of the town kids. I don't mean that in a bad way."

"I think she did some babysitting too," Mr. Porter piped in. "In fact, I'm sure some of the teachers used her services. And they had nothing but praise for her abilities."

"Did she have a boyfriend?" I asked changing the subject.

"I don't think so, at least nobody here at the school. Mr. Porter replied. We usually have the inside scoop on who's dating whom. You know these kids are with us at least seven hours a day. There are some things we know and their parents have no idea about. And because we're not their parents, they sometimes confide in us." He pushed back from his desk and walked over to the window. "This can be a good thing in some situations, but bad in others. I've been in this position for many years and I've heard it all."

He stood staring out the window, then slowly turned to face me. He came back to his desk, sat down, leaned back and crossed his legs. "Last spring, I want to say around the end of April or beginning of May, Becky came into the office on a Thursday afternoon just like she did every week. She was smiling and bubbly. I kidded her about the extra make-up she had on. I told her it looked like she'd eaten a raspberry popsicle at lunch because her lips were so red. She laughed. Then, I said some ink must have leaked onto her fingers and she'd rubbed her eyes because the blue shadow over them was dark. Her smile went away and she shifted her glance away from me. Becky always had a comeback. That day she had none. The reason these things stood out is because she never wore much make-up. She was beautiful without it."

"Now that you mention it, I remember that day too. She did the filing in the bin and left without saying good-bye to anyone," Mr. Bowdin said. "We didn't think much more about it, then the next day she called in sick."

Mr. Porter finished, "And Monday, she was back as though nothing had happened."

Mr. Bowdin reached forward for another cookie. I followed. They were good.

I took a drink of water. "What about her family? I understand they are very involved in the community."

"If you've ever gone to the Scallop Festival you've seen Bob Morgan. Most years you can hear him chanting *drop-the-scallops*, meaning into the fryolators, of course. I think he heads the committee. He's also pretty involved in politics. I don't get involved much, but when he runs an event, seems like I'm always there. He possesses an amazing power of persuasion." Mr. Porter folded his hands together as if to pray. "Did you know he's related to Judge Thompson?"

I nodded my head in acknowledgement. "I actually just found out this morning."

My leg was starting to cramp, so I stood and gave it a little shake. I explained it was an old injury and I needed to move it around a bit.

I paced slowly back and forth in front of Mr. Porter's desk. "How about her circle of friends? Were they a close knit group? Did they all share Becky's personality?"

"They were close. You'll find that when kids belong to a specific group, like cheerleaders. They were all active and, let's face it, in with the popular kids, the jocks and all." Mr. Porter added with pride, "But they were all achievers and good students. That was one of my prerequisites for any student to be a cheerleader or football player or to participate in any school sports program. If their grades started to slip, they were taken off the team until they showed improvement."

I sat back down and tried to settle my leg into a comfortable position. I picked up my notebook and read my notes. "Sorry, I need to review a couple of things," I said. "You said the make-up incident was somewhere around the beginning of May?"

"Yes, or the end of April," Mr. Porter said. From the look on his face he was trying to release the incident from his memory. "You know, I remember something else. It was probably a few weeks later, again during her Thursday afternoon office duty. Her cell phone rang. That was a no, no. I'm very strict about cell phone use during school hours. I only allow it if it's an emergency. She answered before the music signaling the incoming call ended. Then she turned away and moved to a corner near the file cabinet – out of earshot." He rubbed his hands together. "It was short and, judging from the smile on her face, it was sweet. I asked her if everything was all right. She didn't know I was watching her. She froze. Her eyes grew big. She knew she had gotten caught with her hand in the cookie jar."

There was a soft knock on the principal's door. Mr. Porter motioned for Margie to come in. "I was planning to leave at two o'clock today, but I need to get some of these forms ready for the printer, so I'll be here until about four. I'm going to run over to Dunkin's for an iced coffee, does anybody want one?"

Mr. Bowdin reached into his pocket. "My treat. I can't make cookies, but I can buy the coffee. Mr. Porter, Casey what would you like?"

Margie took a small sticky note from the corner of Mr. Porter's desk, slid a pencil out of her pocket, and stood ready to take an order.

"Margie, you're the best. I'll have a medium black. Casey?"

"I'll have a medium iced coffee, cream only, thanks."

"What the heck, I'm going for the calories," Mr. Bowdin said with a grin from ear to ear. "I'll have a coffee coolata with cream and whip cream. Tell them not to forget the cherry!" He chuckled, handed Margie a twenty dollar bill and she was on her way.

When we all sat back down, I said, "I really want to thank you for taking the time to speak with me. Your input has given me new insight into Becky's life. I wish I had known her."

"She was a beautiful little girl, just beginning to blossom into a lovely young lady. Her future was destined to be promising and bright. She was one of those kids that could do anything she wanted to do, if she wanted to do it bad enough." Mr. Porter was interrupted when the phone rang. He let it ring four times before he answered. Margie must have forwarded the calls. He finally gave in. "Good afternoon, Bourne High School, may I help you?"

I tried to pretend I wasn't listening, but I was.

"This is Mr. Porter." He sat quiet listening to the voice on the other end. "No problem, Bob. Today, I'm tied up. I can meet with you tomorrow morning, say around nine o'clock?" Again, silence on Mr. Porter's end. "Fine, I'm looking forward to it." He took a deep breath as he cradled the receiver. "That was Bob Morgan. He wants to stop by to tie up any loose ends with Becky's records.

He really doesn't need to come in. I actually think he wants to. Maybe it will help close part of a chapter in his daughter's life."

"So let's get back to the cell phone day." I wanted to keep the momentum going. "Did you ever find out anything about the caller?"

"No, she immediately shut it off and put it in her pocket. I did, however, remind her of my cell phone rule. She said she was sorry and went back to her filing."

Mr. Bowdin listened intently. Something registered with him. His mouth twisted sideways. He was noticeably biting the inside corner of his lip. Was there another incident he wanted to talk about? "Mr. Porter, do you recall the day several of the girls from the cheerleading squad were standing in a huddle-like position talking quietly so no one could hear them?"

Mr. Porter thought for a minute before answering, "I do, now that you bring it up."

Mr. Bowdin continued, "We had just left a meeting in the second floor science lab. As we got to the bottom of the stairs, the girls must have seen us coming because they stopped talking and pretended to be getting stuff from their lockers. We said good-afternoon and kept on walking. They all responded but Becky. I told you I'd meet you in your office, that I had something I had to check on."

Mr. Porter took a new interest in Mr. Bowdin's story.

"I made a circle around the center classrooms, knowing I'd end up back by the girl's lockers. The only one left was Becky. When I asked her if there was a problem, she said no, but didn't turn to look at me. She had been crying. I detected it in her voice. I let it go, figuring I'd check on her the next day. I did and she seemed fine. It was toward the end of May. Do you remember it? I was convinced something was going on. I'm sure of the date because we were working on graduation plans. In hindsight, I should have paid more attention." Mr. Bowdin was fidgeting with his pant leg.

I imagined a heavy cloud of unwarranted guilt forming over his head.

Mr. Porter stood up and walked over beside him. "You had no idea if there was a problem," he said putting his hand on his assistant's shoulder. "In retrospect, we probably could have made many significant observations. In reality, none of them would have led us to a conclusion that Becky was in some sort of trouble." Mr. Bowdin's head was still lowered as Mr. Porter continued, "You're the best assistant I've ever had. Don't you forget that. Someday you'll be standing here in a deep discussion with your assistant. And I have no doubts, as I have none now, you'll handle whatever it may be with insight and integrity." He moved to face Mr. Bowdin, who was now looking directly at him. At the same time the two men reach out to shake hands, Mr. Porter pulled Mr. Bowdin forward in a fatherly hug.

I felt the pain and emotion being exchanged between them.

As they resumed their positions behind and beside Mr. Porter's desk they shared a smile of professional admiration. "Thank you," Mr. Bowdin said.

The next thing I heard was Margie tapping on the door. I turned to see her trying to balance the coffee tray and twist the knob at the same time. I was closest to the door, so I got up to help. My iced coffee looked refreshing, but that coolata was calling me, next time I'll go for the calories.

Margie handed each of us our drink. "Mr. Bowdin, I believe this one belongs to you, since it's the only one with a cherry on top." We laughed. The break in the questioning was welcomed by all three of us. Once we collected our thoughts, we moved on.

"Thanks, Margie," I said then turned to Mr. Bowdin. "I've always said real coffee, not decaf, is food for the brain and right now I need some. Thanks."

"I agree," said Margie as she turned to go back to her desk and the waiting paperwork.

My mind was spinning. I may have exceeded my authority today by visiting Becky's school. I told Sam I was going to pursue some ideas I had and he didn't object, at least not too much.

"What I'd like to do now is take all the information you've given me and put it into some sort of order, make a timeline, if you will. Hopefully I'll be able to formulate some meaningful clues to help determine what happened to Becky. I'll probably take a trip over to The Train Stop and ask her co-workers a few questions. Anything we've talked about today I know will be kept confidential." I delivered a message without actually making a request. "I need to be careful what I ask in town though. People like to talk. It's like the kindergarten game. The teacher whispers something to the first child and they pass it down the line. When it gets to the last kid it doesn't resemble what the teacher originally said at all."

I leaned back in the chair. It was quiet.

"Will you please keep us informed of your progress?" Mr. Porter took a sip of coffee then continued, "If we remember anything else or find something you should take a look at, do you have a number we can call?"

"Oh, I'm sorry. I should have given you my card when I first came in." I reached for my purse to retrieve a business card and wrote my cell number on the back. Call me anytime. I'll get back to you next week to let you know how things are going."

I stood up and stretched my leg out. "This has been a remarkable meeting for me. I have to tell you, it brought back memories of my principal. He was a great guy to talk to. I always wanted to be a detective. My parents thought I was crazy. I guess I am a little. My principal, Mr. Dorsey, always encouraged me to go for it. He said I'd make a great one because I was a little on the nosey side. I don't wear a shiny-silver or gold badge, my pen is my badge," I said as I neatened my notes and slid them into their slot in my briefcase for safe keeping. "Enough about me."

"Nonsense, you had a dream and you're fulfilling it in your own special way. I'm impressed," said Mr. Porter. "Keep up the good work."

"Thanks." I lifted up my briefcase and purse and draped both straps over my shoulder.

Mr. Bowdin moved toward the door. Mr. Porter got up from his chair and walked around to the front of his desk. "Take care of yourself." He turned to face Mr. Bowdin. "Please let Casey out. I need some time alone to think. Give me fifteen minutes and we'll take a look at tomorrow's schedule."

"Sure thing, see you in a few. I've got to pick up some supplies from the storage room." Mr. Bowdin held the door open for me.

"Casey, I had hoped Becky was killed by a hit and run driver with no personal objective. After listening to you, I don't believe that to be true. Please help find who did this to her. And, thank you for heightening my awareness with the kids. You've made me realize I've got to be more observant and attentive in my surroundings."

We reached the front doors. I shook Mr. Bowdin's hand. "Take care of the big guy. I'll talk to you soon."

My steps quickened as I walked to my car. Now I had information. Now I had background. Now I felt like I really did know Becky.

CHAPTER TWENTY-EIGHT

It was getting close to 2:30 when I pulled into my driveway. I was tired, both mentally and physically. My briefcase sat on the seat beside me. It begged to be opened. With purse on one shoulder and briefcase on the other, I made my way up to my front door. There was a calming breeze gently blowing behind me trying to coax me inside. I moved over to the couch and laid my carry-ins on the floor beside me. The pillow was already puffed at one end, so I kicked off my sandals and plopped down on my back. I stared at the ceiling, watching the fan turn around and around and ....

Suddenly I was awakened. It was my cell phone. The caller ID read *unknown*. I really didn't feel like talking to anyone, but answered anyway. "Hello," I said not even bothering to sit up.

"Hi Casey, it's Sam. You okay?" I detected concern in his voice.

"Yeah, it's been a long day."

"I'm not going to ask you why. Listen, would you like to grab a pizza tonight? If you don't feel like going out, I can pick one up and come over to your place." He waited for an answer.

"What's up Sam?" I asked. "One minute you're reprimanding me, the next you're concerned about what I'm up to, and now you want to bribe me with food?" I laughed. "Make it a double pepperoni and you're on."

"I haven't forgotten. I'll pick up some beer too. See you around 7:00."

My little cat-nap gave me some renewed energy. "Since I gave *Hazel* the day off, I'd better get off my butt and pick up a little." I chuckled, "I wish." It had been a while since Sam had been over. I liked the idea of companionship tonight. Maybe we can do some catching up. I made sure my notes regarding the case were tucked away. If he gave me an opening, I would reach around the corner by the kitchen table and retrieve them.

I scurried around with the dust cloth and dry mop. The place looked pretty good. Now it was my turn. I dug to the bottom of the bureau drawer where I kept my good jerseys. I was looking for the cute peach colored one I bought at the beginning of the summer.

Ah, ha ... found you.

The tags were still attached. I had washed my white shorts the other day. They never got any further than the laundry basket. If I throw them in the dryer with a wet facecloth, most of the wrinkles will come out. It beats ironing.

Even though I took a shower this morning, I decided to freshen up. Why was I doing this for Sam? I missed him more than I thought. The shower felt refreshing. My cell rang as I stepped out onto the bath mat. I hustled to wrap a towel around me and grab the phone before the caller hung up. It was Peggy.

I answered, "Oops, I forget to check in when I got home. Sorry."

"I got a little worried when I didn't hear from you. Did everything go okay at the school?" she said.

"It went better than okay. Mr. Porter, the principal, and Mr. Bowdin, his assistant, were amazing. I made sure to tell them I was not associated with the police department. I told them I was a reporter for the Tribune. We talked. I think, no, I'm sure, I gained their confidence. They were very open with me. I asked questions and got answers. Everything I learned is fragmented right now, but as soon as I get it together, we'll meet and I'll run it by you." I hesitated, not knowing whether I should tell her about Sam. I decided not to.

"I wish Sam would bring you into the case," said Peggy.

"I have a feeling he will. I just hope it's soon." I felt bad not telling Peggy I was seeing Sam in a couple of hours. "Talk to you tomorrow." We said our good-byes, I disconnected the call and went back to getting ready for Sam's visit.

I'm not a perfume type girl, but I do have one that's more fresh than flowery. Just a little spray wouldn't hurt. Actually it might help. I twisted my hair into a roll and secured it off my neck with a flower clip my Mom gave me years ago. She had tried so hard to make me into a girly-girl. It didn't work. She finally gave in to my tom-boy antics. Tonight, Mom would be very happy. I looked really good, if I did say so myself.

Since Sam was bringing beer, I moved stuff in my freezer around to accommodate four mugs. There's no doubt about it, the best way to serve beer is in frosty mugs. I probably should put two more in.

Naw, two each is enough.

It was still early, so I went out on the deck to take in some fresh air. The neighbor's kids were playing in their backyard. I could see them over the fence, but it sounded like a game of hide and seek. I didn't have any brothers or sisters, but when I was young, my cousins lived nearby so we'd play together all the time. Hide and seek was one of our favorites. Listening to the neighbor's kids brought back memories.

Where did the time go? Where have the people gone?

The sky was a mellow blue with no clouds at all. Sunsets over the water are always beautiful. Tonight would be no exception.

"What are you thinking about?" I jumped a mile and turned to see Sam standing in the doorway with his hands on his hips and a shit-eating grin on his face.

"What are you trying to do – give me a heart attack? I didn't hear you come in."

115

"I knocked," said Sam." Nobody answered so I let myself in. You should lock your door. If I've told you once, I've told you a hundred times." He shook his head. "Typical Casey, you never listen."

"Why don't you go back out the door and I'll lock it. Then you can go away, Mr. Smart Ass." I flipped my wrist in a circular motion and pointed to the door.

Sam locked his hands on the door jam and pretended to brace himself for battle. "I'm not leaving without some pizza."

"Okay then," I said. "Guess you're staying."

We laughed.

Sam came over to where I was standing, reached out, and gave me a hug. "Sorry Sherlock, I didn't mean to scare you, but I wasn't kidding about locking the door," he said. "You never know."

Once a cop, always a cop.

"You're early. What's the matter couldn't wait to see me?" I tossed my head in the air as I walked by him, turned, and gave him a flirtatious smile.

"Let's eat outside. Get the dishes and napkins. I'll take two beers and put the rest in the fridge. Did you make some frosties?"

"Can't surprise you with anything, can I?" My eyes shifted to follow his movement. New relationships take too much work. This old familiar one is much more relaxing.

"Nope. Grab the pizza. I'll be right there."

It was going to be a good night.

CHAPTER TWENTY-NINE

It was two am when James rolled over to check the alarm clock. Something had interrupted his sleep. There it was again. He froze. A scraping noise was coming from the living room. Still not completely conscience, his mind was foggy. "Relax," he whispered to himself. The noise stopped. He waited. Could it have been his imagination? The silence was deafening. He swung his legs over the edge of the bed and gently rested his feet on the floor.

There was a flashlight in the top drawer of the night stand. He hadn't used it since last winter, so he hoped the batteries still worked. He slowly pulled the drawer out and reached in to retrieve it. It wasn't there.

What the hell ... somebody's messing with my mind. I'm sure I didn't take it out of there.

There was very little moonlight to direct him. His adrenalin kicked in. Why was he panicking? It was his house. He knew every inch of it. He didn't need that old flashlight anyway.

He quietly made his way to the hall outside of his bedroom. His next step drew a sharp creak from the hard wood floor. Startled, he stopped mid-step and braced himself against the wall. He could feel the accelerated beats of his heart pounding on the inside of his chest. "Damn it."

He wiped the sweat from his forehead and continued his one sided conversation, "What's wrong with me? There's nobody here and I don't believe in ghosts." When he got to the living room, he reached around the corner and clicked on the table lamp beside his mother's rocking chair. She used to keep that light burning all night so they wouldn't be scared. It had made them feel secure. Old habits never die.

Before he had a chance to fully survey the room, the scraping noise resumed. It pierced his ears like a tuning fork. He spun around in its direction. His eyes were round as saucers. His heart changed tunes and beat like a jungle drum – loud and deep. There at the window was the impostor, the charlatan of darkness. The spiny-fingers of a tree branch echoed an eerie howl of repentance on the window pane. He lowered himself onto the rocking chair. The noise stopped and again it was quiet. He lifted his arm and pointed a shaky finger at the window. "That will be the last time you creep into my life," he yelled. " Tomorrow you will be gone!"

It was only 2:30 when he crawled back into bed and pulled the sheet up around his neck. It took time, but eventually he drifted back to sleep.

His alarm sounded at its usual 6:00 am. He thought about calling in sick. Then he thought about Marnie. They had a lunch date.

A light fog hovered just above the ground. It reminded him of the demon who disturbed his sleep last night. He didn't want a repeat performance, so he slipped into a pair of jeans, slid on his sandals, and headed for the garage. No time like the present to take care of that tree branch. It wasn't very thick so it came off quickly. "Done," he said, and returned the saw to the garage.

Less than an hour later he stood in front of the mirror. "Looking good," he commented as he admired his spit shined and polished image. "Let's do this. It's time to eat the donuts."

CHAPTER THIRTY

His morning ritual at Nancy's Donut Shop was uneventful. She was busy with customers the whole half hour he was there. Not much to talk about this morning anyway. Barry didn't even come in. That was unusual. He guessed mornings were different when you have somebody to share them with. He wished it was him with Marnie and not Barry. He caught Nancy's attention when he jingled the bell on his way out the door. He gave her his usual morning nod. She smiled and waved.

A couple of the jurors were waiting for him in the hallway of the Courthouse. "Good morning, you're early today," James said as he leaned down to unlock the door to the jury room.

"It's quieter here than at home," one of the jurors said.

The other juror agreed. "I brought my book, thought I might be able to get in a couple of chapters."

James broke his routine and fixed a pot of coffee. Normally this was the last thing he did. Usually he'd distribute any written instructions on the table in front of each juror's chair in the jury room. Then he'd get his check-in lists ready. After that, he'd unlock the courtroom and snap on the lights. Finally, he'd check the jury box to make sure he hadn't missed any papers or notes the jurors might have left behind the day before. When all this was done, he'd make coffee. He was a man of routine, but not today.

He propped the door to the jury room open and headed for his desk. A faint whistling sound was getting louder. It was Barry. "Mornin', James," he said as he sauntered in.

"Aren't we in a good mood this morning," replied James without looking up. "Thought I'd see you at Nancy's."

Barry puckered his lips and rolled his eyes. "Not this morning. Your little sweetheart fixed me breakfast – a fried egg and bacon sandwich on a bulky roll."

"She's practicing on you. Mine will be the pièce de resistance." James held his thumb and finger to his lips and made a kissing gesture. He leaned over toward Barry and whispered, "I might even get a sweet dessert."

"For breakfast? Dream on, Romeo," Barry laughed. "Hey, we've got some early birds this morning," he said as he poured himself a cup of coffee.

"They were waiting for me." James looked at the wall clock. It was 7:50. The rest of the jurors should be here soon. He rolled his chair over to Barry's desk. "If all goes as planned, this case should be done today or tomorrow morning at the latest. One way or the other, I'm going to see if I can take Friday, either all day or at least the afternoon, off. I'd like to spend some time with Marnie."

"Sure, no problem," Barry answered in between greeting the other jurors.

Like clockwork, the remaining jurors checked in. By 8:30 all were accounted for. James reminded them of their obligation. "The same rules apply, nothing has changed. We are nearing a close. If the attorneys finish their closing statements this morning, Judge Thompson will instruct you how to proceed." James could recite this speech in his sleep. "I'm going to welcome the judge into the courtroom to start the proceedings. In fifteen minutes the assistant Court Officer will escort you to the jury box. In the meantime, if you need to use the facilities, please do so now." With the formalities done, he left the jury room.

"All rise. The honorable Judge Richard Thompson presiding," James announced.

Right on cue, the doors to the courtroom opened and Barry directed the jurors to take their respective seats. At precisely 9:00 am the court was called to session.

"I'll bet you a coffee this case goes to the jury by eleven o'clock," he whispered to James. "Better still, I'll bet you a beer at The Tavern, that the jury returns with a decision by three o'clock."

"It's a sucker's bet, but you're on," James responded. "It's a bet I won't mind losing."

At 11:15, he nudged Barry, "You owe me a coffee." No sooner did he get the words out of his mouth, the prosecution rested their case.

Judge Thompson sat for a minute tapping a pencil on his notepad. "We'll break for lunch until 1:00. When you return, I'll instruct you how to proceed."

James stood up and turned half toward the audience and half toward the jury box. "All rise."

The judge nodded to James, stepped down off his platform, and headed back to his chambers.

James dismissed the jury for lunch.

"What time is Marnie meeting us at Scoops?" Barry asked as they crossed the hallway to the jury room.

"I suggested she be there a little before noon in order to get a table. Since we're out so early, we can head on over. I'm going to make sure the courtroom is ready for the afternoon session. Give me a hand, will you?" James motioned Barry back to the courtroom.

"Everything's set. Let's get going," said Barry.

"Be right with you," James answered. "I've got to get something from my desk."

Barry was half way down the stairs when James caught up to him. "Let's cut across the parking lot. I want to put this bag in my trunk."

CHAPTER THIRTY-ONE

The noontime sun was bright. Barry fumbled in his pocket for his sunglasses. There was a rippled glare coming from the front of James' car. "Hey buddy," he said, "What's wrong with the black Mariah? Looks like something on the right front fender."

James' eyes shifted from one side to the other. "I don't see anything. You know if there was something wrong with my baby, I'd know it."

Barry walked on ahead. James hesitated. Don't panic, he thought.

"Right here." Barry rubbed his hand over the spot in question. "It's in a weird place. Strange, doesn't look like anybody hit you."

"You know what, the other night, I lifted a couple of boxes down off a shelf in the garage. I was balancing on the step stool and the top one slipped off. I knew it hit the car, but didn't notice it had left a mark. The light in the garage is dull, not bright like the sunlight. I guess I should have checked it out better." James felt pretty good about his story. He hoped Barry bought it.

"My cousin has really cast her spell on you. You've always dusted your car for finger prints. And, if anyone got caught touching it, you threatened to cut off their fingers. Now, all you've got is Marnie on the brain." Barry stepped away and continued walking toward *Scoops*. When he realized James wasn't beside him, he turned and asked, "Well, you coming? I'm hungry."

It worked. Barry believed him. He hated using Marnie as an excuse. "Let me put this in the trunk and I'll catch up with you."

Marnie was already waiting when they got there. Scoops started out as an ice cream shop. It was bought by a local family a couple of years ago. There were pictures of ice cream cones, sundaes, and even a banana split professionally framed adorning the restaurant walls. They weren't your run-of-the-mill posters. They were done by a local artist. The cones were done in water colors and the others in oils. The tables and chairs were 50's vintage soda shop, painted in bright yellows, greens and reds. Since the Greenleaf family bought it, an array of specialty sandwiches were added to the menu. There was also a small glass case beside the register that displayed delicious desserts that Mrs. G made from scratch. If you left there hungry, it was your own fault.

James walked over to Marnie and gave her a little peck on the cheek. Barry stayed at the counter checking out the daily specials.

"How's your day going?" James asked.

"I have great news," she replied. "Let's order, then I'll tell you all about it." She left her purse on the table and they walked up to the counter to join Barry.

"I've already ordered," he said. "Mrs. G made meatloaf." He looked to Marnie who was busy reading the menu board. "I always have a meatloaf sandwich with a slice of American cheese on focaccia bread, when I can get it. You don't get anything like it in New York. Trust me, you should give it a try."

Marnie thought for a minute, then gave her order to the girl behind the counter. "Sounds good to me, I'll have the same as Barry, please. Could I also have a Diet Coke?"

"Make that three." James could already taste the home cooking. "Marnie, why don't you go back to the table and I'll bring our sandwiches over. Do you want to split a bag of chips?"

"Sure." She took their drinks and headed for the table.

James could tell from the enthusiasm in her voice she wanted to give them a rundown on her morning.

The guys picked up their food and joined her at the table. She was smiling like a little kid.

"I'm sure glad we have an extra twenty minutes to hear about your morning adventures. I think we're going to need it." James chuckled as he lifted his sandwich to take a bite. "Wow, have you ever had anything so good? He turned toward the counter and gave Mrs. G a thumb up.

She nodded and mouthed a thank you.

Marnie washed down a bite with her soda. "Annie came with me to look at the places her friend had for rent. He owns two duplexes. There's a unit available in each of them." She hesitated, "You'll probably think I'm crazy, but I liked the one closest to the street. It was brighter, but it could have been the time of day. Anyway, he made me a deal I couldn't refuse. The last tenants moved out a week ago. The landlord wanted to clean and paint it before he showed the place. I told him I'd clean and paint, if I could have it immediately. He took a hundred dollars off the monthly rent. Of course, I'm paying for the paint, but that's okay." She tilted her head sideways, and, in a cocky little voice said, "This way I can pick out the colors."

She was like a teenager getting her first car. "I don't need to get a kitchen table and chairs. The last tenants left theirs. They need a little help, but it will do for now. Once I get settled, I can paint them and make some cushions and curtains to match."

Wow, thought James, she's not only beautiful and sexy, but talented too. He looked at Barry and knew what was coming next.

Barry smiled. "Hey buddy, you got some old clothes ready? We just got ourselves a part-time job."

"I was hoping you two would volunteer." Marnie laughed. "I'll pick up some paint this afternoon. I have an idea what I want."

"I bet you do," James said as he drew in a deep breath. "Please don't have me painting hot pink walls with lime green trim. And, make the bedroom a soothing, relaxing shade of whatever." He *fluttered* his eyelashes and looked at Marnie for a reaction.

"Why do you care what I paint the bedroom?" she teased back.

"That's enough. Next, I'll be hearing your dirty little stories." Barry shook his head and smiled. "Remember, she's my cousin."

"Do you want to check the place out after you get off of work? My lease starts today, so I have the keys." She looked at James. "I know this isn't much of a date, but I'll make it up to you later."

"Yeah, yeah … just brush me aside." James got no reaction. He wrinkled his forehead. "Get it? Brush … as in paint."

"Don't quit your day job. Comedy Central doesn't have any openings," said Marnie.

"I've got an idea," said Barry. "Why don't you swing by Kmart and pick up a plastic table cloth, some paper towels and a package of paper cups. We'll pick you up at my condo, then stop for a pizza and a bottle of wine so we can christen the new digs."

James glanced at the clock above the counter. "Yikes, we've got ten minutes. We better head back pronto." He slid his chair out and stood up.

"You guys get going. I'll throw the trash away." Marnie had already started cleaning the table. Now go, so you're not late. I'll see you around 4:30 or 5:00." She leaned toward James and gave him a little kiss on the cheek. "Thanks," she whispered.

CHAPTER THIRTY-TWO

James and Barry hustled across the parking lot and into the Courthouse. They ran up the stairs to the second floor. The jurors were back from lunch waiting to be escorted into the courtroom. James led them in and motioned for them to take their seats. At exactly 1:00, Judge Thompson entered from his chambers. He walked up the stairs and took his place behind his desk. The afternoon session was called to order.

The Judge turned to face the jury, "Over the past three days, you have heard the arguments presented by both the defense and the prosecution. This morning they offered summaries of those arguments for your review. First you need to evaluate the evidence given regarding this case. After careful deliberation, it is then your job, as members of the jury, to arrive at a finding of innocence or guilt. Should you have any questions while you're out, let one of the Court Officers know and every attempt to clarify them will be made." Finished with his instructions, the Judge turned back to face James and nodded for him to proceed.

"If you will all please stand and follow me to the jury room." James motioned with his hands for the jury to stand. He led the group and Barry followed behind. The judge stepped down and went to his chambers.

Barry got two pitchers of water and some paper cups and set them on the table. Several of the jurors poured a drink and sat back waiting for the rest of their instructions. They elected a spokesperson. It was juror number five, Andrew Watkins. He was a thirty-two year old, married car salesman. James studied him. He was nicely dressed, well spoken, and appeared to be well educated.

The twelve jurors were given ballots and told to write their juror number and their decision as to guilty or innocent. After they finished, they passed them to the spokesperson. Both James and Barry hoped the decision would be unanimous. But they knew, that rarely happened the first time around. Barry stood beside Mr. Watkins as he opened and recorded the information written on the ballots. When Mr. Watkins was finished, Barry took the form and handed it to James. Eleven people agreed both defendants were guilty. Only one held out, juror number two, Mrs. Barrows. She only wrote her jury number.

What in the world was her problem, James wondered. Let the discussion begin.

"Mrs. Barrows," Mr. Watkins said, "Do you need clarification on a piece of evidence?"

"No," Mrs. Barrows responded in a very quiet voice. "I need a little time to think." She got up from her chair and moved toward the windows. Nobody spoke. She grasped her hands behind her and rocked slightly back and forth just staring out the window. Still nothing. She paced several times across the back of the room, then looked up at the ceiling with a puzzled look on her face.

Twenty minutes passed when Mr. Watkins spoke. "Perhaps we can talk about the case." He was trying to be diplomatic.

Mrs. Barrows spun herself around. "Are you deaf?" she asked. "I told you, I need time to think." Her voice changed. It was loud and demanding.

"What's going on here?" James looked at Barry. He shrugged. Maybe the bubblegum chewing bimbo would have been a better choice.

James knew it was his cue to inject something … anything. All eyes were on him as he spoke. "Mrs. Barrows," he began, "It's not easy to make a decision that affects another person's life. When you accepted the responsibility of jury assignment, you agreed to hear evidence and make an educated decision regarding the outcome of the case." He saw her eyes start to well up. "If something about this particular case hits too close to home, you have to put that aside. If you have questions, you need to ask them. If you need more time, you certainly have that right. But what you need to do is think about this case and the evidence pertaining to it. Don't bring any outside bits and pieces from an unrelated incident into the picture." James tried to sound comforting, but firm.

Mrs. Barrows nodded. "Thank you, Officer." Ten more minutes passed. She looked at her fellow jurors. "I'm sorry," she said as she sat back down in her chair. "Can we please take another vote?"

Mr. Watkins passed around a second set of ballots. This time they came back all marked guilty. He recorded them on the information sheet and handed it to James. "I believe we're ready to return to the courtroom," he said.

It was 2:30 when James and Barry escorted the jurors back into the courtroom. They took their respective seats and James went to Judge Thompson's chamber to notify him of their return.

Five minutes later Judge Thompson emerged. He took his seat and proceeded to ask the jury if they had made a decision. Mr. Watkins rose to his feet, "Yes, your Honor, we have."

"Please give your verdict to the clerk."

The clerk retrieved the slip of paper from Mr. Watkins and handed it to the Judge. Judge Thompson read it and handed it back to the clerk. She recorded the verdict and handed the paper back to Mr. Watkins for him to read out loud to the court. "We, the jury, find the defendants guilty as charged."

It wasn't a surprise. There weren't any gasps or outbreaks. The Judge set a date for sentencing and the two defendants were put into cuffs and led out of the Courtroom. Judge Thompson thanked the jury for their service and dismissed them.

"I thought we might have a problem earlier," Barry said as he followed James back into the jury room. "I wonder what her problem was?"

"Who cares," said James. "It's over. Let's get things straightened up. I'll take the paperwork downstairs and tell them I'm taking a personal day tomorrow."

"Sounds good to me," Barry said as he gathered up the left over paper cups and scraps of paper. It was always good when a case wrapped up early.

CHAPTER THIRTY-THREE

"It's only 3:30," James said looking at his watch. "Marnie went paint shopping after she left us at lunch. She probably isn't back yet. I have an errand I need to do. It won't take me long, then I'll meet you at your condo."

"I didn't want to say anything in front of Marnie, but would you rather I take my own car to her new place? She'll be happy I'm checking out her new digs, but I think she'd like a little alone time with you." Barry's question took James by surprise. He never really gave it much thought, until Barry mentioned it.

"Thanks, buddy, I'd appreciate it." James' mind kicked into gear. "Did she tell you that Annie invited her on a girl's-night-out? I guess Casey Quinby, Marnie and Annie and are having dinner at the Paddock tomorrow, then taking in the Beach Boys concert at the Melody Tent."

"Yeah, she mentioned it. Annie's a good one for making somebody feel right at home. Actually, I haven't seen Casey since last spring. She's a good kid. Not my type, but I like her. She's landed herself a great job at the Tribune. Did you know she made head investigative reporter? That's probably why she hasn't been around." Barry knew all the gossip or at least he thought he did. "If those three get together, they'll be a force to be reckoned with."

"Why's that?" James asked as he locked the doors to the Courtroom.

"Well, Annie works for the DA's office, Casey is a reporter and Marnie will be working with Annie doing investigative work," Barry said. "No criminal-in-hiding will stand a chance."

"Marnie's going for the interview tomorrow morning. You don't even know if she has the job."

"I saw Annie earlier today and the interview with Mike Sullivan is just a formality. Don't tell Marnie I told you. I'm sure she wants to surprise you later." Barry shook his head and laughed. "Looks like we'll have our own Charley's Angels. Maybe we should call them the Barnstable Beavers? Not!"

James caught himself tapping his foot nervously. He stopped abruptly. Barry was too busy rambling to have noticed. "I'm going to head out now. I'll be back at your condo in about a half-hour or so." James was already part way down the stairs when he called back to Barry, "I forgot to take the trash bag from our office. Would you please just tie it up and set it outside the door? Thanks."

CHAPTER THIRTY-FOUR

James didn't want to talk anymore. He wanted to be by himself. He sprinted across the parking lot. Just as he reached his car, he tripped on a small tree branch. It sent him tumbling against the right front fender. He opened his eyes to see Becky's dent staring at him. He jumped back. His heart was beating out of his chest. Without hesitation he pressed the button to unlock the door. His finger slipped and the alarm wailed. He quickly shut it off and proceeded to push the adjacent button. He looked around to see if anybody was watching. He didn't see anyone. He got in, started the engine, and quickly pulled out of the lot. Instead of turning right onto Phinneys Lane, he took a left toward Kelly's Landing. It was only five minutes away and, besides, he had some extra time. There were a couple of dog walkers in the parking lot and a few families on the beach. He pulled into a space in the front row and opened his windows. He laid his head back and closed his eyes. The sounds of children laughing and having fun echoed in his ears.

Memories ... happy memories.

He didn't hear the car door beside him open. A little voice came from nowhere, "Hey mister, are you sleeping?" Startled, he shook his head and opened his eyes only to see little hands trying to hold on to the open window.

Another voice called from the other side of the car, "Ryan, get over here, right now!" The hands slipped away. He turned to see a toddler, probably no more than three, run to his mother's side. "I'm sorry," she said.

"Don't worry, I was about to leave anyway," James said as he sat upright and started his car. Once he was sure the little boy was with his mother, he slowly backed out and headed to the main road.

He checked his watch. There was still plenty of time. He crossed Route 6A onto Phinneys Lane. About a mile down, he made a left turn onto Bradley Avenue. A James Taylor song came on the radio. He got so into the lyrics, he almost missed the turn into the Stop and Shop parking lot.

"Whoops," he said out loud. He parked and went inside. It had been a long time since he'd bought flowers. He had to walk up a couple of isles to find them. A beautiful bouquet of pink and white carnations with a couple of yellow Shasta daisies, some white and purple alstroemeria and a scattering of baby's breath caught his eye. Since he knew Marnie didn't own a vase, he asked the girl behind the floral desk if he could buy one. Normally, they weren't for sale. She hemmed and hawed a bit, but he convinced her it was a special occasion. It probably didn't hurt that he was still in uniform.

He made his way back to Barry's condo. It was just 4:15. He didn't see Marnie's car. Barry saw him pull in and was waiting at the door.

"She called about ten minutes ago." Barry motioned for James to come in. "She's got the paint and is on her way here. Have a seat. Do you want a beer?"

"Sure," said James. He looked around. Barry really had a nice place. His eyes stopped at Ned's lamp. A smile came over his face.

"It feels like Ned is here with us, doesn't it?" said Barry.

133

James sat, folded his hands, and leaned forward on his knees. He tilted his head down, taking his eyes off the lamp. "I miss him."

"We all do," said Barry.

The door opened and Marnie came in all smiles. "Here I am, you lucky guys. Are you ready?" She was giddy. "Wait till you see all I got done. Not only did I get the paint and brushes, etc., I picked up a couple of neat pictures at Home Goods."

"How can you pick out pictures before furniture?" James asked.

"Easy, I know pretty much what I want. You'll see. It will all fit together perfectly."

James didn't doubt her for a minute. He and Barry finished their beers and the three of them got up and walked outside.

"You guys take the paint and stuff. I'll pick up pizza and beer. Give me the address and I'll meet you there," Barry said, got the address from Marnie, then left.

Marnie and James shifted her purchases into his car. He wanted to surprise her with the flowers, but there was no way she'd miss them. She looked into the back seat, stopped, then turned and wrapped her arms around him. Without hesitation, she gave him a long warm kiss. "You're really special."

"Hold that thought for later. If we don't leave now, we never will." He didn't want the moment to end.

Marnie put her stuff in the back seat and took the flowers into the front seat with her. She hugged them tight.

He backed out of Barry's driveway and headed south on Route 6A toward Yarmouthport. The radio played soft rock. Very apropos, thought James. He glanced at Marnie. Her eyes were shut. She was tapping her fingers to the beat of the music on the side of the vase and quietly humming the song being sung by Kelly Clarkson. When it ended, she rolled her head to the left and whispered, "Thank you."

James smiled. "You're welcome."

"The house is just around the next bend, on the left. There, it's the white one with the dark green shutters and the red geraniums in the window boxes." She raised a hand and pointed to a duplex about forty-five feet in from the road. The house didn't face the road. It was tilted at an angle with the main driveway passing in front. There was a parking spot wide enough for two cars on each side.

"I'm on the left side." They arrived before Barry, so James pulled into the space closest to the house.

"Great location," he said as he opened his door and got out. "Close to everything, yet quiet enough to relax. Something like my house, only I'm a little more in the country. One of these days I'll take you there."

"I'd like that. Let's go inside. I want you to see what you're in for." She chuckled, sniffed the flowers, and got out of the car. As they walked up to the door, she handed them to James. "I need two hands to fumble through my purse for the keys."

"Typical woman," he said almost wishing he hadn't. In his mind, Marnie was far from typical. She was his dream come true.

Just a few obstacles he has to overcome and this relationship will work.

"Found them," she exclaimed. "Now close your eyes and hold on to my belt. I'll guide you in."

James' foot caught on the edge on the door jam and he almost lost the vase he had cradled to his chest.

"Oops," said Marnie. "You can open your eyes now. I forgot to tell you to lift your foot higher than usual. It's an old place. I guess that's part of the ambiance; old doors, high jams, creaky windows and whatever else I discover. At least I'll know if a stranger tries to enter because they'll trip for sure."

He tightened his lips and rubbed his chin as he surveyed the place. His nods of approval made her happy.

She reached forward to take the flowers he still held firmly in his grasp. The only place to set them was on the kitchen table the former tenants had left. She was home. The only thing missing was a glass of wine, a chunk of sharp provolone cheese, a baguette of fresh baked French bread and some soft music playing in the background. She could slip James into the picture, but for this moment she wanted it to be all about her.

"Okay, now that you've got a general idea, let me show you the rest." Marnie took his hand and pulled him toward the kitchen. "The stove and refrigerator are relatively new. Some night I'll keep quiet and let my pot roast do the talking," she said as she set the vase in the center of the table.

"That'll be a challenge."

Marnie scowled, "So what is it, I can't keep quiet or I can't cook?"

"Well, I know you can talk – and the cooking thing, I'll reserve my comments. He quickly redeemed himself. But, if that's an invitation, I accept."

"Moving right along. Follow me, I'll show you more."

Just as they left the kitchen, there was a knock at the door. Marnie jumped a little, then realized it must be Barry. The tour was interrupted when she opened the door for her cousin. The smell of hot-steamy pepperoni and mushroom pizza and a bag of what she presumed to be a couple of six packs took center stage.

"Just in time." She took the pizza from him. "Put the beer in the fridge and I'll set the pizza on the table. We need to get the bags out of James' car. I've got a table cloth, a package of paper plates, some napkins and plastic cups in one of them." They ventured outside to retrieve the stuff they had previously transferred from Marnie's car to James'. Back inside, Marnie said, "Why don't we eat while it's hot, then I'll continue the tour. Cuz, you didn't miss anything. We were headed for the bedroom when you knocked."

"Saved by the knock," laughed Barry. "Sounds good to me, I picked up a bag of chips, too."

James rolled his eyes as he searched the bags for the 'family linens and fine china'. He was smiling inside. He had a feeling of belonging again; belonging to a family. He liked that.

"Wait till you see my color scheme. I'm sure you both will approve. Even if you don't, I don't want to hear it. You better act surprised or pleased, just humor me," said Marnie.

"I can't wait. Actually, I can. I'm hungry," said Barry. Remember I had to smell this from the restaurant to here."

"This pizza is really good. It's darn close to New York style. They're the best, you know," she teasingly said to James.

"I'll be the judge of that," he said back.

"Some good things come from New York. I know you disagree when it comes to the Yankees, but take me, for instance." She was grinning.

"Enough, you two. Let's eat." Barry was ready to start without them.

They each opened a beer and James toasted to Marnie's new beginning.

"Here's to it
Those who get to it
And don't do it
May never get to it
To do it again..."

It didn't take long for Barry to devour the last piece, hoist a beer, and chant, "Let the tour resume."

"Hear, hear!" agreed James and Marnie.

They closed the empty pizza box, picked up their beers, and followed Marnie out of the kitchen.

James stood in the doorway surveying the surroundings. The living room had a beautiful low bow window with a seat. The window itself had a Cape Cod flair with a collection of six by eight inch panes. There was a cobalt-blue sun-catcher attached to one of the panes. "Did you already start decorating with the hanging art?" asked James.

"No, it must have been left by the previous tenant as a welcome to the new tenant, or maybe they just forgot to take it. Whatever the case, I like it. I might even add some more," She motioned the guys to follow. "I think I'm going to look for a couch, a couple of side chairs, a coffee table and one or two end tables." Marnie

137

turned to Barry. "I like the small entertainment center you have. Actually, I want to check out the furniture store you used." She looked at James. "Maybe we could take a ride there tomorrow after I leave the DA's office?

"I've got nothing planned, so your wish is my command," he said.

There were two more windows on the side wall looking out at the parking area. They each had a set of wooden shutters that could be closed for privacy. The floors were wide board pine, scuffed in places, but Marnie thought that enhanced the charm.

She led the guys down a small hallway. At the end was the bathroom.

James nodded his approval. "This is really nice. It looks like it's been updated." There was a nearly new granite top vanity and a cream colored commode with a matching tub and shower enclosure.

On either side of the hallway was a bedroom. Without furniture taking up space, it appeared to be a good size. The one that faced the front of the house had a walk-in closet. Each room had a double window. "I'm going to use the one in the front, mostly because I like the walk-in."

James instinctively walked to the windows and checked the locks. "Just making sure nobody can get in and steal you."

She smiled. "Remember I'm a city girl. Ain't nothing gonna spook this kid and, for sure, nobody's taking me against my will."

"Hey, cuz, you did a great job finding this place."

"You can thank Annie for that. Do you know Charlie at the DA's office?" asked Marnie.

"Yeah, why?" Barry wondered.

"Well, he owns this duplex and the one further down the driveway. I guess he owns another one somewhere else, but this location was right for me. So here I am." In her mind she was already settled in. They went back to the kitchen, opened another beer, and sat down at the table.

James marveled at her self assurance, her self confidence. She's amazing, he thought. "What time did you say your interview is tomorrow morning?"

"It's ten o'clock. Annie is meeting me in the lobby and introducing me to Mr. Sullivan. She said I'd probably be there less than an hour. I'm hoping to start work the middle of next week. Once that's done, I need to check on the bar exam schedule to see when they're offering the next one. Annie said that Mr. Sullivan would probably write a letter of recommendation for me. It will be easier taking the exam soon after finishing school when things are still fresh in my mind."

"Now that we've got the serious stuff out of the way, let's see the paint you picked out," said James as he headed to the living room to retrieve the cans sitting beside the front door.

"Set them up here on the table," she said. There was a bag on the floor just inside the kitchen door. She lifted it to the table. "You'll have no excuse for not starting early. I have all the paint brushes, pans, blue tape and even an opener. I don't think I've forgotten anything."

James looked at Barry. "I thought I took the day off tomorrow. I'm going to be working harder than I do when I get paid."

Marnie stood beside the table with her hands on her hips. "Listen, big guy, you're the one who volunteered – enough of your whining."

"Only kidding," James said.

There were four gallons of paint. Marnie looked at the numbers on the lids. She kept two on the table and moved the other two to the floor. "This is the color for the living room. It was listed on the National Trust for Historic Preservation color chart. It's called Cincinnatian Hotel Hannaford." She opened the can. "It's a dark creamy color with a hint of tan. It will be an easy color to match furniture to." She looked to the guys for approval. Not hearing any objections, she moved on to the next can. "This color is for my bedroom. I love it and the name is perfect." She hid the label on the cover with the palm of her hand. "Would either of you care to take a guess?"

Both James and Barry could care less, but this was Marnie's moment, so they went along with her game.

"Since neither one of you have any decorating skills, let me enlighten you. It's called Romantic Rose; a perfect color to enhance the mood and arouse the senses." Marnie closed her eyes and hugged her shoulders.

James felt the need to change the conversation. "If you want, I can get here early and get a head start. When you're done at the DA's office you can meet me here."

"That'll work," Marnie said shifting her attention to Barry. "What's the name of the furniture store you got your stuff from?"

"It came from Hickey's in Dennisport. James, you know where it is, don't you?"

"I think so. Isn't it the one on Main St. across from the Clam Box?"

"Yep, the parking lot is on the side street. If you go by it you have to go down around the rotary and circle back."

"Okay, then, it's a plan. I'll give you a key tonight and I'll meet you here when I'm done. Maybe we can grab some lunch after I look." Marnie was all wound up.

James wasn't use to being swept up in such a whirlwind, but he liked it. It was new, it was good, and he didn't want it to end.

Barry looked at his watch, then at Marnie. "It's almost 9:30. I know I don't have a busy day tomorrow, but you guys do. We should probably get going. Are you riding home with me or James?" Barry was actually getting bored. Not only bored, but he felt like the third wheel. "I need to stop at the gas station on the way."

"I'll ride home with you then. I need to pick up a couple of things at the little convenience store at the station. You don't mind do you James?"

"Of course not, just don't forget to give me a key." He was a little disappointed, but knew it was better she leave with Barry. "Is there anything else on your to-do list that I need to know?"

"Not tonight, I don't want to scare you away." She laughed.

James and Barry went outside to wait while Marnie took one more walk around her new house. She took a deep breath and whispered, "I think I'm going to like it here." She smiled, shut off the lights, and headed for the front door. She made sure the door was locked and handed James the key. "I'll get a couple made tomorrow. Cuz, I want to leave one with you in case of emergency."

"Sure enough, I'll meet you at the car." He walked away to give Marnie and James a little privacy.

"You know, I'm really loving this place. Now I see why Barry never came back to New York. Tomorrow will be fun. I'm looking forward to the whole day."

"Me too. Now get on your way, Barry's waiting." He set down the trash bag and pulled her close. He didn't want to let her go.

She tilted her head back to meet his lips. "I'll see you in the morning."

Barry waved to James as Marnie got into his car, closed the door, and off they went back to the Village. He watched Barry's car round the corner, then out of sight.

A feeling came over him. One he had never felt before. Was this what love felt like? It had been only four days.

Take it slow – tomorrow will be another day.

CHAPTER THIRTY-FIVE

I must have been tired. I didn't even hear Sam leave. That old comfortable feeling had crept back into our relationship. We were friends; maybe a little more than friends. Neither one of us were ready to commit to an engagement or marriage or anything close to that. We were both wrapped up too tight in our professional lives. We understood that. Maybe someday, but for now, we were just special friends with benefits.

I know it's Friday and a work day, but just a couple more minutes wouldn't hurt. I rolled over and hugged the pillow next to me. The smell of Sam's after-shave lingered. I buried my head and gave my imaginary image an Eskimo kiss, then I pulled back and giggled. It was a fun night, but now I had work to do.

I made myself a cup of French Vanilla and a couple of slices of toast, then headed to the deck. It was a beautiful morning. The birds were singing and the trees were dancing in the gentle breeze that meandered through their branches. It was going to be a great day; I could feel it.

I decided not to tell Sam about my visit to Bourne High School yesterday. I would when the time was right, but first I needed to do a little more research.

My plans for today include a visit to The Train Stop. I know I have to be careful how I approach this. Talking to Mr. Porter and

Mr. Bowdin is different than talking to Becky's peers and co-workers. I could tell them I'm writing a public interest article on Becky. After all, her family is well connected with the community. I can interject a few things I know about her and maybe they'll fill in the blanks. This type of interview is my specialty. It usually works pretty good.

Although I didn't want to get started, I knew I had to. I had a busy day ahead of me and toying with the clock wasn't going to change it. I reluctantly stood up and, with coffee cup and empty paper plate in hand, headed back into the kitchen.

My cell phone rang and I scurried inside to answer it. It was my boss, Chuck Young. "Are you planning to come into the office today?"

"Actually, I am. Are you going to be there this morning?" I said, waiting for his reply.

"I'll be here until 11:30, then I have to head out. I have a Rotary Club meeting at The Riverside."

"Great, I'll be there within the hour. I have something I want to run by you for Sunday's paper."

Without hesitation, I jumped into the shower. I hadn't let the water run, so it was still on the cold side. It felt refreshing though. I thought about the proposal I was going to present to Chuck. I had to sell him on my idea of running an article on Becky. I figured he'd go for it, but he is the boss so I had to get his approval. It would be very short and with not much more information than was already reported. I needed to print some open end thoughts that might trigger questions or guilt in somebody's mind. It's a long shot, but it was all I had.

I didn't bother to dry my hair. I just pulled it back in a ponytail, then threw on a pair of peach colored capris and a white jersey. My sandals were still beside the front door where I had left them when I got home yesterday. I slipped them on, grabbed my briefcase and car keys and was off.

The traffic was still light. In another hour, the beach road would be crowded with vacationers armed with chairs, coolers, and suntan lotion. It would be a race to position themselves in such a manner to avoid the lingering rolls of the waves – yet strategically facing the sun without being blocked by a neighboring family's umbrella.

I pulled into the Tribune parking lot, gathered my stuff, and headed for the employee entrance. I stood by the door swiping my ID without success. It wouldn't open.

Jamie walked up behind me, slid her ID through the security scan, and opened the door.

"Card not working?" She glanced down at my hand and started to laugh. "The last time I checked, my Macy's card didn't have door opening privileges either."

I looked at the red card with the big gold red star embossed on the front. It was my Macy's card all right. I was more than a little embarrassed. "Okay, you got me. Too much on the old brain," I slid the card back into my briefcase, followed her inside, and headed for my office. "Thanks," I called back to her when I was half way down the corridor.

Chuck was just leaving the employee break room with a cup of coffee in hand. "Come on over to my office after you get settled."

I dropped everything on my desk, did a quick check of my piled-up mail, then headed toward his office. I had to pass the break room on the way, so I decided to grab myself a cup of coffee.

Chuck's office door was open. He was sitting at his desk flipping through some paperwork, so I knocked on the side of the door casing before I went in.

"Have a seat."

"Thanks." I mulled over how to present my proposal to him. Just go for it. "I'd like to submit a small article on Becky Morgan to appear in this Sunday's paper. I don't want it on the front page or anywhere very conspicuous. It should be in an area that will be seen by a person who reads all, or most all, of the articles in the paper; somebody who is hungry for news, in this case, about Becky. I'll be very careful about what I include. I'm working on a hunch. I'll make some comments without stating facts, at least ones that aren't already known. I need you to trust my judgment and let me run with this."

He clasped his hands behind his neck, leaned his head back, and stared at the ceiling. "I don't know what you're pursuing." He sat back up and looked straight at me. "And at this point, I don't think I want to know. You're in the position here because of your ability and your work ethic. I've no reason to doubt you this time." He folded his arms in front of him and rested them on his desk. "Just remember, this death is tied to prominent members of the community. Be careful what you say because once it's in print, it can't be erased."

"I understand completely. The Tribune will not be put in jeopardy. My gut feeling tells me there is more to this story than a routine hit-and-run. I'm working on a few leads and need more time to confirm my theory. I'll be using the article as bait. Will you let me run with it?"

"Go ahead," Chuck said. There was a little apprehension in his voice, but he put his trust in me. "What section do you think will promote the most interest?"

"I was thinking of either the local news, specifically under Bourne, or the week in review section."

Chuck wrinkled his forehead pondering the question. "I think if somebody is scouring the paper for an article related to a specific location, and Bourne is the designated location, then I think it should run under the local news. Go ahead and write the copy. I'll call Bucky in production and tell him to expect you within the hour. Take it directly to him."

"Thanks boss. I'll check in with you as soon as I have something definite to report. If all goes well, it will be soon."

I immediately returned to my desk and started writing the article. I knew once it was released, Sam would call and chew me out. It wasn't information he gave me, because he didn't give me any. It was stuff I picked up on my own, although some of the information I had was incorporated into leads he was also working

145

on. He'd be mad, but that was his problem. He wouldn't stay mad for long and besides it was always fun making up.

I finished the article and rushed down to Bucky's office. He was waiting – funny how a call from the boss carries clout. If I had called and asked him to wait for copy, he would've laughed and probably hung up. I handed him the copy and quickly headed for the door. "Bye," I said without turning around. "And, thanks, I really appreciate it."

CHAPTER THIRTY-SIX

It was only eleven o'clock, plenty of time to get to Bourne. My objective was to visit The Train Stop and, hopefully, pick up some vibes from Becky's friends. I should get there right around lunch time. Good excuse, I thought. If I remember correctly, they have good sandwiches. I packed up my briefcase, grabbed my purse, locked my office door, and headed to the parking lot. Jamie was on the phone, so I just waved as I passed her desk.

So far the day had progressed wonderfully. I had plenty of time to visit the Train Stop, ride by the accident scene, then get home, shower and get ready for girl's-night-out. I wasn't meeting Annie and Marnie at The Paddock until five o'clock.

I started down Main Street, figuring I'd jump onto Route 6, get off at the Scenic Highway exit and cut over into Bourne. But when I turned onto Route 28, just before the exit onto Route 6, I was forced to pull over to the side of the road. Up ahead I could see the barrage of red and yellow lights accompanying the blare of screaming sirens. Apparently there had been a bad accident on the ramp leading to the highway. That was my cue to cut back and take one of the side streets that would eventually take me to the service road. It was out of my way, but in the long run it was quicker.

Finally, back on track, I began to plan my strategy. Since I'd be on the Scenic Highway anyway, I planned to pass by creepy Mr. Parker's house. I just wanted to keep tabs on the old guy, after all, he might end up being the key witness to what I already deemed a murder.

There he was, rocking and watching. I wanted to wave, but knew I couldn't. I wondered if he recognized my car. I slowed. Just around the bend was where Becky had been mowed down and left to die less than a week ago. In my heart, I wanted to stop, but again knew better. Even though the yellow police crime tape was gone, this was still the scene of an active investigation. Instead, I said a silent prayer for her and continued on.

The Train Stop's parking lot was full except for two spaces toward the back of the building. Another car was coming in from the other direction, so without hesitation, I accelerated forward and slipped into a space just perfect for my little green Spider. I decided to leave my briefcase in the car and use my mental notebook to record any pertinent information I might obtain from her co-workers.

The only table not taken was in the back corner next to the bathrooms. Since I had no choice, I zigzagged my way in and out of the other occupied tables to reach my destination. It was busy. This might be a good thing. It gave me a chance to look around and focus on the people working there. A young girl with short blonde hair was taking an order from a family of four. The two kids didn't seem interested. They were coloring and occasionally swinging their legs under the table just enough to touch each other. This caused a quiet reprimand from the mom.

Another girl, probably around Becky's age, delivered half of an order to the table next to me and headed back to the kitchen. I assumed to get the rest. There was a dark haired handsome boy with a terrific tan taking orders at the take-out window. He caught me looking at him and gave me a smile. I felt the color rush into my face. I must have been staring.

If only he knew why I was here.

I actually wasn't staring at him; I was trying to get into his head and draw information out.

About five minutes passed when the young blond girl came over to my table. "Can I take your order?" she asked.

"Sure, I'll have a cheeseburger, well done, with lettuce, tomatoes and mayonnaise. Also, could you please toast the roll?" The nametag on her shirt read, Sara.

"You got it. For your side, would you like fries? And to drink?" She asked without skipping a beat.

"Yes to the fries and I'll have a Diet Coke, please."

"Is Pepsi okay?" she looked to me for an answer.

I hesitated, wondering if she was a friend of Becky's. She seemed like a sweet kid.

She repeated the question.

"Oh, I'm sorry, Sara, that will be fine." She nodded and headed back to the kitchen. Whenever somebody was wearing a nametag, I addressed them by the name engraved on it. Usually it created an aura of familiarity.

I continued my survey of the surroundings and the people working. There was an older woman at the cash register. She kept one eye on the register and the other on the patrons. She might be the owner. Whoever she was, it appeared she ran a tight ship.

I had an idea.

Sara was on her way to my table with my Diet Pepsi. I had to make my move now. "Can I ask you a question?" I said as she put my drink down in front of me. "Were you a friend of Becky Morgan?"

Her eyes opened wide then closed. I noticed a tear form in the corners. "Yes, she used to work here."

"I know. Did you go to school with her?"

"I did. We were cheerleaders together for Bourne High School. She was a co-captain." The buzzer hooked to her belt went off. "Your food is ready. I'll be right back."

Damn it. Did I lose her?

Hopefully I can reopen the conversation. The restaurant was half empty now, so maybe I had a chance. I took a deep breath, crossed my arms, and tucked my chin into my chest.

"Did you know her?" Sara asked as she put my burger and fries down on the table in front of me.

"In a round about way, I did." I wasn't lying just stretching the truth a little. I had to go for it. "I'm a reporter for the Cape Cod Tribune and I'm doing a story on Becky. Judging from the interviews I've already done, she was a very smart, popular girl with lots of friends."

"Your information is right on." I could tell Sara was ready to talk, but I knew this was the place.

"Would you like to talk to me about her?" I asked bluntly.

"I get off work at 2:30 this afternoon. That's only an hour from now. Could I meet you somewhere?" she asked.

"If I remember correctly, there's a little coffee shop, Jessie's Java Hut, just up the street on the opposite side of the road. I've got an errand to run, then I'll meet you there just after 2:30. Is that okay with you?"

"Can I bring Shawn with me? He's the guy at the take-out window. Shawn's the star quarterback for Bourne High. He knew Becky well."

"Of course," I said. "And Sara, thank you."

I ate my burger and half of the fries. She was cleaning a table a few over from me. I caught her attention. "Sara, when you get a chance could you please bring my check?"

Her approach slowed. Her face was sad. She handed me the check. "I just want you to know, Becky was special. She was my best friend. I miss her."

"With your help, I'll try to keep her memory alive. Take it easy and we'll talk. See you shortly at Jessie's." I gave her a smile and a wink of confidence.

CHAPTER THIRTY-SEVEN

The Bourne PD was about a half mile down the road. Since I had some time to kill, I decided to stop in to see Peggy. The office was pretty empty. I glanced over to Sam's office, but the lights were off and the door was shut. "Hi there, is this the complaint desk?"

Peggy was deeply engrossed in a report and hadn't seen me come in, so the sound of my voice startled her. She put her hand over her heart, "Are you trying to give me the big one?"

"Why so quiet?" I said looking around. I waved to a couple officers milling around in the back of the room.

"Sam's in a meeting somewhere. He left about two hours ago and said he'd see me later. You know him. His later could be Monday. We've had a couple of fender benders around town and I sent one of the guys to escort Rhonda from Sea Side Marina to the bank to make a big deposit. We've had a few attempted hold-ups within the last couple of weeks, so better safe than sorry. And you, what brings you to this neck of the woods?" Peggy asked as she motioned me to sit in the chair beside her desk.

"I'm glad it's quiet so we can talk. My meeting yesterday with Mr. Porter and Mr. Bowdin from the high school was amazing. I certainly got an insight into Becky Morgan. When we've got more time I'll fill you in. By the way, I haven't told Sam about any of this yet." I stopped to catch my breath. "Right now, I'm just killing some time. I had lunch at The Train Stop. A girl named Sara waited on me. Through conversation, she told me she is, rather was, Becky's best friend. She and a guy named Shawn, who also works there, are going to meet me just after 2:30 at Jessie's Java Hut."

I looked around to see if anyone was watching us. "I don't want to get you into any trouble. As far as any of these guys know, I was in the area and stopped in to say *hello*."

"You're talking to me, remember. Last Wednesday, you told Sam you were still going to conduct your own investigation, so he knows you're up to something." Peggy tilted her head, paused, then added. "You two make a good team. Once you put your heads together, if there's something to solve, you'll do it."

"I don't know how you do it, but you could walk right by the Secret Service, through the front door of the White House, and get invited to tea by the First Lady without getting into any trouble." Peggy shook her head.

"I told her I was a reporter for the Tribune and was doing a story on Becky."

Peggy grinned and rolled her eyes.

"What, don't look at me like that. I'm not lying."

"Make sure you choose your questions carefully." Peggy said. "I know you're looking for specific answers, but you don't want these kids to start a talk chain that could turn bad. Remember, they're hurting too." Peggy was dead serious.

"I completely understand what you're saying. Trust me on this one. I'll keep you informed." I turned to check the wall clock for the time. It was 2:20. "I'm going to head out. Tonight I'm going on a girl's-night-out with Annie. She has three tickets for the Beach Boys concert at the Melody Tent and asked if I'd like to go. She wants me to meet Barry's cousin from New York. I guess she's staying with him until she gets set up in her own place. Anyway, I think Mike Sullivan is going to give her a job in the DA's office doing investigative work until she takes the bar exam.

Annie seems to like her." I stood up. "It will probably be late tonight, so I'll give you a call tomorrow."

"Later," Peggy called as I crossed the room and headed out the door.

CHAPTER THIRTY-EIGHT

I pulled out of the PD parking lot and headed back to Jessie's. The yellow and red, blinking neon sign of a giant coffee cup hung in the window. It would drive me crazy if I had to watch that all day. The place was empty. I took a table as far away from the counter as possible. Since the place was small, the furthest away was still too close for me, but it would do. I was only there five minutes when the door opened and Sara and Shawn came in. They walked to the table and I motioned for them to take a seat. "Do you guys want anything? I'm going to have an iced coffee."

"I'll have one, too," said Shawn.

"Could I please have a strawberry smoothie?" asked Sara.

I went to the counter, placed the order and came back to the table. "First of all, I want to thank you for taking the time to talk to me about Becky. Like I told Sara, I'm a reporter for the Cape Cod Tribune, the head investigative reporter."

Before I could say any more, Shawn spoke up, "Why are you doing a story about Becky?"

"Here's the thing, Becky was the victim of a hit and run, we all know that. What we don't know is who hit her and why they didn't stop or why they haven't come forward." The lady behind the counter signaled to me that the order was ready. "Hold your thoughts, I'll be right back." I distributed the drinks and sat back down. "Obviously, the Bourne PD is actively examining all the information and facts they have to date. I'm working independently." I took a sip of my iced coffee and winced. I'd forgotten to put a couple packets of Sweet-'n-Low in it. "Do you understand what I just said?"

Sara nodded and Shawn said, "I think so." He continued, "What can we do to help you?"

"First of all, can I trust you to keep this conversation between the three of us, at least for the time being? This is important. What you might think isn't pertinent to the case may very well be a vital piece of information. If for some reason, it reaches the wrong ears, we may never know what happened last Sunday night." I waited for a reaction.

Shawn spoke first, "We both have known Becky since kindergarten. I live down the street from the Morgan's. We were like brother and sister. This whole nightmare is tearing me apart."

Sara's lips started to quiver. Shawn stayed calm and put his arm around her. She leaned over and put her head on his shoulder.

"Did it seem like anything was bothering her the last couple of months? Was she having any problems at home or with any of her friends? Did she break up with a boyfriend?" It was the last question I was most interested in. I hoped it was the first one they answered.

"Becky used to date one of the guys on the football team. His name's Kevin Brown. It didn't work out, but they were still good friends. She may have been seeing someone else though. One Saturday last month, she got a ride to work from somebody with a real neat set of wheels. The sun was hitting the windows, so I couldn't see who was driving. When she opened the door, I saw her lean over and give the guy a kiss. He looked like an older guy, so I assumed it was Mr. Morgan. I asked if her Dad got a new car." Shawn sighed. "She gave me a strange look and said it wasn't her Dad, then turned and walked into the Stop. I didn't ask any more about it."

Sara sat quietly until Shawn finished his story. "I remember that day," she said. "Becky was in a weird mood. I asked her if she wanted to go to the Lobster Hut, then a movie after work. She told me she was busy. That was all … she was busy. It wasn't like Becky. We always shared plans and stories." Sara leaned forward on one arm and lifted her smoothie with the other. "We were scheduled to work until 6:00. The Stop actually closed at 4:30, but we were on the clean-up list, that's why the 6:00." Sara took another sip. "Becky asked if she could leave at 5:30. Mrs. Murphy said okay and the next thing I saw was Becky standing around the corner, next to the ladies room, talking on her cell phone. She was all giggly until she saw me. She turned and began to whisper, so I couldn't hear what she was saying."

My mind was spinning. I wanted to record the conversation, but that wasn't an option. I knew as soon as I got home, I'd take out my 3 x 5's and write it all down. I didn't want to forget any of it. "Did you see who picked her up?"

"Yeah," said Sara. "Well, I didn't see the person, but I saw the car. It was a dark color, black, I think. And it was shiny. It was some kind of sports car, but I don't know the different names. It sure was pretty though, something like your car, Shawn. When she saw the car pull in, she grabbed her purse and left without saying a word."

"That sounds like the same car I saw her get out of earlier," he said. "From that day on Becky changed. She became more reserved. She didn't want to do anything with us anymore. The other thing was, she started wearing make-up. Becky never or very seldom wore make-up."

"Did you ever see that car again?" I asked both of them.

Sara thought for a minute, "I did, a couple of times." I'm sure it was the same car. One time it was way in the back of the student parking lot at school. I don't think Becky expected it to be there. She looked around to see if anyone was watching before she darted between cars and quickly disappeared inside. I wondered why she didn't introduce her friend to us. I did ask her, but she practically told me to mind my own business."

"How about last week, was she still acting strange?" I asked.

"She seemed a little depressed. Well, not really depressed, just sad. We did take in a movie one night. I asked her if she was okay. She said she would be. She had to work a few things out."

I remembered the faces at Becky's memorial. Two of them were sitting across from me. "I'm puzzled." I said, "Why would Becky be walking alone on the Scenic Highway on a Sunday night after dark?"

"I don't know. I called her earlier in the day to see if she wanted to go to the Mall."

I knew this was getting hard on Sara. "She said she was meeting a friend so she couldn't." Sara fidgeted in her chair. "Casey, please help us find who did this to Becky. We miss her." Sara's eyes welled up.

Shawn stared at the floor. His face lacked expression.

I reached into my purse and pulled out some tissues and a couple of business cards. I wrote my cell number on the back. "Here's my card," I said handing one to each of them. "I'm going to take the information you gave me today and shuffle it with what I already have. Hopefully, I'll be able to make some connections. I'm sure I will. Give me a couple of days and I'll get back to you. Is that okay?"

They both nodded. We stood up and I extended my hand, "Thanks for your help."

They reached out at the same time. Our three hands were joined together like a team bonding and I was their captain. I wasn't going to let them down.

We left Jessie's. Shawn and Sara waved, then joined hands and headed toward Shawn's car.

Once inside my car, I leaned forward and rested my head on the steering wheel. It was time to share my findings with Sam. This was definitely not a random hit-and-run. The clock on the dashboard lit up when I started the engine. It was already 3:30. As usual I'd have to put the pedal to the metal and take a quick shower in order to meet the girls at The Paddock by five o'clock. That was allowing myself fifteen minutes travel time from my house to the restaurant. It'll work. I'll give Sam a call tomorrow.

CHAPTER THIRTY-NINE

James got up early. He had a busy day ahead of him.

I can't believe it's Friday already.

Marnie had given him his to do list. He knew he wasn't going to get it all done in one day – that was impossible. But working alone, without having to deal with anyone else's chatter, he figured he get enough done to impress her.

Since he'd be driving by Nancy's, a nice hot cup of joe and a freshly baked donut would give him the energy to get started.

The sun was already warming the air. It was going to be a beautiful day. Nancy was busy. He tweaked the bell as he usually did every morning before work when he stopped in for breakfast. She knew it was him without even looking up. The regular door tweak had a different sound than a James' tweak. Without turning around, she raised her arm to wave. "Hello, Jimmy," she said.

Just like a Mom. Always knew the sounds her children made.

He waited until all the customers were away from the counter. Most of them bought stuff to go. "Good morning," he said in a cheerful voice. "It's a great day. No work, at least at the Courthouse; no boss, at least for a few hours; and the best donuts on Cape Cod." He lifted his nose in the air and sniffed the tantalizing aromas.

"I've got your favorites today," said Nancy as she reached high on the third shelf. She slid the tray out and rested it on the counter. "Pick one," she said handing him a dish with her free hand. "Want coffee?"

"Sure do," he said

"Do you want it in a cup or to go?"

He felt that Nancy wanted him to stay. "I'll have my first cup here, then take one to go."

"You've got it." Nancy poured a cup from the pot she'd just brewed. "What are you up to today? Obviously, you're not meeting the governor in that get up." She wasn't used to seeing James in anything but his uniform or looking picture-perfect, like an ad from GQ.

"Nope, the governor will have to wait. Today, I'm working for the princess." He smiled and headed for a table close to the counter. He felt really good. "Hey, Nance, do you have time to grab a cup of coffee with me?" He looked at her with little boy eyes.

She looked around. There wasn't anybody needing anything at the moment so she got herself a half cup and joined James at the table.

"Marnie found a house to rent on Route 6A in Yarmouthport. Barry and I went down to see it last night. It's a two bedroom in a great location. It needs some tender loving care, so today I'm playing Leonardo da Vinci and putting my painting skills to work. She picked out the colors."

Nancy hadn't see James this happy in years. In fact, until Marnie came along, he'd been teetering on the dark side and she couldn't figure out why. "You'll have to take some pictures when you're done. I'd love to see it."

"How about this," James took her hand. "How would you like to see it in person when we're done?" Nancy was like family to him, so he was sure Marnie wouldn't mind.

Nancy beamed as only a mother would, "I'd love to. Give me some notice and an idea of Marnie's taste so I can get a housewarming gift."

"I'll do that." James looked at his watch. Well, I better be off or it will never get done." James got his coffee to go, gave Nancy a kiss on the forehead, and headed down 6A to Marnie's new house.

He parked his car in the same spot he was in last night. He automatically locked his car door, reached in his pocket for Marnie's key, and unlocked her front door. He didn't feel like a stranger. He felt like he belonged there. "Please don't let this be a dream, and if it is, don't let me wake up." He snapped back to reality, then looked around just to make sure nobody heard him. "Duh, I can say whatever I want, there's nobody here."

The paint was still sitting on the kitchen counter where they'd left it. He decided to start in the living room on the wall opposite the front door. He knew she'd be excited to see it done when she walked in. That was his plan.

Her meeting at the DA's office was for 10:00. He figured she'd probably stay and talk to Annie for awhile, then head on down to Yarmouthport. It was 8:30. If he was right, he'd have about two and a half hours to work.

The ceilings were only seven and a half feet tall, so he could reach them easily with the four- foot ladder he'd brought from home. He worked continuously until he finished cutting in the paint along the ceiling line, then stepped back to admire his work.

Painting looks so much better when you want to do it, not when you're forced to.

She did a good job picking out the color. He finished cutting in the other edges along the wall then started to roll the open areas. Before he realized it, he had finished the first wall.

It was quiet, too quiet, he thought. He completely forgot he had brought a portable radio from his house. It was the one he kept in his garage and used when he worked on his car. The music would add a little hominess when Marnie walked in. Actually, it would keep him company until she got there. He found the same soft rock station he had the car radio tuned to.

It only took him a little over an hour to complete his first segment. He continued on the rest of the walls cutting in the trim around the windows and the doors. With that done, he figured he could finish around the ceiling edge too.

He was on the last dip of the brush when the door opened. It was Marnie. Her eyes opened wide. "WOW," she screamed. "You're amazing, simply amazing." She stood in the middle of the room turning in a continuous circle.

"You better slow down. You'll get dizzy. Even more dizzy than you already are." James smirked and made a Charlie Chaplin face. "Besides, judging by the wildness in your voice, the neighbors might think we're having too much fun."

She stood on her tip toes and threw her arms around James' neck, "Thank you, thank you, thank you. How about you wash that paint off your hands and I'll treat you to lunch. You know a working man has to keep up his strength." She bobbed back and forth like a prize fighter trying to avoid his opponents jabs. "Let's head in the direction of the furniture store. After lunch I'd like to take a look. I don't have any furniture in New York, so I'll need everything to set up housekeeping here." She wrinkled her nose and gave him a wink. "Sound good to you?"

"Won't take me but a minute," he said. "Please hand me the hammer in the tool box by the door, so I can make sure the paint lid is on tight."

James headed for the kitchen to put things in order. Since Marnie was going out with the girls tonight, he figured he'd come back and do more painting. After all, he had nothing else to do. Marnie was his new project.

When he came back into the living room, she was measuring the walls with a tape she'd found in his toolbox. "I want to make sure I get the right size couch, then work a couple of chairs into the remaining space. Since there's a ceiling light, I don't have to

162

worry about lamps and that kind of stuff until I get back. Can you please write these numbers down for me?"

After the living room, they moved into the bedroom. "I know I want at least a queen size bed. I think the room's too small for a king." She stood in one spot, turning to study the room. I need to get a bureau and a dresser with a mirror." James folded his arms and leaned against the door jam. She continued, "If I get a queen, then I'll probably have room for two end tables. Okay, I'm ready, let's go."

He followed as she went back to the living room, picked up her purse, and headed toward the front door. "Wait for me."

Once in the car, he turned to Marnie, "I don't know what the future holds, but right now I'm enjoying the present more than you'll ever know." He leaned over and gave her a kiss.

"I think I've uncovered a hidden talent." She raised her eyebrows.

"And what's that, if I might ask?"

"You're a terrific painter, of course," she pinched his cheek in a teasing fashion.

"I'm hungry," he said.

"For what," she said.

He put the keys in the ignition and turned it on. "It better be food or this car isn't moving."

She reached forward to adjust the volume on the radio and they were on their way.

The Clam Box was about a half mile before Hickey's Furniture. "Do you feel like a clam roll?" He asked, as they rounded the corner into Dennisport.

"Do I look like a clam roll?"

"Think you're pretty cute, don't you? I know you're going out to dinner, but that's five hours away. Besides, it sounds good to me and I'm driving, so hold on, we're turning in."

"They sure do a good business here." Marnie remarked looking around. "Are they as good as Seafood Harry's?"

"I think so. They're only open during the season from May to October. They're a big tourist attraction. Usually places that cater to tourists aren't that great. This one is an exception. The same family has owned it for at least forty-five years. Two years ago they had a fire and it burned to the ground. The townies weren't sure if they were going to rebuild. But they did. The new building is an exact replica of the original. We're up. What do you want?" He waited for Marnie to place her order, then added his.

"Let's get a table, they'll call us when the food is ready." James put his hand on Marnie's back and guided her across the room.

He watched Marnie study the pictures hanging on the walls.

"These pictures are new since the fire. Some of them were donated by long time Dennisport residents and other local businesses. Of course, all the original pictures were lost in the fire. It was a shame. Some were irreplaceable."

"Why's that?" she said listening intently to James.

"The Dennis Playhouse is in the next town over. It's America's oldest professional summer theater. They've run six plays or musical cabarets a year for the last 84 years. The opening performance, I think it was around 1927, starred Basil Rathbone. The others I remember reading about were Bette Davis, Ginger Rogers, Humphrey Bogart and Gregory Peck." Marnie was drawn into his knowledge of the arts. "You remember I told you I was a history buff. Well, there's a little taste of it."

"Anyway, back to the original Clam Box pictures. Many of the stars from the Playhouse came here to eat. Old Mr. Butkus would pose with them, then he'd have a buddy of his develop the picture. When he got it back, he'd take it down to the Playhouse for the actor to sign. Each production ran for two weeks, so he had plenty of time to get the autograph. Those pictures were hanging over there." James pointed to a wall at the far end of the restaurant. "Those are the ones that can never be replaced."

"Have you ever seen a show there?"

"I used to have season tickets. I had two, so I could bring a friend. It got so The Tavern was more the in-place and the

Playhouse was passé. I didn't want to go alone, so I gave them up. Maybe you'd like to go some night?"

"Number 42, your order is ready."

"That's us. I'll be right back." James pushed his chair away from the table and headed for the counter.

He came back with a tray full of food.

"By the way, yes, I would like to go to the Playhouse some night." Marnie smiled. She loved theater of all types. She became quiet. A dream-like expression overtook her face. Her mind drifted back to the times she went to plays on Broadway. They were special because they were the only things she did with her dad. He was always too busy for anything else. Many times they'd be accompanied by a client, but that was okay, at least they were together.

James wondered if he should interrupt her thoughts. "Are you still with me?" he said. "We can go on our bed-finding-mission as soon as we eat."

"Smart ass," she said abruptly. "I heard every word you said. I'm looking for furniture. You're helping me find it. Just for your information, it's my bed not ours." She stopped talking and started to eat her clam roll.

"I'm sorry. I don't want to upset you. Can we get back into that happy space we were in a few minutes ago?"

"I didn't mean to get angry with you. Talk of the theater brought back memories of my dad. We used to go quite often, when he'd make time. Enough of that, he's moved on and so have I."

The rest of lunch consisted of idle chit-chat. "I'm looking forward to girl's-night-out."

Before James could reply, Marnie's cell phone rang. She didn't recognize the number that flashed across the screen. "Hello."

A familiar voice on the other end said, "Hi, it's Annie. I figured you're with James and want to run an idea by you. The Beach Boys concert should be over between 10:00 and 10:30. It's a Friday night, so nobody has to get up for work in the morning.

Would you like to go to the Tavern afterwards for a drink or two? I'll call Casey a little later and ask her if she wants to go. I'm sure she will. I have to bring some paperwork over to Super Court, so I'll stop and ask Barry to join us. Why don't you ask James if he wants to meet us there, too?"

"Sounds good to me." She watched the puzzled look on James' face. "I'll see if he's up for it. He's been working his fanny off today. Wait till you see the house. It's looking great. We're on our way to check out a furniture store in Dennisport. A place called Hickey's."

"They have really nice stuff. Gotta go. There are few things I have to get done, then I'm leaving early so I can go home and get ready. I'll pick you up at 4:30. Say hi to James for me." And the conversation was done.

"That was Annie. She wants to know if you want to meet us at The Tavern after the concert for a drink. She's going to ask Barry and she thinks Casey will go too. It'll be fun." She noticed the look on James' face. It was a happy look.

"I'll be there," he said. "I agree, I think it will be fun. Like old times for us, with a new twist added – you." James couldn't help the grin that overtook his face.

"Good. It's going to be a great evening," said Marnie.

They finished eating, threw the trash in the bucket on the way out the door, got in the car, and headed to the furniture store.

There weren't many cars in the lot, so they were able to get a spot right next to the door. "Life is so much simpler here. If I went to a furniture store in New York, first of all I'd have to park in a garage, check my surroundings before I got out of my car, check for the closest entrance, jump out, and lock the door as I semi-ran to get inside the store." She stopped to take a breath. "And you think you want to visit the Big Apple?" She shrugged her shoulders. "I shouldn't knock it that bad. There are some great things to do and some amazing things to see. One of these days we'll go for a weekend and you can form your own impression." Her hand was resting on the door handle. "Let's go inside."

This was all new to James. On cue, he followed her. She had the door to the store open before he reached the top step. "You're not too excited." He gave her a little tap on the butt.

She tilted her head in his direction, "I guess I have to learn to slow down. I'm not used to this pace." She stood just inside the door, biting her top lip as she looked around the store. "Okay, let's head in the direction of living room furniture first. I think it's over there to the left." James hadn't moved when she turned around, "Are you coming?"

"Be right there, dear," he said jokingly.

She scowled, "You're going to owe me an extra glass of wine for being such a brat."

"Moi," he laughed. "Don't you think it's the other way around?"

Marnie didn't respond. She was searching her purse for the tape measure she'd taken from the house. "They have a great selection. Look, there's the same couch Barry has. It's really comfortable."

"I suppose it is." James said. "I've never really thought about it."

"Well, I should know. It's my bed, remember." She walked over to check the tag. "The price isn't bad either. It would be almost double back home." She moved to another grouping. "I like this one. I really want to find something they have in stock. I don't have time to wait for a special order." She went from couch to couch; chair to chair; coffee tables to end tables, then started all over again.

"I guess I'm lucky I didn't have to do any of this. My mom picked out my furniture many years ago and it still suits me just fine." His head dropped slightly down and his eyes met the floor. After a couple of seconds, he said, "But I'm enjoying this, I really am. Let me know when you want my opinion." A happy smile reappeared on his face.

"Am I doing too much talking?" She studied his smile.

"Absolutely not. Wow, did I just say that?" He cringed a little waiting for her reaction. "Only joking." He glanced at his watch and tapped his finger on the face. "I don't want you to rush. We can finish this tomorrow if you want."

"No, I'm okay. I really like this one," Marnie said. It was a sea foam green, overstuffed three-seater. "I think the whole display would fit in size wise and I know the color would be perfect with the walls." The chairs were the same style; comfy and big enough where you could pull your legs up under you and hug the side of the arms. One was a sea foam green and cream plaid and the other was a plain cream color. Both had cream colored throw pillows embroidered with grayish brown and green flowers. The pillows on the couch were made from the plaid material. "I'll be able to get some really light panels for the windows. Since I have those shutters I can close, I don't need to get heavy curtains."

"What about the tables?" James said looking around. "I like the ones in the display over there. Take one of the couch pillows and see it they're the same shade."

Marnie was impressed. She picked up a pillow and headed toward the table he had pointed out. She set it down on the top of the coffee table. "Good job. I like the square style end tables, but I think I'll stick with the rectangular coffee table." She stood admiring her choices. "Don't they have any sales people following your every footstep?"

"Why don't we go over to the bedroom furniture and take a look there before we hunt somebody down."

"Good idea. Um, I think it's in that direction." She pointed to the opposite side of the store.

"I think you're right."

"How am I doing so far? Do you like my taste?"

"You have impeccable taste, my dear. After all, you chose me didn't you?" He nudged her enough that she lost her balance and ended up sitting on the edge of a bed.

"Cute, real cute," she said. "I like the color of the living room tables I picked."

"Who picked?" kidded James.

"It helps to visualize how something is going to look by the bedding the store uses to enhance the display. What about this one?" Marnie was already sitting on the bed testing out the mattress.

"I thought you said it was your bed, not ours." James reminded her of her earlier comment.

She let his remark slide. "I like that one too," said Marnie as she moved down the aisle to another display. "I like this style, but I don't want dark wood. I think the cream color will go better with the wood floor." She walked back to her original choice. This is a queen size bed and the night tables aren't real big, so I'm sure this would fit just fine." She reached in her pocket and took out the paper she'd written the measurements on. "Yep, it'll work."

There were a couple different styles of bureaus and dressers to choose from. Marnie moved from piece to piece; opening drawers and checking the amount of space in each. "I've made my decision. I'm going to take this one here and that one over there. I'm not going to get the mirror. I think I'll look for something different. I don't need that right now." She was pleased with her choices. "Can you find a salesperson for me?" she asked.

There were those little girl eyes again. James melted and headed to the middle of the store in search of the sales desk.

Marnie was sitting in a boudoir chair when James returned with a salesgirl in tow. "I'd like to purchase some furniture and arrange for delivery next week. According to the tags, you have them in stock."

"Okay, let's get the information and I'll make sure." The salesgirl lifted her clipboard and began to write.

"If you don't need me, I'm going to wait in the car," he said.

"That's fine. If there's a problem I'll come get you, otherwise I shouldn't be long," Marnie said looking at her watch.

The sun peeked around the corner of the store as James walked to his car. The rays caught the right front fender.

Damn it.

He didn't need a constant reminder of last Sunday night. Next week, he'd check with the body shop in Sandwich and see if they could fix the fender without having to keep the car more than a day. He knew they had loaners. If anybody asked, he'd say he was having it detailed. Usually, he did it himself, but he'd use Marnie as an excuse again. He knew she could keep him busy. Nobody would question that. He laid his head back against the head rest and closed his eyes.

He jumped when Marnie opened the door and got in. "Oops, I didn't mean to wake you. Signed, sealed and will be delivered next Wednesday." She leaned over, hugged his arm and gave him a kiss. "Thanks for everything you're doing for me. I really appreciate it."

"Now I have to hustle. Annie is picking me up at Barry's at 4:30. That doesn't give me much time," she said while adjusting her seat belt.

James looked at her, "I'm going to stay at your place and do some more painting, then I'll head home, get cleaned up, changed, and meet you at The Tavern after the show."

"Sounds good to me. Since I'm running behind, I'm not going to stop at all. I'm really looking forward to tonight."

They pulled into Marnie's driveway. She quickly got out of the car and came around to James side. "Get out so I can give you a hug."

"I know you're in a hurry, but I just wanted to tell you I had a great time today. I never thought I'd say that about furniture shopping, let alone shopping of any kind," he said as he pulled her close in a tight squeeze. "Now give me a kiss like you mean it and be on your way."

She smiled. She felt comfortable in his embrace. His kiss was warm and tender. She almost didn't want to leave. "See you later. Have fun." She waved and scurried to her car.

He shook his head and started toward the front door.

CHAPTER FORTY

The me-time tonight was long overdue. Dinner and the Beach Boys concert should do the trick. I'm actually looking forward to meeting Barry's cousin. I wonder if she's like Barry – nice, but a little spacey. We'd gone to dinner a couple of times. He's not my type, but; then I'm not sure what my type is. I think Sam fits the bill pretty close.

My first thought, when I got home, was to have a glass of wine and relax a bit. I glanced at the clock.

What are you thinking, girl? No time, get your butt moving.

Fortunately, I'd laid out clothes for tonight before I left for work this morning.

The shower was a good pick-me-up. I felt rejuvenated, ready to party. As I opened the bathroom door, I heard the click of my answering machine signaling a call had come in. There was no need to run naked around the bed. I'd missed the call anyway. It was probably Peggy. I should have called her when I left Bourne.

I slipped into my black slacks and black v-neck sweater. It needed a touch of pizzazz, so I tied a black, white and raspberry colored scarf around my waist. I found the earrings I bought to match and finished the outfit off with a pair of black dressy sandals. I liked the look. The lady in black was on the move.

The beeper on the answering machine was still squawking. Since I'd gotten ready in record time, I circled the bed to check out who called. It was Annie. Oh no, I thought. I hope plans haven't changed. I pushed the button to listen to the message.

"Hi, it's just me," said Annie. "Don't panic, we're still on as planned. I just wanted to let you know that after the show, we're heading to The Tavern for a drink. It's Friday night, we're out, so we might as well make the best of it. You don't have to call me back. I'll see you shortly."

Hmm, I thought. Maybe I'll give Sam a call to see if he wants to meet us. It'll be like the good old days. I dug into my purse for my cell phone. He was number one on speed dial. I never changed it. His phone went straight to voice mail. I was going to hang up, then changed my mind. "Hey, buddy, Annie just called me and said that after the show we're going to go to The Tavern for a drink, being Friday night and all. If you're not busy, why don't you join us? We should be there around ten-ish." I stopped for a second wondering if I should have called. Too late now. "Later," I said and hung up. If he showed, he showed – if not, well, that was okay too.

I grabbed by purse and keys. I caught a glimpse of myself as I passed the front hall mirror. "Looking pretty good, if I do say so myself," I remarked, stopping to check out my reflection. It was the scarf that made the outfit pop.

The traffic was on the heavy side, but I was early, so I didn't bother to weave around the back roads just to save five minutes. There were still a lot of spaces available in The Paddock's parking lot. That was a good thing. If you eat dinner there before a show, they let you park for the night and walk the short way to the Melody Tent. I saw Annie's car parked three down from mine, so I locked up and headed inside.

As always, Tom was standing just inside the door and greeted me when I came in. He came around from his reservation desk and gave me a big bear hug. "It's been a long time. How's everything going?" He stepped back and gave me a polite once over, "Casey,

172

you haven't changed, still as beautiful as ever. Sam was crazy to let you go."

I felt my face flush, "Actually, we're still the best of friends. Who knows what the future might bring." I gave him a little shrug. "You're right, though; it's been far too long. I'll just have to do something about that. How's Linda?"

"She's fine, still my blushing bride. She's seating a big party in the garden room and you know her, after they're settled in, she'll talk to everyone. It'll take her ten minutes or more to get back out front." He smiled and looked over my head to see if she was on her way. "Annie's at the bar."

Another party was coming in the door. "I'll catch you later," I said and headed to the empty seat beside Annie.

The Paddock was a beautifully appointed restaurant, adorned with heavy dark wood and a mirrored bar with stained glass panels on each side. And as the name might imply, it carried a lavish paddock theme throughout – sporting paintings and memorabilia depicting horses, trainers, jockeys and even the Kentucky Derby. A five-foot-six inch replica of a jockey wearing a blue and yellow jersey with the number seven painted on the back greeted diners as they entered. Tom said it was his lucky number, but never said why. Maybe he'd won big at the track with that number. I'd forgotten how impressive it was just to sit and admire the surroundings.

Annie and another girl, I presumed it was Marnie, were sitting at the bar.

When I reached Annie, I tapped her on the shoulder. "Been here long?"

She turned, "Just long enough to order a drink. Casey, this is Marnie Levine, Barry's cousin from New York."

I held my hand out.

"Marnie, I'd like you to meet one of my best friends, Casey Quinby. We've known each other almost since she moved here eight years ago." She shifted her eyes from Marnie to me and back.

173

Marnie returned the greeting.

"Welcome ashore," I said to a smiling Marnie. "You're certainly going to find Cape Cod a lot different from New York. I found it different than Shrewsbury and that's only an hour and twenty minutes away, still in Massachusetts. I had a little head start though. My family vacationed here for as many years as I can remember. Is this your first visit?"

"It is and I don't want to leave," answered Marnie. "In fact, I'm not going to. I'm sure Annie told you, I just graduated from law school in New York. I love the profession, but don't want to practice there. When Barry asked me to visit, I took him up on it, with an ulterior motive in mind. I've only been here one week and it seems like a lifetime."

"Marnie met with Mike Sullivan this morning," said Annie. "She'll be working with us in the DA's office as an investigator while she's waiting to take the bar exam."

"Let me order a wine, then I want to hear more," I turned to see the bartender walking toward me. I didn't recognize him and wondered where Glen, the bartender who'd been there for at least eight years, was.

"Hi," he said. "My name is Ethan. And yours?"

"I'm Casey."

"Pleased to meet you, Casey. Would you like to order a drink?" he said, offering a little wink and a smile.

"Thought you'd never ask," I answered, returning only the smile. "A glass of white zin with a glass of ice on the side would be wonderful. Thank you." He certainly was different from Glen.

"Okay, now that that's done, back to more important things." I could see Annie was anxious to fill me in on Marnie.

"We've got a back-load at the office and Mike was about to place an ad for an investigator. I met Marnie with Barry and James at The Tavern. "Marnie, do you want to continue?"

"Well, my dad is an attorney in New York City. While I was in school, I worked in his office doing all sorts of odds jobs. For the last two years, I helped with investigations. I love the business and

174

got pretty good at what I did. My dad had high hopes of me joining his law firm, but that wasn't in my plan. Even though I was born and brought up in Long Island and the City, I didn't want the fast pace life style my family and most of my friends had bought into." Marnie turned to face the back of the bar. "In a nutshell, when Barry invited me to visit I saw my opportunity to escape. Of course, I'll miss my family and friends, but that's what cell phones and cars are for – I can call or visit." Marnie lifted her glass, took a sip, and turned back to face the girls. "Okay, enough about me for now. Casey, what brought you to the Cape?"

"I'm an only child. My parents both passed away after I graduated from college. I actually celebrated my first birthday on the Cape at Rogers' cottages on Grand Cove in West Dennis. We came down the same time every year with family friends. After the first few years of coming only once a year, my parents decided to make the trip at least four times a year, sometimes, only for a weekend." I felt a wave of nostalgia rush over me. "I fell in love with the lifestyle, everything about it. So here I am."

"And me," said Annie, "I was born and raised a Cape-y and intend to remain one."

We were just about to offer up more stories when a hand brushed across the middle of my back. It was Wally, the piano player, making his way to the corner on the other side of the room. He nodded when I turned to acknowledge him. He slid in behind the piano and positioned his fingers on the ivory keys. "Ever since Willy Nelson played the Melody Tent and began his show with, All of Me, Wally starts his show with the same song," I said to Marnie.

He smiled at us and began to play. "See, I told you."

I looked at the table beside him. "Marnie, see the lady beside the piano? She's Beatrice Bailey, known to all of us as Miss Bea. She's an old vaudeville singer." Miss Bea was busy swaying to the music, tapping to the beat, and sipping what looked like white wine. "See the glass of *white wine*. Well, it's really water, but she

175

doesn't want anybody to know. You want to talk about stories, well, she's got a ton of them, some really funny ones too."

"I think she came from New York City, back in the day," said Annie. "You should hear her sing, New York, New York, and talk about Frank Sinatra. Everybody loves Miss Bea."

She was just getting ready to sing when Tom headed toward the girls. "Your table is ready. It took a little longer than usual, but I thought you'd like to sit in the stable room, so I waited until a table cleared. They're gone and it's all yours."

He balanced our drinks on a tray, turned, and motioned for us to follow.

"This place is amazing," said Annie. "Marnie, wait till you see where we're sitting. It's so comfortably elegant. You're going to love it."

"Thanks, Tom." We sat down and he handed us each a menu.

"Enjoy, Tina will be your waitress tonight. She'll be right by to tell you about the specials. Don't forget to order the escargots." He looked at Marnie and smiled, "They're the best on the Cape. If they aren't, I want to know."

We ordered a round of drinks and, as suggested, a couple orders of escargot. "So," I asked, "What interesting things are happening at the DA's? You said you have a case backlog."

"That we do," said Annie. "Most everything, though, has been put on hold to work on the Becky Morgan hit-and-run. She's related to one of Mike's best friends, Judge Thompson. Do you know him?"

Marnie sipped her wine while she listened intently to the conversation.

"I've met him a couple of times. One was at a fundraiser the paper was involved in and the other was the kick-off for a child advocacy program the court sponsored. I didn't cover either because that isn't my area of expertise, but I did attend the gatherings."

"Isn't he presiding over the Superior Court?" Marnie asked.

"Yes," Annie answered. "You sat in a couple days during a trial this week, didn't you?"

"I did," said Marnie. "James and Barry let me sit in and observe. They did say the Judge seemed distant and preoccupied. He actually ended the trial early one day. They said it was very unusual for him to do that."

"I was at the accident scene. The Bourne PD kept me behind the spectator tape. I wondered why, since I'm usually allowed to observe the scene up close and personal." I set my glass down and leaned forward on the table. "There's something about this case that's baffling me. Truthfully, I don't think it was just a hit-and-run."

Annie spoke softly, but with eyes wide open, "Are you thinking murder?"

Now I had both Marnie and Annie's undivided attention. "Yes, but I'm not a hundred percent sure yet, but I'm working on it. Since it happened in Bourne, Sam is the lead detective." I turned to Marnie. "Sam is my on-again, off-again, on-again boyfriend. Right now we're kinda on-again. I've worked on lots of cases with the area PDs, including Bourne. This time they're shutting me out. They won't talk about it or show me any evidence they've got. Actually, I don't think they have much, but I really don't know that for a fact."

"Marnie, this is one of the cases you'll probably be working on. Usually, we don't get involved unless there's foul play and a person of interest. This one is different. I thought it was because of the friendship between Mike and the Judge. I'm sure that factors into it, but there must be something else too." Annie leaned her elbow on the table and rested her chin in her hand. "Yesterday I was booking an appointment for Mike and noticed he had lunch with Sam on Wednesday before the memorial service for Becky."

"I may be new to the area, but I'm not new to the business. Just from what you two have said, even I can see there's something mulling around under the sheets," said Marnie.

Annie was about to speak, when the waitress stepped up to the table carrying the escargot. "Excuse me, these are hot, so I'll set them down between you. Can I get you another drink?" she said.

I looked up. "Not for me, thank you."

"I'm good," both Annie and Marnie replied.

"We better order, so we'll have time to enjoy before we have to head next door," Annie said to the waitress.

I ordered the stuffed flounder with Newberg sauce and au gratin potatoes. The girls ordered prime rib, loaded baked potato and white asparagus with lemon sauce.

Tom was right, the best damn escargot on the Cape. "Well, Marnie, what's your verdict?"

"Since they're the only ones I've had, I'll have to agree, they are the best." She laughed and proceeded to dip a piece of French bread into the garlic butter.

"Back to business," Annie said in-between bites. "Whatever we talk about tonight regarding this case has to be kept between us. I'm sure you both agree."

"I certainly do," I said. "However, I think we can work together and come up with some answers. I've been doing a lot of pavement pounding. My friend, Peggy, at the Bourne PD met me for lunch on Tuesday. You remember her, don't you Annie?"

She nodded.

I continued, "Well, seems that any talk about the accident is being done behind closed doors. And, Peggy was told not to discuss it with anyone. She told me there was nothing to discuss because they wouldn't tell her anything. She's just as baffled as I am. The only thing she overheard was the mention of a black, late-model car. But, she had no idea what, if anything, it had to do with the accident. The other thing she mentioned was a man named Mr. Parker. He's an old guy who lives on the Scenic Highway, not far from the accident scene. It seems as though he's known well at the Bourne PD. I guess he's always filing nonsense complaints. This time he was seated behind closed doors in Sam's office. Peggy didn't have any idea what the conversation was about."

"I'm ready to start working this case now. I wish I didn't have to go to New York on Sunday, but I have to meet my dad and pick up clothes and stuff," Marnie said. "Mike has me scheduled to start on Tuesday morning. If this is my assignment, I'll play dumb."

"Casey, didn't you say you went to the memorial service on Wednesday?" asked Annie.

"I did. It was quite the service. Sam saw me in the parking lot and practically told me to stay away from this case. He told me to be careful." I shook my head. "Can you imagine. Annie, you know me better than that. Don't tell me not to do something. That only makes me want to do it more."

"Speaking of more, yesterday I visited with the principal, Mr. Porter, and the assistant principal, Mr. Bowdin, at Bourne High School. I tried to get some insight into Becky's life. When I left there, I felt like I knew her. As soon as I get my notes in some sort of order, I'll share them with you guys."

"You're really convinced this is more than a hit-and-run, aren't you?" Annie asked. "You know Casey, if Sam tells you to be careful, then maybe you should listen to him."

"I know Sam cares, but it's in my blood. Investigation is what I know. They didn't make me the head investigative reporter because I cover the flower show or routine auto accidents. This is my job and I'm good at it."

"Okay, okay," Annie said, wishing she could take back her last statement. "I know and you're right."

Marnie wasn't sure if she should say anything. She decided to try to lighten up the conversation a little. "I'm so looking forward to the show tonight. This will be an experience for me. Living in the City, we'd go to shows on Broadway. They were great. It was the getting to them and getting home from them that stunk. It was a real hassle. I can't believe we're having this wonderful dinner, then just walking next door to see The Beach Boys."

"Don't forget The Tavern for drinks after." Annie turned to me, "You are coming, aren't you?"

"Yes, of course. Hey guys, I'm sorry for getting so involved in a work conversation during play time." I raised my eyebrows and rolled my eyes. "Am I forgiven? In fact, we should make girl's-night-out at least a once a month thing, even if it's just for pizza and beer."

"I'm in," said Marnie.

"Not without me you're not." Annie declared.

Our food arrived.

"Oh my God," said Marnie. "This is absolutely wonderful. I know this place won't be just a one-night-stand."

"James and Barry are meeting us at The Tavern." Annie smiled, "They're probably scared to think we've inducted Marnie into a secret sister's sorority. We'll keep them guessing. It's better that way."

"I left a message for Sam, but he didn't call back, so I don't think he'll be joining us. You never know though. I'm sure you'll meet him soon enough. He's a good guy, you'll like him."

"When did you say you'll be back from New York?" I asked.

"I'm leaving here Sunday morning and coming back Monday. I figure if I leave the City around six am, then I'll be here by noon at the latest."

"I should have my notes together and hopefully some updates to report by then. I know you'll be tired, but we could grab a sandwich and do a little talking. I can pick you up at Barry's and swing by the DA's office to get Annie. How's that sound?"

"I like it," said Marnie.

"Ditto," said Annie.

"This meeting of the minds is very interesting. It's like fate put us together. Imagine the three of us working on cases," I said. My adrenaline was flowing. "Do you guys remember the TV series, Lipstick Jungle? It was one of my favorites, just think, that could be us."

We looked at each other and laughed.

"I'll never forget this night," said Marnie.

"That's for sure." Both Annie and I agreed at the same time.

There was silence for the next few minutes as we concentrated on finishing our meals. Annie was getting ready to speak when the waitress stopped by our table. "Tom would like to buy you girls an after-dinner drink."

I smiled. "Thank you, I'll have a white crème de'mint on the rocks. How about you guys?"

"A Bailey's on the rocks sounds good," said Annie.

Marnie ordered the same as me. "I've never had white crème de mint on the rocks before, sounds good."

"My excuse is that it settles the stomach, been using that for years." I glanced at my watch. "You know it's quarter past seven. When Tina comes back, we should get the check and think about heading on over to the Tent."

"Wait till you see where these seats are," said Annie. "A friend of Mike's had them, couldn't use them, and neither could Mike. So, he gave the tickets to me; perks of the job. They're five rows up on aisle four. That's the aisle where the performers come down. And to boot, they're the first three in. Did we score, or what?" Annie took the tickets out of her purse and fanned them in front of her.

"You go girl," Marnie said. "I'm sure likin' this place."

We finished our drinks and divided up the bill. Tom was at the front door. "It was like old times. Thanks, I promise I won't stay away so long. Please tell Linda I said hi."

"Enjoy the show; I hear it's a great one." Tom gave us each a hug as we exited into the parking lot.

It wasn't even a five minute walk, through the gate and maybe a few hundred feet to the Tent. We knew exactly where to go since we'd been there so many times.

By the look on her face, Marnie had created a space in her mind to store this new experience. "This is great. It's like a huge circus tent, only fancy, and it doesn't smell like elephants," she said as she took a deep breath, "Nothing like this in the City. Sometime we should plan a girl's weekend and head for the Big Apple."

"Well, let's do it," I said.

"Let me get settled in and we'll make plans."

Aisle four was half way around the Tent. It was crowded, but then it always was, especially when a group like the Beach Boys played.

"Wait here, I'm going to the box office and grab a schedule of coming events," said Annie as she turned and headed toward the entrance.

"Don't be surprised if her little jaunt to the box office takes her fifteen minutes. I swear that girl knows everybody on the Cape." I watched her hurry down the walkway.

Annie and I had hit it off the first time we met. That was eight years ago. And Marnie fit right in. I knew we were going to be a trio to be reckoned with.

"Annie said you found a duplex to rent on 6A in Yarmouthport? You'll like it there. Close to everything, yet far enough away. Route 6A is amazing. It actually goes all the way to Orleans, then connects with Route 6, and continues to Provincetown. It's a beautiful ride. Now Provincetown, that's a place you'll have to visit."

"Even in New York, I've heard of Provincetown."

"It's a colorful place," I said. "It was originally a fishing village, but it's kind of evolved into an artist's colony. They do have some great shopping and wonderful restaurants. It's a fun place to visit a couple times a year."

Marnie smiled, "It's probably like Greenwich Village. In fact, I remember a couple of my father's clients talking about it. Rick called it P Town. He wanted to open a jewelry shop there, but Emil thought it was too seasonal. I don't remember who won out."

The lights in the Tent blinked. "They're getting ready to start." I turned to see Annie power walking toward us. "Who'd you bump into this time?"

"Nobody special, you know me, I just like to talk," she pushed my arm.

"Marnie, you'll get used to her. You'll have to if you're going to hang with us." I shook my head and moved sideways to let Marnie walk in front of me. "Forward march," I whispered.

"What was that?" Annie said with eyebrows raised.

"Not a thing." I crinkled my nose at her. "Not a thing."

I went in first, Annie second, and Marnie sat on the aisle. It wasn't five minutes later when a voice came over the loud speaker, "Let's all put our hands together and give a warm Cape Cod welcome to the heart and soul of the California surf scene, The Beach Boys.

The applause was overwhelming. We were transported back in time with a nostalgic rendition of Good Vibrations. The stage rocked and the audience rolled. Every eye was glued to the revolving platform in the center. Then came *California Girl's, Surfin' Safari, Little Duece Coupe* – music filled the air.

I watched Marnie's face when the band ran up aisle four, high fiving everybody seated in the end seats. It was intermission. "What a show," she said. "I can't thank you guys enough."

"You're one of us now." Annie leaned over and gave Marnie a hug. "I'm glad you're having a good time. And the best part is they're only half way through their show. Then, we're only half way through our night. Remember we're heading on over to The Tavern."

"I'm with you, girlfriend." Marnie was in awe. "Seeing a show in the Tent is much more fun than in a stuffy New York theater."

"Hey, look straight across from us, in the front row," said Annie. "That person looks familiar. I don't mean familiar like one of our friends, but somebody famous."

The three of us gazed across the stage and at almost the same time, we said, "Kathy Lee."

"And I think that's Frank sitting next to her." I said. "If I'm not mistaken, she's starring in a play at the Dennis Playhouse this coming week. I saw her there a couple of years ago, great job."

"If you want, I think we still have time, we could get a glass of wine."

"Annie, remember the last time we tried to do that. We finally got to the front of the line and the lights started blinking," I said. "Not only did we not get our wine, we just made it back to our seats before Paul Anka came down the aisle."

"Oh, I sure do remember. What a dream he was." Annie looked at Marnie. "He came up the aisle singing *Puppy Love*, stopped right in front of us, and leaned over and gave me a kiss on the cheek. I melted, didn't want to wash my face ever again. I was in love."

The lights blinked again. "See, we never would have made it," I snickered. "Besides we'll have a couple waiting for us later."

Another five minutes went by. The lights dimmed and a pre-recorded rendition of I Get Around welcomed the Beach Boys back to the stage. We clapped and sang along and clapped some more.

The next forty-five minutes were wild with non-stop music. The air jumped and swayed with every note. I closed my eyes and imagined the tent rocking and rolling to the beat. I had come to many shows with Sam. Maybe I can talk him into taking in a couple before the summer is over. "Annie, did you make it to the ticket window to pick up a schedule?"

"Actually, Miss Smarty Pants, I got one for each of us. I can multi-task with the best of them. I schmoozed and carried out my assignment all at the same time."

"Never a doubt, never a doubt," I said. "Sometimes Annie's schmoozing pays off. Somehow her gift of gab has gotten us autographs."

This was new territory for Marnie. "Is tonight one of those times?"

"I tried, but my buddy isn't working security, so you'll have to take a rain check." Annie shrugged her shoulders. "Remember these were Mike's tickets, so I really didn't have time to make the contact, maybe next time."

"Did you have fun playing with us tonight?" I asked.

Just then, the sounds of an ambulance and a police cruiser pierced the air. My head instinctively glanced in their direction. "Sorry," I said. "It's my inquisitive instinct kicking in … like when a master whistles for his dog to come. Well, that's my master, only I'm going to be disobedient and not react to his beckon call. Bad dog, no treat for me."

Annie and Marnie stood laughing and shaking their heads.

"Come on Rover," said Annie. "It's time for you to lead us to The Tavern and sniff out the bad guys waiting to fill us full of liquor and keep us out all night."

"Sounds like a plan to me," said Marnie.

"I just want to remind you guys not to mention anything we talked about earlier regarding the Becky Morgan case. We'll keep that info on file with the Secret Sister's Sorority. Marnie, when you get back on Monday, we'll meet as planned. We can resume our discussion then." I said. "Oh, by the way, I need your cell number."

I floundered around my purse looking for my cell phone. Marnie was already armed with a piece of paper and a pen. "I'll just write it down and you can enter it later."

"Gotcha. One of these days I might invest in a smaller purse." I chuckled. "Not."

We made our way back along the walk to the Paddock parking lot. It was still full. If we weren't going to The Tavern, we'd probably head in for a drink ourselves. "I'll meet you in the Village."

They waved. "See you in a few."

I sat for a minute searching my bag for my cell. It was there in plain sight. "This is so annoying. I do it all the time." I turned it on and checked for calls, Sam's in particular. None, he hadn't called. But then, I'm not surprised.

I knew it would take less than fifteen minutes to get to The Tavern. Since I didn't want to get there before Marnie and Annie, I decided to make a quick stop at the convenience store just down the street to get a package of gum … always good to have for the ride home after a couple of drinks.

CHAPTER FORTY-ONE

The road to the Village was dark. The muted glow of the moon and the haze it created emitted an eerie feeling of uneasiness.

"Yikes." I swerved to avoid what appeared to be a small person walking along the side of the road. He or she was dressed in dark clothes and not paying one bit of attention to my car coming up behind them. Is this what happened to Becky? Maybe it really was an accident. Now, I was second guessing myself. My mind drifted back to the conversations I had with Becky's friends. Something wasn't right, but I couldn't put my finger on it. No, it wasn't an accident. I was sure of that.

I was glad to see the lights of The Tavern. Fortunately, there was a parking space in front. Annie must have parked in the lot behind. The space was small, but so was my car. I maneuvered into the opening, careful not to bump the fancy black car in front of me or the silver pick-up behind me. It was right under one of the lamplights in The Tavern's courtyard. As I walked away, I glanced back and smiled at my little green Spider; a spotlight on beauty, I thought.

I hadn't been to The Tavern for awhile, but looking around, things hadn't changed any.

"Casey, we're over here." It was Annie. It sure didn't take her any time to get settled in.

"Hey, girl," I turned to see Barry get up from his chair and head my way. "It's been a while. How ya doin?"

"Staying busy," I said. "Yeah, the old place hasn't changed. What's new with you?"

"Pretty much the same. So, you met my cousin, Marnie?" he said motioning me toward the table.

"I have. We had a great girl's-night-out. You guys might be in trouble, we plan on having one at least every month, maybe every week. You'll never know what we talk about when you're not around." I squinted and gave him a shadowy stare, then laughed.

"You'll never change, Casey Quinby. Always the Sherlock Holmes entrance and the Alfred Hitchcock exit … forceful and mysterious … leaving us wondering who, what and where."

I pushed my shoulder forward, threw my head back, and tossed my hair. "You're being a tad bit dramatic, I'd say."

"James, look who the cat dragged in." Barry sat back down in his chair.

James stood up, "It's good to see you again. I understand a dangerous trio was formed tonight." He leaned forward, smiled and gave me a kiss on the cheek.

"It'll be dangerous if I don't get me a glass of wine soon," I said looking at the waitress who was headed in our direction.

"The Beach Boys were unbelievable. We got a schedule of upcoming shows. Maybe we can all go to one. It'd be fun," said Marnie. "Once I'm settled in, there're so many things I want to do. And things I want to see, all while I'm studying for the exam, of course." Marnie, in her excitement and flare for the dramatic, waved her hand in front of her, knocking a full glass of wine off the end of the table. "Oops, I'm bad. But, I didn't hit anyone." We laughed and the waitress brought another glass.

We'd been laughing and talking about stuff we used to do, when I felt a tap on my shoulder. I turned quickly to see Sam standing behind me. "Hey, lady, do you mind if I pull up a chair? I was just in the neighborhood and thought I might find some action here."

My heart skipped a beat. I hoped nobody noticed. I cocked my head and smiled, "Not at all, but, only if you promise not to keep your hands to yourself."

"James, Barry, good to see you guys again. Same old, same old happening at the Courthouse? And, Annie, always a pleasure, staying out of trouble, I assume?"

"Nothing has changed, but I wouldn't have it any other way," said Barry.

James hesitated answering Sam, hoping Annie would chime in.

"It's no fun staying out of trouble. You know me better than that." Annie laughed.

"Sam, I'd like you to meet Barry's cousin, Marnie Levine," I said. She came for a visit and decided to stay. Now she's going to be, or should I say is, one of us. She starts working at the DA's office on Tuesday. She just graduated from law school and is going to take the Mass Bar Exam."

"That's going to make a dangerous trio; an investigative reporter, an assistant to the DA, and a lawyer. Watch out guys – we don't stand a chance."

"You got that right, Sammy," said Annie.

Sam ordered a beer and slid in beside me. It was like old times. And, as for Marnie, it felt like she's been part of us forever.

"Where you been, Sam?" James asked.

"It's been busy. The normal summer influx of tourists have petty crimes up, but lately there's been some troubling ones. We're investigating the 'accident' ... 'not accident' ... hit-'n- run that happened last Sunday night on the Scenic Highway." Sam shook his head. "It's a stumper and we've got very little to go on. Our biggest break hinges on an old guy who sits in his rocking chair on his front porch and observes the cars that ride by his house. He's got a photographic memory for detail. The problem is jarring that memory and getting something specific from him. Hopefully, you'll see our results sooner than later. This case will be hard for Judge Thompson since it involves a relative.

189

Obviously, he'll have to excuse himself from it. But it's still his Courtroom and it will hurt, I'm sure."

James felt his whole body tense up. His eyes darted around the table. Everybody was listening intently to Sam. "I'm not looking forward to that day. It gives me the willies to think about it." Beads of sweat formed on his forehead. He used the beer for an excuse to leave. "Duty calls, I'll be right back."

"Thanks for the info," said Barry.

Thank goodness, nobody's in here, thought James. Who was this guy Sam was talking about? He splashed cold water on his face, careful not to get the front of his shirt wet, then reached for a paper towel. The dispenser was empty. "Damn it," he said and retreated into the stall for some toilet paper. A bad combination, water and toilet paper; it stuck in little pieces on his hands and face. He heard the outside door handle turn and quickly closed and locked the stall door. He shook his hands in a rapid fluttery motion to air dry what water was left. With that done, he brushed the paper bits from them. Now his face. The outside bathroom door closed. James quickly moved from the stall to the mirror over the sink. He was okay. His color was normal and his pulse rate had slowed. His paranoia about having toilet paper chicken pox was gone. "I can do this," he whispered then headed back to rejoin his friends.

"I came here right from the station and could use a little food before I have another beer. Anybody up for some fries?" asked Sam.

"Sure," said Barry. "How 'bout some wings too?"

"Sounds good," Sam turned to get the waitress's attention. "We'd like to get a couple orders of cheese fries. Actually, make it one cheese and one regular and also, two orders of wings with a couple different sauces on the side. Annabell, I remember you don't like cheese and hot sauce. See, it hasn't been all that long. I can still remember things besides blood, guns and violence." He looked at me.

I knew exactly what he meant and, boy, was he right. My whole body tingled.

Marnie, who had been sitting quietly back in her chair leaned forward, "I was wondering if I could ask you guys a favor? Since I have to go back to New York on Sunday, I was hoping we could all grab some supper tomorrow night. Actually, I'd like to suggest the place too."

"Pushy, isn't she," Barry laughed. "What's the idea you've been planning for the last half hour? You think I didn't see the smoke coming from the top of your head? I knew something was up."

"You don't have to go if you don't want to," Marnie tightened her lips and folded her arms. "But, if I know you, and I do, you'll be the first one ready and out the door. Anyway, be still and let me present my case."

"A true lawyer in the making," said James nodding in agreement.

"I'd like to go to Seafood Harry's. Those fried clams will keep my taste buds aroused till I get back on Monday."

"I'm in," I said.

Everybody agreed. "What time is this shindig going to happen?" Sam asked.

"Whatever's good for everybody. We'll be working at my place most all day, more painting and cleaning. That includes you too, Barry."

"There she goes, worse than a wife." He grinned, "Of course, I'll be in Yarmouthport. The faster we get it done, the faster I get my couch back." He rolled his eyes, "Only kidding, cuz. You know you can stay as long as you want." He made a mimicking gulp, "Yikes, did I just say that?"

Sam looked at me, "I've got to go into the station in the morning, but should be finished by 3:00 at the latest."

"Works for me, too. I've got a few things to do in the morning, then I can be ready anytime." I knew Sam could read me like a book and for that reason I avoided eye contact.

191

Thankfully, Annie chimed in, "Why don't we meet there at seven o'clock?"

We all agreed.

The waitress hovered over Barry's head with a plate of chicken wings in one hand and an array of sauces in the other. "Don't back up or you'll be swimming in teriyaki mixed with ranch," Annie said.

He moved to one side. "You can set those down right in front of me. I'll take the first one to make sure they're okay." He reached out faster than a jack rabbit before anyone could say a word.

In between the finger licking and frequent gulps of beer, he managed to blurt out an audible sentence. "Casey, are you working with Sam on the Bourne case? Usually the dynamic duo is scavenging around like Batman and Robin when there's something big happening."

Before I had a chance to answer, Sam spoke up. "I'm flying solo on this one at the moment. Doesn't mean we won't combine our efforts in the very near future. After all, Batman could never exist without Robin."

There was that rush of adrenalin again, flowing through my body. He was going to work with me. At least that's what he was telling our friends and in the very near future. That future needs to be now. He needs to know everything I've been working on, and, in turn, I need to know what leads he has. It would have been nice if he'd talked to me before now. My article on Becky is scheduled for this Sunday. I have to talk to him before that. It was his fault I wrote the article in the first place.

Barry pursued the topic, "I bet that was the center of conversation during girls-night-out dinner. Can you picture these three teaming up together in hot pursuit of a murderer? The poor guy."

James' eyes moved around the table studying faces for a response. "First of all, what makes you think it was murder?" he said. "And second, why does everybody always assume it was a guy? Don't you think a female is capable of committing violent crimes?"

"Well, yeah, of course a female is capable of the same crimes a man is. I wasn't singling out a specific gender. We know that better than John Q. Public. We see it all the time." Barry wrinkled his brow, "Hey, buddy, didn't the wings agree with you? You're disposition certainly soured fast."

Annie reached over Marnie and gave James a friendly arm punch. "Let's change the subject. Don't let the job get to you. Remember, it's only a job."

He nodded.

"How about one more round, then we'll call it a night. I want to make sure my painters get some sleep. Grouchy painters are the worst to deal with." Marnie snickered and gave James a wink.

"Hope you're planning a big house-warming party. I'll make my famous Mama Annie's sausage calzones … to die for … no pun intended."

It was late. I could feel my eyes fluttering. "I'm done."

Sam agreed. "I'll walk you to your car. I didn't see it in the lot. You out front?"

"I am." The other four decided to finish the pitcher of beer then head out. "See you tomorrow."

Annie raised her mug, "It was a great night. I know our first girls-night-out won't be the last."

Sam reached down and took my hand. It felt good. "Know what, Sherlock, I think we better talk. How about I stay at your house tomorrow night? We shouldn't be too late. After all we're only going to *Seafood Harry's*. Get your stuff together tomorrow and I'll bring my notes when I leave the station. If you want, we can start before we go to supper. I'll stop by my place and get ready, then be in West Hyannisport around 4:30."

That's my Sam – a man direct and to the point. "Sounds fine to me," I said. "See you guys tomorrow."

We left out the front door and crossed The Tavern courtyard. My baby was where I'd left it, shimmering like a jewel under the soft glow of the lamp light. The same black car was parked in front of me. I didn't think about it earlier. It was James'. The light from the full moon blinked on and off behind the passing clouds. It bounced off the sleek dark finish. My eye caught a glimpse of something out of place on the front right fender. As fast as I saw it, it was gone; just my imagination running ahead of me. I decided not to mention it to Sam, at least not now, and especially since we'd been drinking.

I loved it when he wrapped his arms around me. It was a safe feeling, even though I knew I could take care of myself. My head was nestled so close to his chest, that I could hear his heart beating. "Sherlock, we'll resume this position tomorrow. You okay to drive home?"

"Of course, you know me, old hollow leg."

My eyes met his. "Okay then, get in your car and get going. I'll see you tomorrow afternoon." Before he let me go, he gave me a long passionate kiss, bopped me on the fanny, then guided me through the open car door.

The ride home seemed shorter than usual, probably because I was thinking of Sam and not my outside surroundings. When I pulled into my driveway, I felt a wave of darkness move in around me. The bulb in the porch light must have burned out. What made it worse were the intermittent flashes of moon beams peeking out between the clouds and tree branches. It was spooky.

I scurried to unlock my front door, snap on the hall light, and just as quickly as I had unlocked the door, I locked it behind me. The slits in my eyelids were getting smaller. What a great night. For awhile, I left the job behind me. Right now, all I want to do is sleep.

CHAPTER FOURTY-TWO

Marnie knocked on Barry's bedroom door. "Up and at 'em."

The coffee was brewing and a store bought box of donuts was sitting open on the kitchen table when he came out.

"These sure didn't come from Nancy's," he said reaching in to get one of the small powdery treats.

"Nope, I bought them the other day. We don't have time to make pit-stops on the way to Yarmouthport. It's 8:30. I'm going to give James a call."

She only punched in four numbers, when there was a knock at the door. Barry walked across the room to answer. "Well, look at you, an already christened painter's shirt with matching pants."

"I was just calling your cell phone – mental telepathy. Or is it … great minds think alike?"

"Whatever," said James as he sat down in the chair next to Marnie.

"Want a cup of coffee?" Barry got a mug from the cupboard.

James yawned, emitting a deep, hollow breath. "Don't mind if I do."

"We've got fifteen minutes and we're out of here. Just think, I'll work you like slaves today, we'll go out and eat whole belly clams tonight then, you two won't have to see me for almost two whole days. You'll both be able to catch up on your beauty rest or anything else I've kept you from."

In exactly fifteen minutes, Marnie grabbed three styrofoam cups off the counter, filled them with coffee, instructed the guys to each take one, picked up her purse, and headed for the door.

"The little general has spoken," Barry whispered. "Years of training, being an only child and all."

"I heard that."

They piled into Marnie's car and off they went.

It was a typical July morning on Cape Cod. A gentle breeze blowing off the bay kept the temperature at a comfortable seventy degrees. There wasn't a cloud in the sky. Once the sun fully realized its potential, the muggies would creep in and distribute their nasty little sweat beads.

There wasn't much traffic on 6A. It was still too early for the tourist beach goers.

Nancy's parking lot was busy though. "Good thing I picked up the gourmet Hostess delights. Look at the cars. It would have cost us an hour of paint time."

"Good thing I like you," said James. "Besides you're driving and I don't want to rile the driver, could have some dangerous results."

"Maybe that's what happened to the Morgan girl. Maybe there were two people in the car that hit her. Maybe they were bickering and didn't see her."

"Barry, stop with the maybes. I'm sure Sam and his team will find out what happened. Casey has also been investigating some theories on her own. I understand when those two work together, they come up with some amazing results. I think I overheard Sam tell Casey to get her notes together so they can do some comparing this afternoon before we go out to supper. I'll be glad to get this moving thing out of the way, so I can get my feet wet in the DA's office, then, perhaps I can work with them."

A knot formed in the pit of James' stomach.

Should I keep the conversation going?

He didn't want to say anything or ask a question that would trigger an adverse reaction. The girls had been out the night before. Maybe Casey had confided in them over dinner? Maybe not – maybe he should let sleeping dogs lie. There were those maybes again.

"Today, let's let anything related to real work stay at work," Barry said. "We've got a lot to do. Let's have some fun doing it. Talking about work stuff will make the day depressing, and heaven knows, paint talk is so much more pleasurable," he said with a bit of sarcasm.

For once James was relieved at Barry's suggestion.

"Okay, boys, we're here."

Marnie unlocked the door and went inside. Barry and James carried bags of household items she had purchased yesterday into the kitchen. James stepped back into the living-room, folded his arms and surveyed his surroundings. "This place is really starting to shape up. The paint job is professional, if I do say so myself."

"Don't bother saying so. Self-praise is not always the best." She stood with hands on hips looking at him through squinted eyes. She leaned forward and punched his arm. "But, just for the record, you did a damn good job."

"Ouch, I'm going to claim workman's comp. Or better still, sore arm, can't-lift-a-paint-brush syndrome."

Barry shook his head and headed back to the kitchen to get started. "We've got a job to do. Missy, here, isn't going to let us rest until it's done."

CHAPTER FORTY-THREE

It felt good to sleep in for a change. This week had been stressful, to say the least. I shuffled into the kitchen and popped a French vanilla K-cup into my Keurig. My body still wasn't ready to accept proper posture, so I leaned my elbows on the counter and watched the coffee drip into my cup. The aroma aroused my sense of smell. That was the only one working at the moment.

My stomach let me know it was still trying to dissolve the last remaining bits of chicken I'd consumed last night. I needed those chicken wings like I needed another hole in my head. That was then ... this is now. I certainly wasn't hungry.

My daily Tribune was waiting patiently on the top step outside the kitchen door. With coffee in hand and newspaper tucked under my arm, I opened the sliders to the porch and headed toward the table. It was bright, so bright I contemplated going back in for my sunglasses. Instead, I changed seats.

I scanned the paper. Usually the Saturday edition was full of weekend events being held mostly for the benefit of the tourists. There was a chowder festival at noon on Ocean Street. It was usually a pretty good take, even though you had to wait in long lines to get a small sample. Last year there were seven restaurants competing for votes for the best chowder, most of the time the Black Cat came in first. I have to admit, I agreed. Guess I won't be taste testing this year.

What a day. There wasn't a cloud in the sky. Two little squirrels were running relay races across the backyard. It was fun watching them. Not a care in the world, I thought. They ran up the big maple in the corner, then, jumped on the top of the fence. It aroused Buster, my neighbor's dog. He was loud. His barking could raise the dead.

There's a few things I need to do before Sam shows up. He said he'd be here around 4:30. I went back inside and pulled out the vacuum.

My briefcase was resting against the wall beside the kitchen table where I'd left it yesterday afternoon. I cleared the table, made myself another cup of coffee, and proceeded to empty it of its contents. Most of my notes were on 3 x 5 file cards. I used a recipe box to organize them and categorize the evidence I'd worked on to date. I could tell though, this wasn't going to be an ordinary recipe box case.

On the last case Sam and I worked, I'd bought a white erase board so we could develop a time line and add or delete information as it became pertinent, or not. Since I figured it would become an important tool in our info-merge, I headed to my closet to retrieve it.

"I think I slid it behind the shoe caddy in the corner." Talking to myself was a trait I developed years ago when I became my own room-mate. Yep, there it was. When I reached forward to pull it out, it slipped out of my hand, and the corner landed full point down on my right big toe. "Ouch!" I yelled. There was blood all right. I'm such a baby when it comes to this stuff, but somebody had to tend to it, and that somebody was me. I grabbed an old tee shirt, wrapped it around my foot, and hobbled to the bathroom. Before I let go of the shirt, I damped a facecloth. I wasn't sure if I was going to use it on my toe or my face. I can handle an accident scene, a murder scene, an autopsy, or help if somebody else gets cut, but the sight of my own blood always makes me queasy. My big toe was throbbing, but not yet ready to fall off. After I played nurse, I headed back to the closet to face my attacker and clean up the messy assault scene.

It was one o'clock when I finished organizing my notes. I pushed the table against the wall to create a place for the board to rest. My kitchen looked like a mini squad room, lacking only the electronics used to project images onto a screen.

The idea of working with Sam again on such an important case sparked excitement in my veins. We make a good team. His suggestion that we brainstorm on a case so secretive gives me goose-bumps. I was ready. I know I have information he needs and he has information I want.

My mind must have traveled in space. When I got out of the shower, my clock read 2:30. I'm surprised I didn't run out of hot water. A half hour had passed and I don't remember solving anything. "Guess I needed that time to clear the cobwebs and start fresh."

Since we're only going to Seafood Harry's for supper, I decided to don a pair of jeans and a jersey. I wrapped a new bandage around my toe, slipped into my old reliable sandals and headed for the kitchen.

CHAPTER FOURTY-FOUR

I had just finished re-reading the two interviews I'd done, when I heard a car pull up beside my house. I glanced outside to see Sam taking a box from his trunk. "Need any help?" I asked.

"Yeah, this one isn't heavy," he said as he handed it to me. "I've got a another small box and a couple of notebooks."

He was really ready to dive right in. "Looks like you brought everything but the kitchen sink."

"You wanted to be a part of this." He put the books down on the counter and gave me a kiss. "Got any coffee? Let's make this a real squad room. You know the guys can't operate without a coffee in hand. Just don't make me one of those sissy flavors. A manly brew will do."

"Okay, Mr. Manly, whatever you say." I curtsied and proceeded to make us both a coffee; mine was French vanilla, of course.

"What I'd like to start with is information about the accident scene. Up till now it has been classified." Sam reached for one of the notebooks. "The very first picture will set the stage for the investigation." He flipped the book open.

I gasped ... something I usually don't do when working a case. In front of me was a picture of a young girl, face down in the dirt. My heart stopped. Along the full length of her body was a tire track. How it missed her head was a mystery. I felt my eyes well up.

"You okay," Sam reached over and put his arm around me. "You're theory of murder is right on. Becky Morgan was the victim of a double tragedy; the first being a hit and run, whether accidentally or on purpose, and the second appears to be a deliberate act with the intent of committing murder. We have a partial tire tread imprint. The question is: Was this done by one vehicle, or two?"

"Oh my God, I didn't see this coming at all." I took a deep breath and turned to Sam, "Why did you wait so long to let me know?"

"Casey, you have a unique way of investigating. I've always given you credit for that. I wanted you to approach this case using your own methods. After today, I'm sure you'll understand why. I'm confident we can combine our efforts and come up with some answers that we can further pursue and get a conviction. The little Morgan girl deserves that, as does her family and the community. This was a gruesome, brutal crime, and, rest assured, it will not become a cold case."

I looked back at Becky's picture. "All right, where do you want to begin?"

Sam flipped through some papers, then turned to me. "Why don't you tell me when and where you started your time-line. Then I'll jump in and run with it from our end. We should take it slow and analyze everything. Hopefully, you'll have a partial clue that will mix with ours and give us something concrete to go on."

"I actually have notes starting right from the scene of the accident. It's really hard for me to refer to it as an accident. But, here goes. As you already know, I wasn't allowed across the police tape. That baffled me."

"Casey, don't get ahead of yourself. You can't interject facts that you know now into information you recorded on your initial notes. I need to look at things through your eyes, because my eyes are obviously missing something."

"Gotcha." I reached for my folder of pictures. The first couple were from the accident scene. "I don't think these will be of much help since they're not close-ups."

Sam went to his photo folder. "Besides the photo of Becky you've already seen, I have ones of tire tracks, matted down brush, both before and after the body, and a couple of foot-prints after the body."

"A couple of footprints?" My heart beat faster. "Does that mean the person who ran over her, stopped his or her car, and got out to check to see if she was still alive? Or do you think the prints may have been there before this all took place?" Now I had questions.

"Since Becky Morgan was the daughter of a prominent Bourne family and the relative of the Superior Court Judge, you know we were directed by the Chief to make this case our number one priority. So Monday morning, our guys in charge of fatals tried to recreate what happened using several different scenarios. Judging from the distance between the footprints and the tire tracks, the angles the footprints were to the tire tracks, and the pressure applied to heal and toe imprints, these footprints were made by somebody exiting a vehicle from the driver's side. It appears that person didn't walk over to the body, but rather observed it from the vehicle. Also, we know it was a car rather than a truck because of the size of the tread. We're assuming they didn't hang around long, fearing they might be seen by a passing motorist."

"Wow, you've got my think tank swirling like an overactive Jacuzzi."

"Monday afternoon we had a visitor at the station. Do you remember old Mr. Parker?"

"Sam, before you go any further, I have to tell you something. I know Mr. Parker came to the station to talk to you." I waited for a response. There was none. "I don't know everything you talked about, but I do know he said something about a dark, late-model car."

"I figured you knew when I watched you survey the parking lot at Our Lady of the Highway. You were a lady on a mission. What you didn't know is, I was doing the same thing. Unfortunately, we both came up empty."

"Yeah, now every dark, late-model car I see draws my attention. I could be surrounded by a royal blue Lamborghini, a lemon yellow Maserati, a fire-engine red Ferrari and a black Ford Taurus and the only one I'd see is the Taurus. Even James has a dark, late model car. How sick is that?"

"Let's get back to Mr. Parker. He's a fixture on his front porch. We should give him a radar gun and let him catch speeders coming around the bend before his house. He'd do it just for the thrill of it."

"I've ridden by several times trying not to be conspicuous. For sure, there he was … every time … just rocking and watching. I was afraid he'd tell you he saw a little green sports car cruising his house. You'd know right away it was me."

"Some life," Sam shrugged his shoulders, folded his arms, and leaned back in the chair. "What you don't know is, he reported seeing two cars. And, by the way, one wasn't yours. They were both dark. The first one was newer, fancier and very shiny. He didn't know the make though. About a week before the accident, Saturday to be exact, he was sitting on his porch and this car came speeding around the bend. He didn't recognize it. Said he'd never seen it before. Then, about ten minutes later, it came back the other way. This time it was traveling much slower. He said he went inside at 12:30 to get a coffee, a sandwich and his glasses. Then, Mr. clock-watcher said he was back in his rocker at 1:30. He had brought his newspaper out with him, but hadn't started to read it when the same dark car came back around the bend. This went on a couple more times throughout the afternoon. He knew the license plate was Massachusetts issue."

"He's a strange little person." I said. "I can't imagine living my life on an upside-down pendulum, moving in slow motion, back and forth, in a tiny measured space. Actually, if you think about it, it's pretty sad." I did a reality check when I caught myself rocking in my chair. "Okay, okay, sorry about the side thought. Let's get back to business. You said Mr. Parker saw two cars?"

"That's what he said, but let me finish about the first car."

"There's more?"

"That whole scenario took place on Saturday. Then on Sunday, he was back on his perch again, teetering like a vulture ready to spring on its prey, when the first car returned, this time heading toward the bend. He stopped rocking and watched it disappear. He said he was caught off guard, again with no glasses. He went inside, only for a few minutes, long enough to get a pad of paper and a pen. His objective was to get a make and model of the car and, if he got lucky, a license plate number."

"I can paint the picture. His feet planted flat on the floor-boards to keep him from rocking, the pad of paper resting securely on his lap, and his fingers firmly wrapped around the pen ready to spring into action at the turn of a wheel. You didn't mention his glasses. Did he forget them again?"

"Sherlock, this isn't an episode from *Castle,*" Sam said, knowing I was always glued to the TV on Thursday nights to watch Rick Castle help fight crime with prose from his pen. "But, I have to admit, you painted a pretty accurate image. Mr. P said it was 3:30."

"And he knew this, how?" I asked.

"The *Mr. Frosty* Ice Cream truck passed his house. He said you could set your watch by the truck's schedule. Every Sunday, during the summer, at precisely 3:30, the mesmerizing jingle, *Hooray for Mr. Frosty*, played loud enough to warn parents it was popsicle time." Sam shook his head. "He didn't miss a trick."

"He gave us plate numbers all right, but from every dark car he could. One of the numbers was even from Detective Martin's unmarked. Some of the numbers were partials. We ran whatever we could, but nothing panned out. He told us if it was 1954, he could tell exactly what make and model every car that rode past his house was, even without his glasses. But, none of the cars sold today stood out. All he knew was, people drove too fast and that irritated him."

I had hardly touched my coffee, but Sam's was gone. "I'm going to get a water. Do you want another coffee, or beer, or anything?"

"Yeah, I'll have a water, too." Sam shuffled through some papers. "Ah, here it is; the report we took from Mr. P on Monday. Read this section here, I'll be right back."

My mind was still sorting through the information Sam had just given me, but I turned my attention to the report. Mr. P reported seeing car number one following behind the ice cream truck. In his haste to get the plate number, he leaned forward and in doing so inadvertently let the pad of paper slip from his lap. He reached down, but not in time. When he got back up, he noticed another dark car following car number one. He had no reason to question car number two until he saw it again an hour later ... then a half hour after that ... then in another half hour. The third time he observed car number two, it was following car number one again.

"So, what do you think?"

"Bizarre," I said and went back to the report. "Mr. P went on to say that, although car number two appeared to be following car number one, it kept its distance." I looked at Sam. "That tells me car number one didn't know it was being followed."

"Bingo," Sam sat back down. "This is where we're at. It's pretty shit sure there were two cars. And, that both of them were involved in some way with the accident."

"What doesn't fit is that all this took place a week before the accident." I said.

"If you read further in the report, you'll see that Mr. P reported seeing car number two on at least fifteen different occasions during the week. Not just once or twice a day, but five times in one day within one hour – three different days. Also, it was approximately the same time each of the days; early evening. On Saturday, both cars were back and again on Sunday morning."

"If Mr. P saw car number two so many times, why couldn't' he give you more details to identify it."

"Who knows. We've asked him that several times. You remember he's pretty old, but he's all we've got. I do believe there were two cars involved in the accident. And we will figure it out."

"Wow, okay now it's my turn." I looked at the clock on the wall over Sam's head. "We have to meet the crew at 7:00. It's 5:30, so we've got about an hour before we need to leave. I'll start and then we'll burn the midnight oil when we get back. Sound all right to you?"

"Let's do it." Sam put his paperwork into a pile while I took my 3 x 5's from my recipe box.

"Since I didn't know the Morgan family, I did some background checking. I won't go into any of that, because you already know what I'd say. You also know, I went to the memorial service. But, what you don't know is why. I did check out the parking lot and found nothing. I went to the service, however, to observe her family, friends, and all others in attendance. I wanted to get a feel for their grief. I wanted to watch their reactions when the casket was rolled down the aisle. I wanted to study their facial expressions. I wanted to find anything I could use to help me understand why this happened."

"And did you?"

"Yes and no. It was heartbreaking. You know that, you were there." I closed my eyes and looked away. "When I left the church, I made a promise to Becky Morgan. I promised her I would find the person who did this to her. From the get-go, I thought this was murder and not just a random hit-and-run. My instincts were right."

Sam put his hand on my shoulder, "This is a tough one in a lot of ways."

"Why was she walking along the Scenic Highway after dark on a Sunday night? It's dangerous enough walking there during the day, but at night – come on. She wasn't a stranger to the area. So why? I asked myself. My take is that she was meeting someone or someone dropped her off there. And because of the location, no houses or street lights, she didn't want to be seen with the other person – or, the other person didn't want to be seen with her."

"I'm with you."

"My first stop was Bourne High. Even though school is out, usually the principal or some of the front office personnel are still working. Fortunately, the principal, Mr. Porter, and his assistant, Mr. Bowdin, were both there. I showed them my ID from the Tribune and they let me in. After a brief explanation as to why I was there, Mr. Porter invited me to his office. It was very enlightening. The last couple of months before school ended, both Mr. Porter and Mr. Bowdin noticed a change in both Becky's appearance and personality."

Sam's wrinkled face created a questioning scowl. "Was she getting into trouble, or causing problems for any of her classmates?"

"No, it wasn't that. She went from bubbly to withdrawn; from a young innocent girl with childhood still in her veins to someone hiding in a dark, secret world. She started wearing make-up, heavy make-up. She was caught using her cell phone during school hours. When Mr. Porter confronted her, she became strangely quiet. Did you know she was a cheerleader?"

"Since there were a group of girls dressed in cheerleader uniforms at the memorial, I figured she was."

"Later, you can read my notes about the meeting at the school." I slipped the 3 x 5's behind the divider I'd labeled Bourne High interview.

"Thursday, after you left, I headed into the office to meet with my boss. I had an idea I wanted to run by him." I winced before I continued. "You're probably not going to like it, but it's too late now."

Sam stood up and walked over to the counter. He turned in my direction and I could see he was uncomfortable. "I'm afraid to ask what you have up your sleeve."

"There's going to be an article in tomorrow's paper about Becky's case." I tried to avoid eye contact with him. I kept talking, but busied myself by throwing away our empty water bottles and straightening the chairs. "Don't get bent out of shape. It's basically the same information I put in the first article only written with different words. I know that sounds stupid, but bear with me. My plan is to jog the emotions of a murderer. So much so, he may return to the scene or make a verbal slip to someone. We know this was no accident. We want him to know that. Does that make any sense to you?"

"It does, but it can be dangerous. I don't want you running interference alone. Do you understand me?

"Yes sir. Hey, it's twenty to seven. We're late." I grabbed my purse and headed for the door. Sam followed without saying a word.

CHAPTER FORTY-FIVE

"I know I said we were late, but don't pretend we have a blue light on the roof of the car. Can you slow it down? I don't know what's racing faster ... you or my heart."

"I always knew I had that effect on you."

I reached over and pinched him. "You know exactly what I mean. I'd like to live long enough to have some fried clams."

He gave me a little wink, then changed the subject. "What's with this sudden romance between James and Marnie? Didn't he just meet her last Monday?"

"Yeah, you know the old saying, love at first bite ... I mean sight." I made a biting motion with my teeth. "Who knows with James. I've never seen him as infatuated with a female as he appears to be with her. For that matter, I don't think he's ever really had a girlfriend. It always seemed a little strange to me. I mean, he's a good looking guy, has a great job, and owns his house, and seems pretty stable. I even wondered if he might be gay. But then, I never saw him show affection to a guy either."

"Well, as long as he doesn't put the make on you or underage girls, or worse, boys, I don't really care what he does. I know he had a pretty tough childhood. Maybe he has a hard time getting close to someone for fear of losing them."

Sam had a point. I hadn't really thought of it before. "They seem happy." I said. "He's been with her every day. I wonder what he'll do while she's in New York for a day and a half."

I caught Sam's tell-tale glance. "I've heard she's good at writing to-do lists. Maybe she'll give him one with enough stuff to keep him busy all day tomorrow. It will keep him out of trouble anyway."

"Enough, I like her. We had a great time last night. The girl talk flowed like a babbling-brook running wild through uncharted territory. You would have had a field day trying to decipher all that was said. Come to think of it, better you don't know. Wait till she starts working with Annie and the three of us become a team. You'll be in trouble then."

"That's an understatement. Oops, I missed the turn. See what happened, your fault, the team talk distracted me." Sam turned around in the general store parking lot about a hundred yards down the street. "Do you think you can keep the team talk to a minimum tonight?"

"Maybe," I said as Sam pulled into an empty parking space beside Barry's car.

Seafood Harry's was busy. After all it was a Saturday night in the middle of the summer on Cape Cod. Since we were late, I figured the rest of the crew had already gotten a table, so we entered from the side door. No sooner did Sam open the door and I stepped inside, a familiar voice announced, "It's about time you got here."

I looked to my right to see Barry waving us over.

"Hi to you too! It's only five after seven. Have you already ordered?" I said looking over the empty table top.

"He's his usual give me food piglet. I just got here myself and was given the same warm greeting." Annie looked over her eyebrows at Barry.

"See, Barry," said Marnie, "We didn't need to get here fifteen minutes early. Oh yea, I forgot, you said something about getting here early to get a table."

"Well, we got a good one, didn't we?" Barry again being Barry.

James chimed in, "Why don't we order, then we can continue this intellectual conversation."

"I'm going to have the usual," said Sam. "Casey, what do you want?"

"I think the same, only onion rings instead of fries."

"Annie, what would you like?" asked Barry. "It's my treat."

"I appreciate that, just remember, I'm not furnishing the dessert."

"Always a smart ass," he took her order and followed Sam to the counter.

"Last, but not least, do you want the same as the last time we were here?" James said to Marnie.

"Exactly, you've got me hooked on …."

James left to join the guys before Marnie finished her sentence. Sam looked back over his shoulder at the girls. He could see Marnie had definitely bonded with Casey and Annie. The three were huddled together in what appeared to be continuous light conversation. Their words shaped smiles and produced quiet laughter.

The guys returned, each carrying two beers. Annie lifted her bottle, pointed the neck toward Marnie and said, "Let's toast to our new found friendship, a safe round trip, and your new job."

"Hear! Hear!" they all said in unison.

"So Casey, did you and Sam work on the Morgan case at all today?" asked Annie.

Casey turned to see Sam's reaction before replying. "We've started comparing notes. It's scary how we have different takes on the same scenario. Then after talking about them and dissecting our thoughts, we come to the same conclusion … at least most of the time."

Sam piped in, "We've only scratched the surface, but, the harder we scratch, the deeper the cut, and the faster the information spurts out."

James felt the tension build up inside. He took a long drink of beer trying to put out the fire that burned deep in his chest.

Stay calm.

When Sam and Casey team up, the results are deadly. He had to find a way to separate them long enough to create a diversion.

"A penny for your thoughts," said Marnie.

James was quick with his reply. "You've worked me to death. At the moment, my mind isn't doing much thinking at all." He smiled. "Actually, that's a lie. I was thinking of how I was going to enjoy my day of rest." He squirmed in his chair. Maybe if he joined in the conversation, they wouldn't notice how fidgety he was. He was about to ask Sam a question, when the waitress set a tray down on the table beside them. The timing couldn't be better. Food is the all time great silencer. He remembered how his mother would give them cookies when she craved silence, even if it only lasted a couple minutes.

"Anybody up for a softball game tomorrow? The Bourne PD is playing Wareham PD in the semi-finals. Yours truly is the starting pitcher." Sam continued, "We're using the Bourne High School field. Admission is free. They've got two dollar dogs, three dollar burgers, chips and ice cream. Everything we make is divided between the two town's youth programs. It starts at 2:30."

James wanted no part of Bourne High School. He had picked Becky up there a few times and didn't want to rekindle old memories. "I've got some things I need to take care of around my own house tomorrow. If I get them done, I'll come on by." He knew damn right well, he'd never show.

In between bites, Barry said, "I'm going fishing with my neighbor and a few of his friends. Six of us chipped in and chartered a private boat. If the blues are running, we'll have a feast next week. Marnie, have you ever had blues lathered with mayo and cooked on the grill?" Even though he had just devoured a heaping dish of whole belly fried clams and onion rings, his mouth was salivating at the thought of grilled blues.

Annie shook her head, "It's no wonder the buttons on your shirt are popping. Do you think of anything other than food?"

"Not usually," said Barry. He threw his hands in the air. "What else is there?"

"I can't eat another bite." I ripped open a wet wipe and attempted to clean the grease from my hands. "That was delicious. If I keep eating like this I'll end up looking like a beached whale that's done nothing but graze while on a three day cruise."

"We should get going," Sam said to me. "There's still a lot of ground to cover when we get home, or should I say to your house."

"What house?" I said. "My kitchen looks like a mini squad room. This was a welcome break, but we've got a long night ahead of us." I got up and Sam followed. "Marnie, have a safe trip and I'll see you Monday afternoon. Don't forget to call me when you get back. Hopefully, I'll have some new information to share."

Sam and I waved as we headed out the door. Once inside the car, he turned to me and said, "Annie was quiet tonight. Not like her. It's usually hard to shut her up. I felt there was something she wanted to talk about, but not in front of everybody. What do you think?"

"I think you're right." I pursed my lips and sat back in my seat. "I'll give her a call tomorrow and see if everything's okay. We did talk about the Morgan case last night. And, as I'm sure you're well aware, it's the highest priority case on the DA's log. Maybe she stopped by her office to re-read whatever they have on file."

"I'm going to tell you right now, they don't have much," said Sam. "I had lunch with Mike the other day and he indicated that this whole thing has him puzzled. He said in his thirty years in the business, he hasn't seen a case that's so public, yet so secretive. If it was a robbery, he said it would have been an inside job. We both feel it's very scripted, only neither one of us can put our finger on the why."

"It's scary cause anybody could be her killer ... even one of her closest friends." That was something I didn't want to think about, but knew in the back of my mind, it could be a strong possibility. "Not that I have any information to substantiate that, but we need to consider the odds," I paused, then added, "I'm glad we're finally working together." I unbuckled my seatbelt as Sam pulled into my driveway and slide sideways to give him a hug.

"Come on Sherlock, we've got work to do."

"I know, but all work and no play makes Sam a dull boy." I winked. "But then Sam has never been a dull boy. So let's get going so we can finish the work and who knows what game we might end up playing."

He pulled me close and we walked in unison to the back door.

Everything was right where we left it. There was no reason it wouldn't be. "I'm making me a cup of coffee. You want one?"

"At least one," he said, as he took a seat at the table.

I handed Sam the 3 x 5's from my box, "Here's the report I did on the interview with Mr. Porter and Mr. Bowdin. Take a look at it and see if anything jumps out at you."

I busied myself at the counter, glancing occasionally at Sam trying to read any changes in his facial expressions. There were none. I could see he only had a few cards left so I asked, "Well, what do you think?"

"I think the human interest and background info combined with what we're hoping are relevant facts will give us a handle on what really happened. It's the whodunit that's going to give us agita."

I carried the coffee to the table and sat down, ready to get started. "From the school interview, I found that she had a part time waitress job at The Train Stop." I slid the schools 3 x 5's back into their slot and flipped to the divider marked Train Stop. "I wasn't sure what or who I would run into there, but you know me ... leave no stones unturned." I fanned down a few cards, "Here," I handed Sam the next four. "I started a conversation with a young girl who was waiting tables. Her name is Sara. As luck would have it, she was a friend of Becky's. And, better still, she was willing to talk to me." I watched as Sam continued reading. "You finish reading what I wrote and then we'll talk."

I didn't want to interrupt him, so I quietly got up and walked into the bedroom. It was going to be a long night. I slipped into a pair of yellow and black stripe Joe Boxers, threw on a black jersey, and went back to the kitchen.

Sam looked up. "Yikes, a giant bumble bee has escaped from the hive." He held his arms up in front of his face. "Don't sting me, I'll give up." Within seconds he had me in a bear hug.

"Knock it off. Don't forget, I am the queen bee in this house." I stood with my hands on my hips trying to act like the voice of authority. I tried to keep a straight face. Of course, I couldn't and we both burst out laughing.

"This is good reading, Sherlock," Sam said as he settled back down. He patted the chair beside him, motioning for me to sit. "I've got some comments, then questions. First of all, I read a feeling of sincerity into Sara's character. On the other hand, I'm not feeling the same way about Shawn. I can't pinpoint why, but there's something not right."

"When I first went to The Stop, I caught him staring at me a couple different times. I just figured he was curious, maybe wondered if I worked in the area, or for some reason, looked familiar. Anyway, after I talked to Sara, it seemed as though she had several small conversations with him before she came back and asked if it was okay if he came with her to talk to me. Of course, I said yes. While we were at the Java Hut, he did appear a little anxious, but I figured it was the nature of the conversation. After all, he said he grew up with Becky – that they were like brother and sister."

"Sometimes brothers and sisters become too close." Sam sighed. "Monday morning I'm going to do a little more checking on this guy. I'm thinking they may have dated, after all she was the co-captain of the cheerleaders and he's a big shot on the football team. Like Anthony and Cleopatra, those two characters usually end up playing huggy bear and kissy face. At least they did when I was in school."

"You speaking from experience?" I said.

"I was on the baseball team. We didn't have cheerleaders. Doesn't mean I wouldn't have tried, but I didn't have the opportunity."

I reached over to the sink, grabbed a dish towel, and snapped it over his head. "I bet you didn't."

Sam looked at his watch. "It's almost midnight. Let's wrap up for the night."

"I've got a question though. I want to know about Mr. Parker. Do you think he'd recognize either one or both of the mystery cars? Have you thought about having him sit with the department's sketch artist? I know he usually does faces, but maybe we could get him to try auto recognition." I raised my shoulders in a questioning gesture.

"You know what, Sherlock, that's not a bad idea at all. Paul Penny is doing them now. I'll ask him Monday. If he can't, then I'll check with the Sheriff's department. Their guy has been with them for over twenty-five years and really knows his stuff. They nicknamed him Mugsy."

"I sure would like to sit in Mr. P's rocker and see the world from his eyes. Maybe I could envision the two vehicles he talked about – watch them round the bend – over and over and over again. Have you been to his house?"

"So now you have ESP? And no, I haven't been to his house. I can see Monday morning is going to be busy. We've put all the puzzle pieces we have in place." Sam tugged on my hand. "What do you say we give the old brains a rest?"

"I thought you'd never ask," I said easing myself up from the chair.

He checked the locks, I shut off the lights, and we headed toward the bedroom.

CHAPTER FORTY-SIX

The dew sparkled like diamonds reflecting the early morning rays of the sun. Sam was already up and in the shower. I lazily lifted my body from the bed, slipped into my robe, and shuffled my way to the kitchen.

As usual, there wasn't much in the fridge for breakfast. Living alone didn't require frequent trips to the market. Pop tarts, cookies or, when there was milk, an occasional bowl of cereal were my in-house morning staples. Of course, though, I preferred to grab a gooey, chocolate frosted donut at Dunkins on my way to work. It would be nice if we could go to Cozy Cupboard for some eggs and pancakes. I'm sure I'll get the lecture about how unhealthy my eating habits are. I'm going to ask anyway.

I decided to wait for Sam on the back deck. A warm, gentle breeze carried an ever-so-faint smell of salt air. I closed my eyes and took a deep breath. Days like this reminded me of why I live on the Cape.

"Hey, Sherlock, I checked your fridge for food and there's nothing in there I want to eat. I suppose you want me to take you out for breakfast?" Sam leaned against the house, crossed his arms and shook his head.

"Who me?" I grinned. "It took you long enough to ask. I'm going to take a quick shower, so why don't you make yourself a cup of coffee."

Twenty minutes later I joined him on the deck. "I'll wait till we get to Cozy Cupboard for my first cup. Let's go, I'm starved."

Since it was Sunday morning, I knew it would be crowded, but they move right along – after all it was just breakfast. "There are a couple of empty seats on the porch. I'll meet you out there," I said.

Sam gave the hostess his name, then joined me outside. "She said it should only be about ten minutes, fifteen at the most. Be right back."

The Tribute Sunday paper box was partially visible from where we were sitting. Sam reached in his pocket for some change. "I need another quarter ... got one?"

"Yep, here, catch." I flipped it in his direction. "Good job, I hope you do as good in your game today."

I slid my chair closer to Sam's. "Look under local news." I had no sooner gotten the words out of my mouth, when the hostess appeared. She sat us at a table for four. "How convenient," I said. "Why don't you lay the paper out so we can both read the article." Obviously, since I wrote it, I knew what it said. Sam was a hard guy to read. He'd make a great poker player ... except he wasn't a gambler. It was a short article and he took much too long to read it.

"Well, did they spell some words wrong or are you stumbling over my thoughts?" Before he could answer, the waitress was back, paper and pen in hand, ready to take our order. "Coffee, small orange juice, and, let's see, I think the Sunshine Special. I'd like my eggs over medium. I'll have the pancakes instead of toast and the sausage patties instead of bacon." I finished ordering and laid my menu down. "You're up," I said.

"I suppose I'll have what she ordered, only I'll have the bacon."

"I don't believe it. Mr. Healthy is breaking down and eating like a human for a change. What happened to the yogurt and granola or the scrambled eggs and wheat toast?"

219

"It's your fault. You zapped all my strength last night. I'll work it off at the game this afternoon. What about you?"

"I might take a bike ride. Maybe I'll clean the house. Who knows, you might even see me at your game. I promise I won't root for Wareham."

"You got that right!" Sam said and went back to his reading.

"Are you reading my article or did something else catch your eye?"

"Your article … I like it. You basically said the same thing as before, but used different words and mixed up the timeline a little. It's just enough to get somebody thinking the authorities know more than they're letting on. Let's hope he or she starts to over think and makes a slip. This person also knows you wrote the both articles, therefore he or she might wonder how much you actually do know. Like I said before, be careful. Don't do anything foolish. And, if you need me, call. You got it?"

The scary part between Sam and me was that he could read me like a book. My pages were flapping and needed to be turned. I was sure the answers we were looking for were not even a chapter away. "I'm glad you found part of the Sunday paper worth reading. There's only one more article I want to write and that's the one that will bring closure to the Morgan family." "That's my girl," said Sam as he folded the newspaper and put it in the chair beside him.

Sam looked up to let me know the waitress was on her way with our food. "When you get a chance, we'd like some more coffee," he said. "Thanks."

"Now let's eat. I have to admit this breakfast really looks good."

CHAPTER FORTY-SEVEN

The parking lot for the Scenic Highway bike path was almost empty. It was still early. The canal was to my left and the highway, even though I couldn't see it, was to my right. It had been a few years since I'd ridden the path, so my mental distance meter was rusty. I knew at some point I'd have to venture off to come up behind Mr. Parker's. What I wasn't sure of was what type of terrain I had to cross to do so. I unsnapped the straps that held my bike in place and lifted it off the back of my car.

I remember the day I bought my shiny royal blue and silver, top of the line mountain bicycle. Sam bought one too. We were going to ride from Bourne to P Town, stay a couple of days, then pedal back. I have no idea what we were thinking. It took a good hour and a half to drive, let alone ride a bike. It never happened. Maybe I can get him to think about it again. Only this time we'll drive the bikes down, then use them for local transportation. He might go for that.

I locked the car, secured my sun glasses with a head strap, put on my helmet, dropped my bottle of water into its holder, slipped on my mini backpack, and positioned myself to begin my quest.

The path was clearly marked in quarter-mile intervals. Two miles out, I stopped to determine my location. I guess-t-mated the railroad bridge that spanned the canal looked somewhere around four miles away. By my calculations, I wanted to turn off long before that, probably in another mile.

Fortunately, just beyond the three miles marker, the terrain to my right didn't appear too dense. I took a pair of binoculars from my backpack and surveyed the area I was about to ride into. The security of the pavement soon turned into scrub brush, dirt, and picker bushes. Thank goodness I had the foresight to wear long jeans and pack a long sleeve jersey. They'll keep my battle scars to a minimum. Was I doing the right thing? I probably should have told Sam what I was planning. What am I thinking? For sure he doesn't need to know. He'll be tied up for hours. Besides, he said he'd get back to me tomorrow after researching the stuff we talked about last night.

I must have gone at least two miles in, when, all of a sudden, I came to a clearing. I stopped abruptly. Damn it, about forty feet in front of me was a gigantic cranberry bog. I took a deep breath and got off my bike to take a better look around – out came the binoculars again. I did a ninety degree scan of the horizon. Just as I was about change direction, I caught a glimpse of a tiny object protruding out of the ground. It was tiny because it was far away. I concentrated on the area, moving very slowly, examining the surrounding vicinity. Mr. Parker's house was situated on an isolated section of the highway. About a mile one way or the other, there were a couple more houses, but his was the only one in that particular section. Across the street from him was an abandoned tree farm, so even though he was on the Scenic Highway, it was a pretty remote area. There had to be something I could find that would let me know I was headed in the right direction. My mind was drawing a blank. I found a large rock a couple of steps away so I sat down to figure out my next move.

Casey, Casey, Casey.

I shut my eyes and tried to picture what was around Mr. P's that would help me confirm the location. That's it … the tower. I jumped to my feet, grabbed the binoculars and moved them a little more to the right. There it was. The outline of the Bourne water-tower beckoned me to continue. Mr. Parker's house was approximately a half mile from the tower. "Yeah," I said out loud. "Is this what Columbus felt like when he sighted land?" Now all I have to do is cross the bog.

Since the berries aren't harvested until the fall, there were no workers around. I remember reading about one of the bogs down Cape that would offer a working tour. For a nominal fee, they'd let people experience using an old fashioned scoop to harvest the berries. I always thought it would be a cool thing to do. It's still on my list. I'll get to it one of these days, but for today, I have to navigate around this one. If I go around the exterior perimeter, it will take me forever. On the other hand, if I'm careful, I can cut across the narrow strip that divides the bog in half. The whole idea is not to fall in.

The strip is about a quarter-mile long and three-feet wide. I took a long drink of water and I was off. The ground was soft, especially along the edge where the water had permeated the soil. If I wasn't careful, I was in for a sponge bath complete with deep red cranberry bath beads.

It was tricky to maneuver my bike over the uneven land. It didn't make a hill of beans difference how careful I was. My right foot got caught up in a hidden hole and I was down for the count. My bike went one way and I went the other. I got up and brushed myself off. It looked like I had slid into home plate and had the skid marks on the side of my jeans to prove it. My hands, my right arm, and the side of my face were evidence I had had some kind of an encounter with nature. My right sneaker squished a little and my right leg was wet. At least I could change my shirt. I knew there was nobody around, so I quickly removed my Red Sox tee and replaced it with the clean one in my backpack. I was still somewhat of a mess and hoped Mr. Parker wouldn't mistake me for a homeless person looking for a handout.

This whole sneaking in the backdoor idea was beginning to make no sense. At the time I planned it, I wanted to make sure nobody anywhere on, or around the Scenic Highway saw me.

Now, I wondered if my thinking was straight from a CSI episode. Sam will certainly say it was.

I felt like I was walking on a tight-rope, but I finally made it. Now I could see Mr. Parker's house clearly. His truck was in its usual parking space on the side. The half-shells of two lobster boats on the other side served as a reminder of Cape Cod's finest cuisine, even though they probably hadn't seen one of those little snappy critters for years. Obviously, I couldn't see if he was on the front porch because I was approaching from the back. But why wouldn't he be? He was always there.

I decided to change my plan. If I came out just above his house, on the same side and rode the short distance to his house, it would only take me a few minutes. That way I could stop to talk to him and hopefully start up a conversation. I was probably dreaming, but what did I have to lose?

I found a clearing that led to the street and headed out. I could see the rocker, but there was a problem. It was empty. I went back to the clearing and waited ten minutes before I tried again. Same thing, no Mr. Parker. I had no choice but to knock on his door.

This was becoming a daytime nightmare. I walked my bike to the back of the house and leaned it against a beat-up old yard chair. It was quiet – like somebody hit the mute button. The three steps leading to the back door were rickety. Each one seemed to creak louder as I made my way up to the little landing at the top. My heart raced faster than Super Saver when he won the Kentucky Derby last year.

There weren't any lights on inside, but it was early so he probably didn't need them. The curtains on the door were pulled back, leaving about a six inch opening. There wasn't a mud room so the door opened directly into the kitchen. I cupped my hand around the sides of my eyes and rested my forehead against the glass. From what I could see, nothing was out of place. Everything appeared normal.

"What was that?" I jumped back. Out of the corner of my eye, I saw a squirrel running through the yard trying to catch up with his buddy, who was already half way up a tree.

Steady yourself.

This isn't the time to talk out loud. If there is anyone around, I just blew my cover. Not smart.

I steadied myself and with a firm hand, knocked on the door. Nothing. I knocked once more. Again, nothing. My instincts told me to leave, but my inquisitive mind would have no part of it.

There was a window to the right of the door. I looked around to make sure I was alone, then went back down the steps and headed toward it. I could see from where I stood, it was only about four-feet from the ground. Just a little peek, I thought. The glass was dirty, making it hard to see things inside. I made out the silhouette of a table, four chairs, and a buffet with outlines of vases or some kind of stuff on top of it. The walls were covered with pictures, but it was impossible to know of what or who. Still no sign of Mr. Parker.

The house was small, I figured it to be six rooms – four down and two up – a typical Cape Cod design. I'd already seen two of the rooms. I tried to visualize the layout. The living room should be in front of the dining room and a bedroom, usually the master, should be in the front left corner of the house. That would be in front of the kitchen. Trying to look into those windows could cause a problem since they can be seen from the street. The ones in the front of the house were definitely out.

There was a side window in the bedroom. I decided to try this one first. Fortunately, there was a huge Rhodie in full bloom growing beside the window. A perfect cover, I thought. I gingerly moved up close. This glass had recently been cleaned. Everything appeared to be in its place, even the bed was made. The door leading to the front hall was open and from this angle I could tell that the door to the front porch was closed. One more room to go.

As I backed away from the bedroom window, I caught a glimpse of the rear end of a car passing slowly in front of the house. Did they see me? I wondered. Even worse, I know it was a dark color – maybe black. I slipped back behind the Rhodie and leaned against the house. I closed my eyes and took a deep breath. I've come this far, I can't turn back now. The whole thing was probably a figment of my imagination. After all, there are lots of dark colored cars and his house is on a main road.

Compose yourself.

I found myself silently issuing instructions.

I repeated the window peeking caper one more time on the other side of the house. This time I half expected to see Mr. Parker sitting on his couch with a cup of coffee watching TV. Nope – nothing. I didn't linger. There wasn't anything for me to hide behind. As I rounded the corner to the back yard, I felt like I was being watched. I glanced over my shoulder and again caught the tail end of a dark vehicle passing. This time in the opposite direction. Smarten up girl, they're not looking at you.

Okay, I had to make a decision. Based on the facts that Mr. Parker's truck was parked beside the house, he wasn't in his rocking chair – I peeked there too – and it appears he's nowhere inside. I'm going in. There's a chance he might be upstairs, but my gut feeling told me he hasn't been up there in years.

I carefully reached for the door knob and gave it a gentle turn. It wasn't locked. Way too easy, I thought. I slowly opened the door and stepped inside. "Mr. Parker," I called out. Just like the knocks, there was no response. I tried again. "Mr. Parker, are you here?" The silence was deafening.

There was no smell of coffee or breakfast or anything. For that matter, there weren't any signs of life either. I flipped the light switch on and stood with my back against the wall, letting my eyes survey the room. Three quarters of the way around, I noticed a door and assumed it led to the basement. It was open a crack, but there wasn't any light coming through.

There's definitely a problem here. I should call Sam, but he's got that big game today. It could be nothing. I'll just check it out and report to him later.

"What's this? Blood?" I knelt down to touch one of the spots. It was tacky and did appear to be blood. The drops weren't fresh, but they weren't dry either. They were close together and led to the cellar door. I stood up, took a deep breath and walked to the door. Carefully, I opened it as wide as it would go. "Mr. Parker, are you there? No answer. "Is anyone down there?"

There wasn't a wall switch, just a pull string hanging from a ceiling light. The bulb must have been burned out because no matter how hard I pulled, nothing happened.

I wish I had a flashlight ... and a gun.

I held onto the railing and felt my way half way down. Fortunately, there was a little sunlight trying to penetrate the windows on the east side of the house. Somewhere, there had to be a couple more ceiling lights.

Once my eyes adjust, I'm sure I can find one.

CHAPTER FORTY-EIGHT

What's going on here? I can't move.

My feet were tied together and my arms were behind my back, bound and secured, and somehow attached to the dowels of a chair.

The last thing I remember was hearing a noise coming from the kitchen, stepping off the bottom step, and not finding the floor. My head hurt. Actually, my whole body hurt. I must have fallen and knocked myself out.

Wait a minute.

I'm so confused. The only thing I know for a fact is that I'm tied up. Mr. Parker must have been hiding somewhere in the cellar. When I fell and knocked myself unconscious, he seized the opportunity to restrain me. After all, I'm an uninvited guest in his house. I must have scared the old guy. When he comes to check on me, I'll explain this whole situation. I'll tell him to call Sam.

My breathing was deep. I tried to stay calm, hoping it would all be over soon. My head drooped down in front of me. My eyes stared at the floor. The basement was cold and nasty and smelled like moldy dirt.

My left ankle throbbed. I tried to wiggle it around, but it hurt too much.

Please don't let anything be broken.

My mind flashed back to the Academy and the fall that ended my career as a police officer.

I closed my eyes and prayed everything would be different when I opened them.

It wasn't.

I was scared, but frustrated that I had allowed myself to get into this situation. After a bout of feeling sorry for myself, I slowly lifted my head and looked around. There wasn't much to see. It looked like a bunch of boxes in the far corner.

Whew, the things stored in them must smell good.

It appeared that a table of some sort and a few chairs were being stored along the wall. That's probably where this chair came from, I thought.

Since I wasn't against a wall or in a corner, I had to turn my neck one way, then the other to see what was behind me. My first attempt was to the left. There was nothing.

"Why wasn't Mr. Parker coming back for me? And why am I talking out loud?" I needed to hear a voice, any voice, even mine.

The angle of my chair and the lack of agility in my body made the fourth corner almost impossible to see. Impossible, though, is not a word in my vocabulary.

If I push a little with my right foot and do tiny body bounces, I think I can maneuver around enough to see what's in the last corner.

Conquering the fear of the unknown is worth the pain.

My eyes flew open wide. The pain temporarily left my body. With all the strength I could muster, I swiveled forty five degrees to the right. The shock of reality reared its ugly face.

Please don't let this be happening.

The shadow of a limp body was sitting upright in a chair in the far corner. It appeared to be bound the same as me. "Oh my God, it must be Mr. Parker."

Panic set in. If that's Mr. Parker, then who did this to me and, obviously, whoever did this to me also did it to him. My cell phone was in my pants pocket. Somehow, I had to get down on

229

my side and try to squeeze it out. Since Sam is the first name on my speed dial, I needed to feel my way to the number one.

It felt like a couple of hours had passed since I first came inside. It must be somewhere around noontime. Sam usually takes his cell off his belt when he plays softball. The game is scheduled for two o'clock so, hopefully, he's still got his phone with him. I rocked the chair sideways just enough to cause it to lose stability. I came down on my side harder than expected. "Ouch." The floor was damp against my skin. "Yuck, I don't like this at all." I wiggled and squirmed until … pop! There it was. I flipped onto my back, then over to my left side. I shimmied my body around until I could grab my cell between my hands. My fingers studied the raised buttons. When I was sure I'd landed on the right one, I kept one finger on it. The send button was on the left. I pushed it, then the number one. I didn't hear a dial tone or a connecting ring. And God knows, it was so quiet, I could have heard a pin drop, even on the dirt. I tried again. Nothing. My cell felt cold and damp, but everything around here was cold and damp. "You've got to be kidding. When I fell into the bog, my cell must have gotten wet. So, I can't call out and I can't get any calls in."

I had to free myself. The throbbing in my left ankle was back. "Mr. Parker, please talk to me."

CHAPTER FORTY-NINE

"Mornin' Sam," said Peggy. "You're here early today."

"I need to get some stuff sorted out before everyone's problems start knocking on my door. Hey, since you're here early, I could use your help."

"You've got it boss. Let me get my notebook and something to write with and I'll be right back." She started out the door then stopped. "Coffee?"

"Sounds good to me, thanks," he said. He leaned down to retrieve his briefcase.

Ten minutes later, Peggy returned with two mugs. She slid one across the desk to Sam, then, settled in ready to take notes and get started on whatever her assignment was going to be. She figured it had something to do with the Morgan case, since that was Sam's major focus these days. "You pitched a mean game of softball yesterday. Once again Bourne retains its championship." Usually this would bring a smile to his face, but not this time. "I thought I might see Casey there."

"I did too. So you haven't spoken to her within the last couple of days?" Sam looked up from his desk and focused on Peggy. "I know you two have gone back and forth regarding the Morgan case. And you know Casey, always the Sherlock. I probably should have confided in her long before I did, but that's water over the dam. She did a lot of investigating on her own and, of course, came up with some very interesting and pertinent information. When I left her Sunday morning, I expected her to meet me at the ball field. She must have gone rogue and checked something out on her own." Sam's eyes were back scanning his paperwork.

"Do you want me to call her?" She could see the apprehension building on his face.

"I tried earlier, but go ahead."

"I'll be right back." She headed for her desk to retrieve her cell. It was seven in the morning. Casey usually isn't up and functioning much before eight. Peggy hit speed dial five. It rang six times, then, went to voice mail. She tried three more times, each time leaving a message to call as soon as possible. She tried her land line, nothing there either. Peggy put her cell in her pocket, took a deep breath, tried to cover her nerves, and headed back to report to Sam.

He watched her walk toward him. "No luck either?"

"No, but you know Casey, half the time her cell doesn't work because she forgot to charge it." She didn't tell him about trying the land line. He'd probably done that too.

"Please shut the door. I need to fill you in on something." He cupped his hands behind his head and leaned back in his chair. "I don't know how much Casey has told you about her investigation." He hesitated, then, continued. "Did she tell you about The Train Stop and meeting up with a couple of Becky's friends?"

"Yes, she did." Peggy knew she had to be straight with him.

"Well, she had some suspicions about the boy, Shawn. She didn't feel his remorse was real. Sara, on the other hand, seemed genuine. In fact, Casey thought his sincerity was an act in front of Sara. This sent up a red flag. And when Casey puts up a red flag, you better watch which way it's blowing. Are you following me?"

"I am, and I don't think I like where it's going." Peggy's full attention was broken by a knock on the door.

Detective Bill Martin stood outside waving an envelope in his hand. Sam signaled him in. "Hey, boss, this was just delivered from crime lab and since it's marked URGENT, I thought you would need it right away."

Sam took the envelope from Bill and nodded, indicating that his job, for the moment, was finished. "I'll talk to you later. Don't plan on leaving the office before seeing me."

"Gotcha, if there's anything you need just ...."

He stopped when Sam motioned for him to leave and close the door.

Peggy watched Sam open the envelope. She could see pictures, but wasn't sure of what. He had them tilted and the glare from the window made them unclear. She hesitated for a minute, then asked, "What are the pictures of?"

"When Casey and I started putting our information together, things began to fall into place. My information and her keen perception narrowed the missing puzzle pieces from twenty spots to three. Take this picture. Study it and tell me what you see." Sam slid it across the desk to her.

Goosebumps climbed up and down her back. "I see a young girl with tire tracks close beside her and also up her whole body."

"Do you notice anything about those tracks?"

"No, am I supposed to?"

"Okay, look at these next two pictures. Same tire tracks, but blown up." Sam must have been getting the right reaction because he was satisfied with Peggy's response.

She puckered her lips and blew out a quick puff of air. "They're made from entirely different tires. Are you saying there were two cars? And, it appears that the first one didn't really run her over, maybe just knocked her sideways. But the other one, made sure he or she finished the job."

"That's why I wanted you to examine the photos. I needed untrained eyes to tell the story. And you did." Sam sighed. "We have an office full of trained detectives and nobody, including me, saw this coming. I'm afraid Casey saw it and is trying to piece it together on her own."

"Do you have any idea who?" Peggy asked.

"I've got my suspicions, but before I can divulge that information, I have to be sure. Right now, I want to find Casey."

Before Detective Martin could raise his hand to knock, Sam motioned him in. "Peggy, keep trying her phones and let me know the minute you talk to her."

She got up from her chair, motioned Bill to sit down, and left without closing the door.

Sam got up from his desk, closed the door, and walked to the window. He stared out, not seeing anything or hearing anybody.

"Sam, are you okay?" Bill started to get up.

"No, but sit down," said Sam as he walked back from the window and sat down himself. We have a situation and I'm trying to figure out our next move."

"I have a report you need to see immediately," said Bill. "We just got the weekend sheets from the Scenic Park Patrol. Since you were busy, I went over them."

Sam stiffened. His face lost all expression.

"I recognized the description of one of the over-night vehicles parked in the bike lot." Bill looked at Sam, then continued. "I ran the plate number to be sure. It came back registered to Casey Quinby."

Sam leaned forward on his desk, secured his elbows in front of him, and dropped his head into his hands. What had she done? Why didn't she wait for him? Where was she?

"I called patrol. They said she had a bike rack secured to the car, but there wasn't a bike on it. I told them to search the bike path to see if she may have fallen and gotten hurt. I just got off the phone. They said they'd take their ATVs out and scour the area. I'm on direct line with them, so as soon as they have any information, they're going to call."

"Bill, I need a few minutes alone."

"I understand, boss. I'll be at my desk if you need me." Bill wished he hadn't been the one to break the news to Sam.

Sam took the rest of the pictures from the crime lab out of the envelope and laid them on his desk. He put the ones from the scene together on the right side and then the other four on the left. The three page report detailing the findings sat square in the middle.

Once he got his thoughts together, he called Peggy and Bill back to his office. Peggy brought her notebook. Sam filled Bill in on what he'd discussed with Peggy earlier. "Since you're the only two who know where we're at, anything I show you stays right here."

They both nodded.

He turned the pictures so they were facing them. "I showed Peggy the pictures on the left this morning. Bill, I want you to take a look at them very carefully and tell me what you see."

"The tire tracks – we completely missed this the first time around." Bill shook his head. "What now?"

"Well, remember Mr. Parker mentioned something about seeing two cars on several different occasions, one always following the other. They were both dark late models. But, we had no makes or license plate numbers. We should have put more stock into the old busy-body's observations."

"That still leaves us nowhere," said Bill.

"Casey and I got together with our notes Saturday. She's pretty good at finding hidden evidence. She filled me in on what she'd been doing and I compared it to what we've been doing. To make a long story short, she interviewed a couple of the Morgan girl's friends. I use the word friends loosely. One, I believe, was and the other was at one time."

"You're losing me, boss. How did Casey find these kids?"

"Trust me, she did her homework. If we had confided in her from the beginning, she'd be sitting here with us now. I'm sure of that." The worried look on Sam's face said it all.

Sam continued, "Yesterday, on my way to the game, I drove by the Train Stop to see if Shawn was working. From the description Casey gave me, he was. I decided to make my own observations, so I picked up a newspaper, sat at a table, and ordered breakfast."

Bill listened, while reading Sam's report at the same time. "Was the girl, Sara, there?"

"There wasn't anyone that matched her description," said Sam. "I assume she wasn't. I'll tell you, though, if Shawn's involved you'd never know it. He's a pretty cool character. The only thing I caught him doing was checking out any young girl who'd come in with or without a family. I mean he undressed them with his eyes. I know he's only seventeen and that's somewhat normal, but some of the leers weren't."

For the last fifteen minutes, Peggy had sat quiet, just listening and taking notes. Finally she looked up from her notebook, "Sam, this is all very interesting, but where is it all leading to."

"Hold on Miss Peggy," Sam took a deep breath, "there's more."

"My car was parked next to what I assumed to be the employee lot. When I left I noticed a dark, late model vehicle on the far end. It was out of sight from the inside of the restaurant, so I decided to take a closer look."

"Still, Sam, a dark, late model car doesn't prove anything." Bill got up and paced in front of the desk.

Sam sat straight up, "It does when the license plate number is registered to Shawn Waldon."

Bill sat back down.

"I had my tread kit in the trunk, so I took a chance and rubbed the tire. They appeared to be new or fairly new, so I was able to get a very clear print." Sam's eyes moved several times back and forth from Bill to Peggy. "Hold that thought, because I'm going to back up to Friday night."

"Casey, Annie and Marnie had a girl's-night-out. Afterward, they headed for The Tavern to top the night off. James and Barry were already there. I got there about ten minutes after the girls. Some discussion came up about the Morgan case. I guess the girls talked about it earlier." Sam hesitated, not quite sure how to finish his sentence. "James appeared edgy. I detected an aura of controlled nervousness."

Bill piped in, "You're not saying you think James is involved or knows something, are you?"

"It's no secret, he's not my favorite person. I don't know why I felt this way, but I did. Call it intuition, but at this point, I wasn't comfortable. Casey and I left a little before the others. We said our good-byes and headed out the front door. I know we'd been drinking, but, she kinda paused just before the end of the courtyard path. For a slight minute she stared at James' car. There was a strange, squinty look on her face … almost like she was studying something. After I got her strapped in and on her way, I decided to check it out, just to satisfy my curiosity."

"My car was parked two in front of James. I knew they had a half pitcher of beer left, so I figured I had at least ten minutes. When I checked out the front of his car, I noticed a spot on the right front fender. It wasn't really a dent, but it felt like it could have been. I took the tread kit from my truck and took a rubbing."

"Does Casey know you did this?" asked Peggy

"No, I didn't tell her." He drew in a deep breath. "I was with her Saturday night, but until I had something concrete, I decided to wait. This morning I sent both rubbings and the tire pictures from the accident scene off to the crime lab to determine if there is a match. Hopefully, we'll get an answer real soon."

The silence was interrupted by the Pink Panther theme song playing on Detective Martin's cell. "Martin here. Are you sure?"

Sam's heart raced.

"I'll call you right back." Bill laid his cell down on the desk. "They didn't find anything to indicate Casey had an accident or any kind of a problem along the bike path. They're waiting for further instructions."

Peggy saw the stress build. "I'll be right back, I'll get us some coffee."

Sam watched her walk across the office. "She's a good friend of Casey's. This is hard on her too. The fear of the unknown always induces stress."

"Let's concentrate on Casey. We know her last stop with her car was the bike lot. I know she never puts the rack on the car unless she's taking her bike somewhere. Since the rack was empty, it leads to the obvious conclusion, she went for a ride. The question is where? And what did she have up her sleeve?"

"Boss, I've got an overhead map of the bike path. It's the one we used when that little kid went missing last summer. I'll be right back." Bill headed toward his desk.

Bill and Peggy were back at Sam's door at the same time. "Sorry it took so long, I made a fresh pot."

"Thanks," Sam reached for the cup Peggy offered him. "I need something to stimulate my brain."

Bill put the map on Sam's desk. The three of them stood over it without saying a word.

Sam finally spoke, "If something happened to Casey's bike, she would have walked it back to the car and taken it home. The entire path is bordered on the left by the Canal. The terrain on the right side varies. There's thick brush with lots of picker bushes. That area is too thick for anyone to walk through. There's several spots with low, sparse, grassy like plants where, over the years, bikers have worn down and made into resting pads. First, we should identify and circle them."

Bill knew the area well, so he was able to quickly identify the areas Sam requested.

"Now, look at each one separately. If we draw lines from each spot heading away from the path, let's see where we end up." Sam took a pencil and a ruler from his desk and began to draw the find lines.

Bill hated it when Sam talked about find lines. The last time they used them, the find at the end of one the lines wasn't good.

"I'm going to draw all the lines in, then we'll go back and work on the areas one at a time." He was careful to use the same number of lines in each 180 degree semi-circle. Consistency, Sam would say. He was meticulous in his investigations.

After he finished his last find line, he sat back and took a huge swallow of coffee.

"Bill, why don't you call the Park Patrol back and tell them we're working on a theory and will let them know their next move within fifteen minutes."

"Sure thing, boss." Bill stepped outside the door to make the call.

When he returned, Sam continued, "These x marks indicate a cranberry bog or bogs. Most of the land between the bike path and the highway has been farmed bogs for years. It's almost impossible to cross them without waders."

"Since this is growing season, there won't be any workers around. Those are pretty desolate places until harvest starts. If I remember correctly, there are very narrow strips of land between the bogs. They'd be hard to walk on, let alone walk with a bike."

"Bill, this is what I need you to do." Sam was in speed mode. "Call the Patrol and give them the coordinates of these cleared pads we've circled. Tell them to head straight back away from the path until they come to the bogs. Then, I want them to call us. Have them hooked up to line nine. That way I can put them on my speaker phone."

This time Bill stayed at the desk and made the call. "They're on their way."

"We'll continue studying this map until we hear back from them," said Sam. "Let's move our focus to the highway. We'll identify landmarks starting west to east." He pulled a magnifying glass from his side drawer.

The three of them hovered over the map, studying and surveying the area without saying a word.

"Peggy, make sure you get all this down." Sam cocked his head to see her already writing.

"This area here is the center of Bourne Village," Sam said pointing to the furthest point west. "I don't think she'd be there. First of all, that's got to be at least eight, maybe ten, miles away, through some rough terrain. And second, if she ended up in the center, there'd be lots of people to help her. There's a gas station, a few houses, and that place across the highway is a tree farm. This is where the highway starts to get rural." Sam pointed to a spot on the map. "There's a stretch of nothing, then, according to the map, one of the bogs comes up real close to the highway."

Bill shook his head. "It must be a dormant section, because I've never noticed it and I travel that the highway all the time."

Peggy wrinkled her face in deep thought. "I think they sold off part of the bogs some years ago. This section had a couple of bad seasons and went bust. You know what, I think Mr. Parker owns that bog. Now that we're talking about it, I remember my parents saying something about the sale of the *highway bog*. That's what they called it. I didn't care, so I didn't pay much attention."

"That makes sense," said Sam. "This next structure is Mr. Parker's house. Then, if we follow the highway, it curves to the left and just a few hundred feet down the road is where Becky Morgan was killed."

Bill's cell rang. "Hold on. I'm transferring you to line nine and putting you on Sam's speaker phone."

"Detective, this is Sgt. Miller. We're in place at the beginning of the bogs. I have six units ready and waiting for your instructions."

Sam answered quickly, "Did anybody notice anything, anything at all, in the area between the clearings and the bogs?"

"Negative, Sir."

"Is there any way to cross the bogs without actually going into them?"

"For the most part, no," answered the Sergeant. "There are, however, a couple of very narrow strips alongside bogs two, three and four. They'd be difficult to maneuver, especially with a bike. Although, my ATV 3 did notice about twenty feet in, the ground appeared to be darker, almost like it had been disturbed. I told him not to check it out until I spoke with you."

"I'm assuming your ATV 3 was referring to bog number three?" Sam asked.

"Yes, Sir."

"You need to stay your positions and I'll get back to you."

Bill picked up his phone, released the speaker, and told the Sergeant. they needed to check something out and would call him right back.

Sam had already started to extend the lines jutting out from bog number three. His eyes opened wide. The third line in from the right led to Mr. Parker's house. "She didn't. She wouldn't."

"I'm afraid she would," said Peggy.

"Let me think a minute. I'm not sure what my next move is going to be. We need to be careful. I don't like how this is shaping up." The stress was visible on Sam's face.

"Bill, you and I are going to meet with Sgt. Miller and his patrol. Can you please get him on the line for me?"

Within seconds a voice came over the speaker, "Sgt. Miller here."

"Detective Martin and myself are leaving as soon as we hang up. Leave your ATV 3 on the scene and send a couple of the other guys to pick us up in the parking lot. I'd like you to stay at bog number three with your officer. Don't investigate the area until we get there."

"You got it, Sir."

CHAPTER FIFTY

Sam and Bill were about to leave the station, when one of the office clerks ran over to them. "This was just delivered by courier. It was marked urgent so I thought you'd want to see it before you left."

Sam stared at the envelope. The return was stamped CRIME LAB – CONFIDENTIAL. He motioned Bill and Peggy back into his office, and, without sitting down, emptied the contents onto his desk.

"Bill, please lay these pictures out, while I read the report."

Sam broke the silence. "The news isn't good. Both rubbings are perfect matches for the tire pictures we took at the accident scene. I'm now officially changing the wording to murder scene. Peggy, make an entry to that effect."

"My hunch was right," he continued. "The first car to hit Becky belonged to James. I believe that he may have tried to kill her and make it look like an accident, but didn't have the guts to actually run her over. The second car, the one that actually ran her over, according to the autopsy report, was the cause of her death. Those tire tracks came from a car that belonged to Shawn Waldon."

"Bill, have a black and white pick Shawn up for questioning in the murder of Becky Morgan. Tell them to keep him in lock-up until we get back."

242

"Peggy, stay in my office and keep this phone open. I'll call you as soon as I find anything or if I need you to look something up." Sam folded the map and put it in his pocket. He took his 9mm from his bottom drawer and instructed Bill to do the same.

Bill quickly went to his desk, retrieved his service revolver, and secured it in its holster.

"Sam, what about James?" asked Detective Martin.

"I'm going to call Barnstable PD from the car and ask Detective Kennedy to go over to Super Court, in an unmarked, and pick James up. I don't want to cause any unnecessary commotion at the Courthouse." Sam's eyes were moving wildly as he spoke. "I'll have them bring him to Bourne. When we get back, we'll question him. Until then, the bastard can sit in a holding cell. It'll give him time to think or, if the big man chooses, he can cry like the coward he really is." Sam's anger and aggravation were starting to wear thin.

CHAPTER FIFTY-ONE

Sam and Bill grabbed an unmarked and headed toward the highway. "We're going to check out the area before Mr. Parker's house on our way to the bike lot." Sam took the map from his pocket and handed it to Bill. The traffic wasn't heavy, but they had to ride the break-down lane in order to go slow enough to identify the defunct bog.

Bill's eyes were glued to the side of the road. "There appears to be a clearing up ahead. See it, just beyond that group of scrub pines."

The small clearing was camouflaged by low brush and a slight dip about five feet in from the shoulder. "There's no question this spot has been used repeatedly as a pull off." Sam eased the unmarked over, but not completely into the clearing. "I want to take a look. It's been pretty dry, so if somebody used this area recently, we should see some fresh prints."

"Boss, check this out," said Bill. He squatted down to examine several indentations in the dirt. "I think you better grab the camera."

Sam flipped the trunk open, took the camera out, and walked to where Bill was. He saw it on the first glance. "Somebody's been walking a bike here. And, judging from the crispness, it wasn't that long ago." He looked around half hoping to see Casey pop out from behind a tree, but knew it wasn't going to happen.

There were several spots in the clearing with bike tire marks and footprints. They all appeared to be made from the same bike and person.

"Bill, look over here, auto tire tracks overlapping the bike tracks."

"I see them, Boss. A car was the last mode of transportation to use this clearing." Bill reached up for the camera and began snapping pictures from several different angles.

"Do me a favor and take a picture looking into the bog, then come out to the road and take one in the direction of Mr. Parker's house." Sam said. "Also, give Sgt. Miller a call and let him know we'll be there in about five minutes." Sam was rambling.

Bill knew what he was thinking.

The bike tire imprints were Casey's. What worried Sam the most were the other tracks.

"We'll find her." Bill put his hand on Sam's back. "Let's get going."

"That's strange," said Sam. "Mr. Parker isn't on his front porch."

"He probably took a pee break. You know, he can't sit there 24/7," said Bill. "We'll check it out on the way back."

Sam agreed.

Casey's car was still parked in the lot. Her empty bike rack was an eerie reminder she was missing. The two ATVs were waiting at the beginning of the path. The detectives strapped themselves in and the park officers took off to the location where Sgt. Miller was stationed.

Sam, Bill and the Sergeant walked over to the spot in question.

"There's no mistake about it, the dirt here has been disturbed recently, and, by somebody on a bicycle. I have no doubt it was Casey. It looks like she caught a soft spot and slipped down into the mud. When she went left, the bike went right. She may have gotten scraped up a little, but I don't think she was hurt bad. If you

245

look a little further up, you can see she started walking again with her bike at her side."

Bill snapped several pictures, then, used the telescopic lens to scope the landscape. "Boss, take a look out over the bog at about one o'clock. Do you see the water tower? That's around the corner from Mr. Parker's. She must have used that to determine her direction."

"We know she made it through the bog to the clearing next to the highway." Sam let out a sigh of despair. "Why didn't she wait? She's so impulsive." He turned and walked back to the ATV. "I know we can't cut through the bog, but is there a way around it, so we can come out directly across from here?"

One of the officers replied, "I know this area well. If you want, I'll take you there."

"Okay, but, if I knock three times on your back, I want you to stop and shut off the engine. Sam turned to Bill and the Sergeant. "You'll need to follow my lead. I have a hunch."

They were almost all the way around when Sam knocked three times on the officer's back. Immediately, they stopped and cut the engines. There was a silence that would scare the dead.

Bill knew exactly why Sam had stopped. Off in the distance to the left, they could make out the shadow of a car. To the right, there was the outline of a house. There was nothing but brush and trees in between.

"Bill, I've got a bad feeling," said Sam. "The car is parked in the clearing we just left. And the house to the right is Mr. Parker's."

CHAPTER FIFTY-TWO

The creaking noise ... there it was again.

I tried to take comfort in the fact that the house was old, and, well, maybe, it had gotten windy outside. After all, I don't know how long I've been here. The sounds of the night creeping in through unsealed windows added a spooky touch to an already haunting nightmare.

Stay calm. Make a plan. Don't panic.

If somebody is lurking around upstairs, it's only a matter of time before they come down and I have to be ready.

First of all, I have to shimmy around, just a little ... enough to see the stairs. Obviously, the person who tied me up knew they left me sitting on all fours. When they see me sideways on the floor, they'll know I came to and probably tried to get loose. Hopefully, they'll think I fell over and lost consciousness again. That's what I want them to think.

There's definitely somebody else besides Mr. Parker and myself in this house. The creaking turned into footsteps ... slow and calculated. I couldn't tell if the person was big or small, fat or thin, male or female, young or old. This feeling of helplessness is a characteristic I won't accept. My heart's pounding so hard, I'm afraid it's going to pop through my chest.

Sam, please, please come through that door.

247

It's not often I pray, but at this moment it seemed like the right thing to do. I closed my eyes and asked for God's help. I whispered to my mom and dad to protect me. I figured my only chance was divine intervention. Nobody, but those looking down, knew where I was.

I wanted to scream out to Sam. I wanted to tell him I loved him. Now he'll never know.

I'm no closer to knowing how Becky was killed. But, I must have hit a nerve with somebody or this wouldn't be happening. There's a person out there who thinks I know more than I do. And, I think that person is upstairs in the kitchen trying to decide what to do with me. He or she killed once. He or she will do it again. I was sure of that.

The more I tried to free my hands, the tighter the rope got. The bindings were starting to hurt.

A new noise drifted down the stairs, slithered across the floor, and rested uncomfortably in my ear. I closed my eyes, trying to unlock my sound bank. It had a definite pitch to it. Well, not really a pitch, but it was something common. Something I hear all the time. I got it. Somebody was on the other side of the door, ever so slowly turning the knob. I knew when it turned a full 360 degrees the door would open.

The sun must have moved to the west side of the house. The natural light that tried to penetrate the small cellar windows was almost gone and the windows on the opposite side were blocked with cardboard.

If ever I wanted to be an actress, now was my time to audition. My part was to play dead or at least unconscious and hope my attacker would leave.

The knob noise stopped. I could see a thin line of light hugging the left side of the door. The line slowly got wider and wider … enough for the person waiting on the other side to pass through. I watched. It seemed like an eternity. Finally, a shod foot made its way off the landing and onto a step … then down another one … and still another one. I could see up to the knees now.

The feet were large and the pants were more masculine than feminine. I assumed the person was a he rather than a she. I took in a deep breath.

He descended a couple more stairs, then stopped. Nothing.

Now I could see up to his chest. He was tall and appeared to be in good shape. His jersey was neatly tucked into his pants. From the reflection of the kitchen light, it looked like he was wearing jeans. The jersey had some kind of logo or wording or a picture on the front.

He turned slightly as though he might go back up. It was in that split second, I recognized the logo. It was a Nike swoosh mark. I closed my eyes. I had just seen that same shirt or one like it. When … where? I couldn't remember. I couldn't pull up the picture.

He shifted back to his original position and took another step down. Just one more step, I thought, and I'd see his face.

The anticipation of his next move switched my thought process into slow motion. One foot came up and gently found its place one step down. He repeated the process one more time.

My eyes opened wide and an uncontrollable gasp rushed from my mouth. I froze. The jersey belonged to James.

He stood staring at me.

My fingers moved back and forth trying feverishly to loosen the knots still binding my hands. I had been rendered incapable of defending myself. Is this how I was going to die?

James sat down on the bottom step and buried his face in his hands. I thought I detected a slight whimper over the deafening sound of my heartbeat.

Without warning, he jumped to his feet. His face became sour … mean. His voice dropped an octave and he began to shout.

"You bitch. You took it all away from me. Nobody cared about me and I didn't care about anyone. All those young girls, they were toys. They let me re-live my lost childhood. They didn't want anything but a good time. And I gave it to them. They had no idea who I was. Then came Becky."

"James, you don't need to do this. Let me help you."

"Shut-up and listen. You need to know why you're going to die." He crossed the floor and stopped in front of Mr. Parker. "Just like him."

"Becky pushed me. She found out who I was. She invaded my privacy. It was none of her business. If she had told anyone about us, I would have gone to jail for statutory rape. I didn't rape her, but I don't expect you to understand."

He folded his arms and walked to the other side of the cellar. After a few minutes, he returned. "I didn't want her to suffer, but I didn't want her to live. I figured a clean hit and run would appear to be an accident. I'd be free and nobody would know what really happened."

"Then came Marnie. I finally felt good about myself. We hit it off. I thought I might have a future with her."

He had that look again. "Then came you and your, I'm better than you, cop boyfriend. If you two minded your own damn business, this wouldn't have happened."

The longer I kept him talking, the longer I stayed alive. "This stuff is our business. Let me tell you something. You didn't kill Becky Morgan. All you did is knock her down, maybe unconscious. There was somebody following you last Sunday night. That person brutally ran her over. The only reason they missed her head is because it was cocked to one side." James turned his back to me. Now I was scared. I couldn't read his expression and had no idea what to expect next.

"It's too late." The thunder in his voice was deafening. "My life is over and so is yours." And with that, James dropped down beside me.

The James I knew was gone. The person hovering over me was the shell of a lost, deranged soul. I felt the fingers on my right hand slip sideways and the rope that was holding them drop. I screamed and with all I had left in me, swung my right arm around and caught him square in the eye. He winced and fell back.

I yelled as loud as I could. But, before I could flip over to free my left arm, his hands were around my neck.

Now he was doing the yelling. An animal like sound echoed off the walls.

I felt my life slipping away.

The last thing I remember was more yelling … and faces … and more faces … then nothing.

CHAPTER FIFTY-THREE

"Casey, it's okay, I'm here. Casey, can you hear me? Please open your eyes." Sam was sitting on the floor holding me in his arms, gently rocking me back and forth.

I could hear him, but I was afraid I was in a place between life and death. I didn't want to tip the scales in the wrong direction, so I stayed as quiet as I could.

"She's going to be okay, Boss," said Bill. "I called for an ambulance. They should be here any minute."

I wanted to sleep, but I wanted to let Sam know I was okay. He had my right hand cupped in his. I gently wrapped my fingers around his thumb and gave it a little squeeze.

"Sherlock, you sure gave me a scare." He leaned down and gave me a kiss on the forehead.

I opened my eyes and smiled. "Can we go home now?"

"You're going to the hospital to get checked out. I have to go to the station, then I'll come by as soon as I can to pick you up."

"Sam, I'm really okay. I'd like to go with you to the station. Please, let me put closure to this whole thing. Remember we're a team."

"All right, if the EMTs say you're okay, you can ride with Bill and me. In the meantime, do you think you can walk up the stairs?"

"I'll give it a try." Between the bike ride, the hike through the bogs, and the fall off the cellar stairs, my body was hurting. But I wasn't about to let Sam know that. Before I went upstairs, I turned toward Mr. Parker. "He's the hero in this case. Without him we had very little to go on. Becky might have ended up in the cold case files. Know what, Sam, I'd love to have his rocker. I could imagine him sitting there, keeping an eye on me, keeping me safe. It would never be empty."

"I'll see what I can do."

I gathered my composure and with Sam behind me, made my way up to the kitchen.

The EMTs said I was okay to go, so without further hesitation, I was out of there.

Sam's unmarked was still parked in the bike lot, so one of the black and whites gave us a ride to get it. "I'll have one of the guys drive your car to the station. Your bike needs to stay at Mr. Parker's house until they're finished taking pictures."

We passed Mr. Parker's house on the way back. Now a crime scene, it was cordoned off with yellow police tape. The coroner's office was backing up to the front porch. And the rocker sat empty. It was sad.

Sam slowed as we passed the clearing where James' car was parked. A black and white was posted, waiting for the police tow truck.

"Want a coffee?" Sam said turning slightly to see my reaction. "I'll stop at Dunkin's."

"I sure do. I'll have a French Vanilla and a jelly donut. Remember I haven't eaten since yesterday." My mouth was watering.

"We've probably got about three hours ahead of us. Afterward, we'll grab something to eat." Sam pulled into Dunkin's parking lot. "Bill, my treat, what do you want?"

"Just a coffee, regular. I think the Mrs. wants to go out later." Bill got out of the car. "You stay with Casey and fill her in."

Sam handed him a ten dollar bill. "Remember, my treat."

"Fill me in on what?" I said.

"We picked up Shawn Waldon for the murder of Becky Morgan. It seems he enjoyed a reputation of being a ladie's man. Becky dated him for a short time, then, she broke it off. He discovered the affair she was having with James and confronted her. She denied it. That's when he started to stalk her. He was a sick puppy."

I was puzzled. "How did you know?"

"Your notes gave me my first clue. When we confronted him, he cried like a baby. The big man on campus couldn't handle it and spilled his guts."

"As far as James, he'll be charged with attempted murder and leaving the scene of a hit and run in the Morgan case. Now, we'll add, the murder of Mr. Parker and assault with the intent to commit murder on you."

"How did you know where I was?" I asked.

"We followed your trail, starting from your car, across the bogs, and to the back of Mr. Parker's house. The Park Patrol assisted us with their ATVs. About three quarters of the way around the bogs, we saw James' car parked in the clearing. From that point, we approached the house by foot. I saw your bike leaning against the back porch."

"How did you get in without either one of us hearing you?"

"James was yelling so loud, we took a chance. The back door was unlocked and the cellar door was open and the rest is history. It's a good thing he was so into himself. We heard most of what he said."

I wrapped my hands around my cup and leaned back in the seat. "Ah .... French Vanilla, my favorite."

EPILOGUE

"Hi, Casey. I'm just crossing the Bourne Bridge. I know I'm running a little late, but there were a couple accidents and some slow traffic. When you get this message, give me a call. I hope we're still on for lunch. I'll give Annie a call."

Marnie waited until she got over the Bridge and around the rotary before she tried Annie. She had programed Annie on speed dial before leaving for New York. Annie was number three. Her finger must have slipped and hit two. Casey's voice came back over her earpiece. "Oops. Casey, it's only me again. I was trying to reach Annie. Talk to you later."

She decided to pull into the Speedway Gas Station to make the call and, while she was there, fill up her car. She glanced at her watch. It was 1:23. Annie probably already went to lunch, she thought. She called anyway.

Annie answered. Her voice was distant. "Hi," she said. Then there was silence.

"You there?" Marnie asked.

"Yeah, I'm here."

"Is this a bad time?" Marnie questioned. "Want to call me back. I'm getting gas at the Speedway, just off the Bourne rotary then, I was going to head toward the Village."

"Are you coming over to the office?" asked Annie.

"That was my plan." Marnie felt something was wrong. "Is that okay? I tried to reach Casey, but I had to leave a message."

Annie's voice cracked. "Marnie, we need to talk."

"Are you all right? What's happening?" Marnie hesitated, "Is Casey all right?"

Annie started to cry. "She will be."

The Cape Cod Tribune

Becky Morgan Remembered

By CASEY QUINBY

Too young for stress...
  Too old for dolls...
Caught somewhere in between...

Fourteen days ago, the life of sixteen-year-old Becky Morgan was cut short by a tragic hit-and-run accident as she walked along the Bourne Scenic Highway.

Tragic ... yes ...
But an accident ... no

In life, I'd never met her, but in death I knew her well. Her legacy survived long enough to lead me ... to help me uncover the inner hurt that led her down the path of stolen innocence. Her faith and love of family surrounded her. It was a lone intruder who pierced her world and tugged at her inner being. Without him, she never would have been alone on the highway. He led her there, but it was another who took her away.

Eleven days ago, we gathered at Our Lady of the Highway in Bourne for a celebration of life. A life, Becky's life, that will live on in the hearts of all who knew her and all who didn't. Her captivating smile, her willingness to help, her desire to succeed, and her love of life, in general, will be passed on through her family and friends. They will remember and she will live the rest of her life through them.

257

46415067R00148

Made in the USA
Middletown, DE
30 July 2017